UNCOVERING THE LORD

Courting a Curious Lady, Book 1

Lexi Post

Dragonblade Publishing, Inc. is an imprint of Kathryn Le Veque Novels, Inc.
P.O. Box 23
Moreno Valley, CA 92556
ceo@dragonbladepublishing.com

Produced in the United States of America

First Edition May 2024
Trade Paperback Edition

ARE YOU SIGNED UP FOR DRAGONBLADE'S BLOG?

You'll get the latest news and information on exclusive giveaways, exclusive excerpts, coming releases, sales, free books, cover reveals and more.

Check out our complete list of authors, too!

No spam, no junk. That's a promise!

Sign Up Here

www.dragonbladepublishing.com

Dearest Reader;

Thank you for your support of a small press. At Dragonblade Publishing, we strive to bring you the highest quality Historical Romance from some of the best authors in the business. Without your support, there is no 'us', so we sincerely hope you adore these stories and find some new favorite authors along the way.

Happy Reading!

CEO, Dragonblade Publishing

Additional Dragonblade books by Author Lexi Post

Courting a Curious Lady Series
Uncovering the Lord (Book 1)

Marrying a Mabry Series
Stealing the Duke (Book 1)
Painting the Earl (Book 2)
Revealing the Viscount (Book 3)

Acknowledgments

For my wonderful husband, Bob Fabich, Sr., who has always accepted me exactly as I am, faults and all.

For my awesome sister, Paige Wood, who helped me brainstorm Teddy and Elsbeth's story and then helped me fine-tune it after it was written.

I can't say enough about my critique partner, Marie Patrick, who lets me go on and on about my stories as I try to figure out what's next or how to fix the inevitable problems.

A special thanks to my Lexi's Legends, Bette Read for the Portugal cave name, Kim Mangels for gentlemen's names, Lisa Staebell-Fishback for a stalagmite column name, and Charlene Whitehouse for the *SeaSprite* captain's name.

A very special thank you to my wonderful and talented friend Ross Martineau, who lives in Portugal, for his help with my Portuguese. His adventures are truly inspirational.

All these people and more made writing this story a group effort and a lot more fun!

Author's Note

If Lord Teddy Mabry seems familiar, it would be because he was introduced in *Stealing the Duke* (Marrying a Mabry Book 1). I heard from so many readers who wanted him to have his own happily ever after that I had to write it. I hope you enjoy.

The Courting a Curious Ladies series was inspired by two of my three favorite books of all time, Louisa May Alcott's novels, *Little Men* and *Jo's Boys*, published in 1871 and 1886 respectively. These were the next two books after *Little Women,* and I fell in love with Jo's school for boys. In Alcott's novels, there were a dozen boys as well as a few girls, all of whom go through the trials and tribulations of growing into adults. In *Stealing the Duke,* Lady Joanna sets up a school for ladies of the peerage modeled after Oxford and Cambridge. It's called the Belinda School for Curious Ladies.

Uncovering the Lord is specifically inspired by the character of Demi Brooke from Alcott's novels. Demi was a studious boy who many adults hoped would become a minister, but instead he became a journalist. He is also looked up to by the other boys though he is not the eldest, simply because he is caring and intelligent. So too is Lady Elsbeth Rawley of Astor. And while her mother wishes her to continue her geological studies for a couple more years, Lady Elsbeth has other plans, especially after making a rash promise to the other ladies of the school in order to help them all.

On a geological note, the Dragon Caves of Mallorca still exist today. At the time the story takes place, only two of the four had been discovered, which is too bad because I'm quite sure Lady Elsbeth would have loved the underground lake in one of caves discovered after she visited. On another note, I do need to be clear that the second cave, Caverna de Pedras Perdidas, with the oculus in Portugal, is fictional, though Portugal has some very lovely caves like it along its shoreline.

CHAPTER ONE

London
April, 1817 – Midseason

LADY ELSBETH RAWLEY allowed her partner to escort her back to Dowager Countess Astor, who was not only an instructor at the Belinda School for Curious Ladies, but also her mother. With her mother were the two who governed the school she loved, her cousin James Huntington, otherwise known as the Duke of Northwick, and his wife, Joanna, who was resplendent in a striking red gown, her usual single black curl falling to her shoulder.

After thanking Mr. Lansing for the dance, Elsbeth studied him as he walked away before turning to her ever-watchful parent and family members.

Joanna winked at her. "And is Mr. Lansing a mudstone or more fluorite?"

She gave the question some thought. Categorizing the men she met by the rock found in England helped her keep them straight in her judgment. "I haven't decided. I believe he may be a mix of obsidian and linsenerz."

Her mother's blonde brows rose. "Now that's a new combination."

She looked over the room, finding the man in question. "Yes, well, as I just met him a fortnight ago, I have not had much on which to judge as of yet."

James frowned, his blue gaze incredulous. "Tell me you do not compare the gentlemen of the *ton* to rocks."

She glanced at the laughter in Joanna's hazel eyes before giving James a cheeky grin. "But I do. If they must compare us to flowers, I see no reason not to compare them to rocks."

Her cousin opened his mouth to object, no doubt for some length, but she was anxious to exit the room, so she quickly addressed her mother. "I'm going to join Dory on the terrace for some cooler air."

Her mother perused the ballroom, her gaze stopping on Lady Dorothea Ansley standing next to the terrace doors in a pretty sky-blue dress that set off her mahogany hair. Then Lady Astor's focus moved across the room and once again stopped as she narrowed her eyes at Alice Ansley, Countess Preston and frowned, never happy with the woman's lack of watchfulness over Lady Dorothea, her daughter. "Very well, but do be back inside before the next dance ends or I'll come find you."

Elsbeth winked, a habit she'd copied from Joanna. "I know you will."

Joanna tapped her on the arm with her fan, stopping her. "Tell Lady Dorothea her book by Thomas Hobbes arrived yesterday. I haven't been able to find her all evening."

She wasn't surprised. Dory tended to stay with Sophie, who willingly listened to her ramble on and on. "I will." Giving her mother a quick smile, she made her way to Dory, not a little puzzled as to why there was a gathering of the Curious Ladies in the middle of a ball.

"Come." Dory hooked her arm in hers. "Eleanor called the meeting. It must be important. She's already waiting with Sophie."

Once they'd traversed the terrace, Elsbeth lifted the lavender skirts of her dress, and they hurried down the steps to the garden below. She noticed her fellow students near the far hedge, their white gowns standing in stark contrast to the darkness behind them. Eleanor's bright-red hair was like a beacon while Sophie, with her brown locks, appeared as almost a shadow. There was a lady missing. "Where's Georgina?"

Dory waved, as if Georgina's absence were of no immediate concern. "She was asked to dance. I will tell her everything, but she made me promise no votes without her."

Elsbeth gave the Huntington abbreviated nod. "Of course." They had made a pact early in their first year at the school that if anything affected them all, they all must have a say. Though the term had finished in late winter and they were already halfway through the following season, she still enjoyed her classmates' company at concerts, lectures, exhibitions, plays, balls, and of course, tea. The school had been a welcome reprieve from the inanity of the season. Now with friends, she found the season much more enjoyable.

"There you are." Eleanor Dulac blew air out from between her lips, a clear indication her patience was at an end. As the oldest of them all, she seemed to be always in a hurry, which often resulted in something being broken.

"Elsbeth was dancing." Dory shrugged. "We came as soon as we could. Georgina's been partnered, so we can't take any votes."

"Votes aren't going to help this time." At the irritation in Eleanor's voice, Sophie Howard, who spoke very little, silently laid her hand on Eleanor's arm.

The woman seemed to calm. "It's just terrible. I don't know what to do."

"Perhaps you should explain." Sophie gave Eleanor a tenuous smile. "Worries are often a lighter burden when shared."

Elsbeth felt her stomach tightening. Eleanor was rarely this upset. "Yes, please let us help."

"I don't think there *is* any help. My mother told me not ten minutes past that if one of us from the school doesn't marry before the end of the season, she won't allow me to attend any longer."

Dory gasped, and all eyes turned toward her. Dory's mouth opened, but no words came forth, which was telling in and of itself. What Sophie lacked in speech, Dory made up for in spades.

"Dory?" She patted the woman's cheek lightly. "Are you ill?"

Closing her mouth, Dory shook her head and then nodded. "Maybe I am. My mother said something similar to me before we left for this ball. She must have shared her feelings with Lady Dulac."

Eleanor's eyes rounded. "And you didn't think that important enough to share with us?" Her pitch rose until poor Sophie covered her ears.

Elsbeth let go of Dory and put her finger to her lips. "Shh, it would be best if no one overheard us."

Eleanor crossed her arms and scowled at Dory but didn't say anything.

Dory, on the other hand, had colored considerably. "I'm sorry. I forgot by the time we arrived. I promise, if I had remembered, I would have told you all."

Her friend's inability to stay on topic made conversation difficult for her, which Dory usually handled with great poise unless it hurt one of the Curious Ladies. Then she couldn't seem to do enough to apologize.

She patted Dory's arm. "There is no harm done, as it would have only been a couple of hours sooner that we would have learned of this. What's important is that we determine our best course of action in response to this new information." Though she wasn't the oldest, for some reason, the other ladies looked to her in times of crisis, and this was most definitely a crisis.

Eleanor threw her hands up before letting them fall to her sides as she looked at each of them in turn. "And what possible course of action is there? We all know that no one is going to propose to *me* this season. The only people I've danced with have been my cousin and Mr. Jenson." She didn't elaborate, daring any of them to suggest that Mr. Jenson was a suitable suitor.

No one spoke, so Eleanor continued. "That means someone

else must marry or we may all be pulled from the school."

Sophie's brows lowered and she clasped her hands tightly before her. "My mother will do what everyone else does. None of us may be able to return."

"What if we had the duke talk to them all?" Dory grinned. "You know how impressed they are by him. I believe that's why my mother agreed originally. He told her he would put it about that we are the top candidates for wifehood."

Eleanor shook her head. "My mother already indicated that his endorsement was obviously not enough. She quite despairs of me ever attracting the attentions of a man younger than my father."

Though no one said anything about that, they all quietly agreed. Elsbeth didn't think it best to dwell on that predicament. "Then we simply need one of us to marry."

"But who?" Dory held her hands out to her sides. "You, Sophie, Eleanor, and I are in our second season. And as of yet, none of us have had any interest shown in us."

Eleanor grinned. "Actually, Elsbeth, you have. You had Lord Mabry dancing to your tune."

Teddy. Even as she thought of him, she missed him. He may have been far too young in actions and deeds, but he did have a good heart. "Yes, but as you saw, he wasn't as ready for marriage as he thought."

"That's true." Dory's disappointed face suddenly brightened. "What about the new lady? I saw her the other day. She's very pretty and has a lovely accent."

"You met Mademoiselle Lissette?" She was a bit envious that she hadn't been the first. She liked to welcome all new students.

"I did. She will definitely turn heads. Her hair is as black as midnight, her skin incredibly pale, and her eyes are a deep brown. I imagine she'll have offers right away. She's from France and lived through the war. I heard she dressed as a boy to hide from the French soldiers. I imagine she's quite happy to be in England. Did you know that there's a great shortage of food over there?

Why, some of the people are actually *starving*. Daniel Defoe said that those without food in their belly are more prone to—"

She touched Dory's arm. "We're talking about someone marrying."

"Of course. Thank you."

Eleanor waved her hand at Dory. "The new lady won't help us. We don't go back to Silver Meadows until *after* the season. Someone must be engaged *before* then."

Sophie spoke up. "Could we *all* simply try to attract a husband?"

"No." Dory shook her head. "If we leave it at that, then we will all expect someone else to succeed and not try hard enough. No. One of us must make the sacrifice for the rest."

As much as Elsbeth wished it weren't so, Dory was right. And as the one everyone looked to, that meant she must make the sacrifice. As much as she enjoyed her studies at the Belinda School for Curious Ladies, she had always had such knowledge at her fingertips because James owned two extensive private libraries. While her classmates had had little exposure to such subjects as philosophy, literature, astronomy and so forth, she had grown up studying them. Since she'd seen her friends transform with just one year at the school, she was quite certain they needed it far more than she did.

"I will do it."

Sophie's eyes rounded, while Eleanor nodded. But Dory turned Elsbeth by the shoulders. "Are you sure? Maybe Georgina would like to?"

As much as she would have liked to retract her offer, there was no getting around the fact that she had the best chance with so little of the season left. "No. Georgina came to the school late, and she should be able to attend another year if she wishes. I will do it."

"You can't."

At Sophie's pronouncement, they all looked at her.

"Why can't I, Sophie?"

"Because you are leaving in a fortnight for Spain. Surely, you don't mean to cancel your trip? I know how much you've been aching to see the Dragon Caves."

Her stomach suddenly felt as if she'd eaten a sandstone. It had taken months to convince James to let her and her mother travel to Mallorca. Since his last relative who'd traveled overseas had not returned, he'd been adamant that she not go. In the end, she'd had to enlist Joanna's help to finally convince him. Sophie was right—she had to go.

"Then I shall just have to be quick about finding a husband when I return." She smiled confidently, though she felt anything but confident. There were three or four men who had shown an interest in her, and two may elicit more tender feelings from her. Of course, now, her feelings may well not matter.

Sophie's brow knit. "Are you sure you wish to do this? I know my mother would be willing to allow me to at least borrow a book or two from Her Grace's library."

Her heart melted at Sophie's offer. "That is so lovely of you. But I want you to continue your studies." She paused as she concocted a lie for Sophie's benefit. "This trip will be the culmination of my studies while you're just starting your journey. I am happy to make this small sacrifice for you all."

"Oh, Elsbeth." Dory pulled her close and gave her a hug.

There were hugs all around and not a few tears.

"Elsbeth, it's time." At her mother's call, they all turned. "Come, ladies. We are not at school. You must all come in before the supper dance is to start." Her mother waved at them to follow her, and they moved toward the terrace doors as one.

Elsbeth's feeling of happiness over helping her friends began to turn into a mudstone in her belly. What if she couldn't convince a man to marry her? What if she was being too selfish by going on her trip? What if her future was miserable because of her promise? Even as these thoughts settled, she arrived in the spot where her mother had so recently stood.

Lady Georgina Bridgeman stepped out just as they reached

the door. Her lithe form barely blocked the light from inside. "There you all are. You must tell me what I missed."

Eleanor opened her arms wide. "You missed that Elsbeth is saving us all."

Georgina cocked her head, her eyes rounding. "Oh, you must tell me."

Eleanor excitedly summarized the problem and solution.

Georgina gave Elsbeth a wide smile. "You are truly wonderful."

Dory linked arms with her. "Yes, she is."

Elsbeth smiled weakly, shivering even as they strolled into the overheated ballroom.

CHAPTER TWO

Mallorca, Spain
Late May 1817

LORD THEODORE MABRY, Viscount Mabry and heir to the Earl of Lansdowne, frowned as yet another palm branch attempted to hit his face. Holding his arm up to protect his eyes, he pushed through the green foliage, not willing to lose his guide.

If someone a year ago had predicted he'd be traipsing through the countryside of Mallorca, Spain to crawl into some devil's pit in search of supposed dragon teeth for a wet nurse so she'd travel to England with him and his infant daughter, he would have thought them bound for Bedlam. Yet here he was on that very quest.

He'd only been a father for three months, yet already he found himself willing to do anything for his little girl, even search out dragon teeth so that Senorita Consuela could wish upon one for a safe voyage. He'd been fortunate that Francesca, his late Spanish wife, had already enlisted Consuela before her illness because as he'd discovered while looking for another wet nurse to travel across the sea in order to avoid such superstitious non-sense, there were none.

It appeared that Senorita Consuela, having lost her baby over two years ago, had become a wet nurse and had very honorable references So, if dragon teeth were needed to get the woman to brave the ocean, then dragon teeth he would find, whatever they actually were. If his Spanish was correct, they were not true dragon teeth, but some kind of animal teeth.

His other option was to wait for Marianna to be weaned, but now that he had her in his life, he wanted to share her with his family. He had yet to tell anyone of his sudden marriage and new baby girl. It felt as though a year had passed since he'd received the letter in Marseille from Francesca that he was to be a father and begging him to attend her. She had been his very first woman upon coming to the Continent and only because of that had he remembered her.

He grimaced even as he ducked beneath a mastic tree branch. He was not proud of his time spent abroad before receiving that letter. After his failed proposal to Lady Elsbeth, he'd sworn off love, determined it was only for the weak, and spent his time enjoying women, drink, and the nearest festival. His lips quirked. How little he knew what the innocent, round, blue eyes of a baby could do. Not only had his daughter healed his heart, but she'd proven he could indeed love very deeply.

"Señor Mabry, we are almost there." His guide's reassurance was a relief. He'd started later than he'd planned because he hadn't wished to wake Marianna. Now, the sun was high in the sky and the temperatures had risen. He was thankful he'd left his waistcoat and tailcoat at home. The landscape was not conducive to formal dress. Even his linen shirt felt warm, and he'd tossed his cravat a mile back. If he was lucky, a wild goat would take it.

He grinned. His good friend Señora Bello, with whom he was staying while on the island, did not like goats. He, however, thought they were funny, and they tended to follow him around. The *señora* had warned him he might attract a few in the wilds, and yet he hadn't stumbled upon any. Then again, Señora Bello also said that people only traveled to the Dragon Caves to face their greatest fears, and that wasn't about to happen, either. He wasn't afraid of underground spaces or the darkness, as he'd proven when sneaking below Paris to the catacombs to hide from an angry husband.

His guide, Mateo, stopped and looked about, his dark brow furrowed, his brown, bushy mustache wiggling.

All he could see were oleander bushes, sago palms, and a date tree just ahead. Though the greenery was pleasant to look at, he could see no cave.

Mateo suddenly turned and smiled, pointing to his right. "We are here."

They had arrived? He looked to his right but saw nothing.

"Here. Here." Mateo waved him closer.

Taking the final steps to stand next to the man, at first, he still didn't see anything, but as he looked closer, he noticed what looked like a rock ledge about twenty feet above them. It was covered in tiny, green plant growth and above it were more trees and bushes. Pushing aside the palm fronds, he moved closer and halted. Beneath what he thought was a ledge was a wide opening split in half by a column. No wonder it had taken him so long to find a guide who knew the way to the Cuevas del Drach. Everyone had wanted to take him to Ham's Caves, which were far better known.

"*¿Sí?*" Mateo grinned at him.

He looked back at his guide and smiled. "*Sí.*"

The man opened the lantern he'd carried and lit it, then handed it to him. "You go. I'll wait here."

He wasn't surprised Mateo didn't plan to go into the cave. From the way Consuela spoke, he had a feeling she and other locals truly thought a dragon might be inside. Accepting the lantern, he turned toward the opening and entered. As he walked into the darkness, the lantern's glow illuminated a wide cavern that curved to his left. He moved forward cautiously, not even sure how far he'd have to go to find skeletal teeth, when the light showed a floor-to-ceiling rock formation directly in his path. A vague memory of his years at Oxford niggled at his brain. He was sure there was a name for it. Moving around it, he carefully meandered between what appeared to be half columns. They were formed by dripping water, but beyond that, he couldn't remember.

He grinned at the darkness. There was someone he knew who would love to see these formations: Lady Elsbeth. He'd never forget her surreptitiously picking up rocks and slipping them into her reticule the one time he'd managed to walk with her at Hyde Park. She was most assuredly married by now, possibly to one of his mates, though he preferred not to know whom.

Despite the fact that there was no vegetation due to no sunlight, the cave itself was not particularly cold, but just cool enough to be a relief from the midday sun. Continuing into its depths, he held the lantern aloft to look for dragon teeth, but the immense columns and half-columns distracted him. The half-columns rose up from the floor and down from the ceiling like spears. It was another world beneath the ground and a painting of Hades, the ancient Greek version of hell, flashed through his mind.

Shaking off the uncomfortable thought, he carefully walked in farther, lifting his lantern so as to view the walls, tops of the short columns, and anywhere else that might hold a dragon tooth. He should have asked his guide if they were fossils or skeletal. Maybe simply breaking off one of the spears would do. The whole cave appeared to be the inside of a dragon's mouth with thousands of long teeth. Would Consuela know the difference? His instinct said she would, so he continued.

He stopped for a moment to listen in case a sound might give him a clue as to where to find what he sought. He stared up at the ceiling towering over forty feet above him. If the teeth were up there, it would take more than a day to retrieve them. He could clearly hear drops of water, which was no surprise, but there was a slight, scraping noise coming from deeper in the cave. Could it be an animal? He hoped the "dragon" was not an animal, as he refused to kill one. But perhaps the animal was in a den where he could find an old skeleton. She did say the teeth would be yellow, having seen two in her entire life.

More optimistic now than when he'd started his trek, he moved toward the sound, still being careful where he stepped. He didn't want to frighten the animal. Then again, he didn't wish to be bitten. Quickly, he thought back over his limited knowledge of Mallorca wildlife, but if it was a cave dweller, he was unfortunately ignorant. At least there were no bats, which there would have been in an English cave.

As he drew closer to the sound, he heard shuffling in addition to the scraping. The nearer he came, the larger the animal sounded. He halted. Perhaps he should have brought a pistol. He didn't wish to wrestle with an angry beast.

A sudden crack filled the cavern. "Dash it all!"

At the feminine voice, he started. Someone else was in the caves? She was obviously not happy. Immediately, he moved forward faster, anxious to assist whoever had found herself in a predicament. Surely, she would not be in the cave alone, but as he listened, he heard no other sounds. Even the scraping had stopped. That worried him. It was fortuitous he was in there or a slip could turn deadly if left alone.

He saw the shadow on the cave wall first, which sped up his steps. She was on the ground in front of her lantern. He didn't want to scare her, or she might slip farther. "Do you need help?"

She sat up at his voice, which was a relief. "Who's there?"

He finally slipped between two columns and found her. Her blonde hair lay down her back to the dirt as she sat on the ground, her back to him. "Do you need help?"

She twisted around and gasped. "Teddy?"

He halted, his heart stopping as he gazed at Lady Elsbeth. He shook his head, as if the face he perceived to be hers would change, but it didn't, and he sucked in a breath. This was the woman he thought himself in love with. This was the woman who'd broken his heart. That very organ began to pound, and he had to swallow twice to get his voice to come out. "Lady

Elsbeth?"

Her lips turned up into a brilliant smile beneath her button nose and her blue eyes lit with pleasure. "I can't believe it!" She scrambled up and stepped up to him, both hands held out. "What are you doing here?"

He stepped back out of self-preservation. "Me? What are *you* doing here?" He glanced at her dress, which was covered in dirt, as were her hands. She even had smudges on her face.

The Lady Elsbeth he'd known had always appeared perfect. She'd been poised, respectful, and kind. Ever dressed in either clean pale pinks or lavenders with every golden-blonde hair in place, she'd looked to be the epitome of a debutante. Her face had always been a bit rounder than the average young lady's, but her high cheekbones, small nose, rose-colored lips, and expressive, almond-shaped eyes had given her the appearance of the ideal lady. She was far from that now, which made her appear much too human and imperfect for his comfort.

She pulled her hands back and brushed them against each other. "I know, I probably look like a street urchin." Her smile faltered a bit as she tucked strands of hair behind her ear. "But look at you."

Her gaze roamed from the top of his head to the toes of his boots. His body heated at her perusal and sweat began to form along his temples and the back of his neck.

"You're taller, and I do believe broader." She judged his shoulders and the appreciation in her eyes had his gut tightening.

"I've been gone well over a year." He tried to keep his voice even, but a bit of irritation slipped in.

"Of course. It has been a very long time." She chuckled. "Last I heard, you were escaping Paris in the dark of night. I did hope to one day see that city, but the Dragon Caves have been my priority." She rolled her eyes. "You have no inkling how difficult it was to persuade James to let me travel here to Mallorca."

At the mention of the Duke of Northwick, his cousin Joanna's husband, he stiffened. The man had not liked his pursuit of Lady

Elsbeth. "Is the duke here? Where's your mother? Tell me you are not in here alone."

She waved off his comment as if it were unimportant. "The duke, here? My cousin would rather give up his library than travel by ship." She pointed upward with one finger. "My mother is above with our guide."

That her mother had left her in the cave had his protective instincts surging. "You should not be alone in here. What if you fell? What if I were someone else? Tell me you weren't afraid the moment you heard my voice."

She had the decency to look abashed. "To be honest, I was. Mother and Alvaro were supposed to be watching the entrance. I'm surprised they didn't see you."

He wasn't. The foliage was thick by the entrance and he hadn't seen her parent or her guide. "It's not safe. Even if they had requested I not enter since you're without a chaperone, you still could be hurt in here. Would your mother come looking for you? I know your guide wouldn't."

Even as she listened, he could see her mind working. She likely wanted to defend her actions, but there was no excuse for such risk. He didn't even want to contemplate why he was so upset when none of it should have mattered to him. She'd had no use for him back in England. He should have no use for her at all. "I will be happy to escort you out."

Her eyes rounded. "But I'm not done."

Irritation burned through him. "Yes, you are."

She stared at him in stunned silence, her mouth open. Finally, she closed it and frowned. "You've changed."

He swallowed an angry laugh. "You have not." Though the truth was, she had. He folded his arms, waiting for her to realize she had no choice. They stared at each other for a good minute before she released a heavy sigh. "Very well. Let me gather my tools."

She turned before he could comment and bent over to put a number of items into a small box, but he couldn't tell what they were since her body hid her actions. Unfortunately, her position presented him with a nice view of her backside, and he quickly looked away. He simply refused to ogle a woman who had no feelings for him. Even the courtesans of Paris had revealed their desire for him was no more than that. They had not pretended feelings they did not have.

"I think that's all." She took a final cursory glance. "If I missed something, I'll be back tomorrow."

He didn't like that but refused to become more involved than he already was. Holding his lantern aloft, he waited for her to approach. "Follow me."

She winked, much like his cousin Joanna, which tugged at his heart. He missed his Mabry cousins.

"If you must know, I've been coming here for the last fortnight." She waved her hand toward the exit. "I know the way in and out far better than you."

A fortnight? "What have you been doing—" He held up his hand. "No, wait. Allow me to guess. You've been collecting rocks."

Even with only the glow of the two lanterns, her blush was obvious. "It's not just collecting rocks." She opened her arm, holding the lantern out to the side, illuminating more of the fantastical landscape. "I'm studying these stalagmites and stalactites. These two caves are filled with them. I cannot imagine a better place on Earth to truly understand such unique and old formations."

Despite her enthusiasm, his mind focused on a single word. "Two? Did you say two caves?"

She stepped around him and started walking as if she needn't worry about tripping on an outcropping and falling onto a young stalagmite. "Yes. There are two caves. I started at the back of the second and have been working my way forward. I worked much faster in the beginning, but now that I'm almost to the entrance, I've been able to truly enjoy the details and intricacies of these formations. Do you know that when a stalagmite and a stalactite meet, they form what's known as a 'column'?" She pointed to her right with her lantern. "There's one, right there. I nicknamed that one 'Guardian.'"

His step slowed. She named the rocks? Shaking his head, he quickly caught up.

"Of course, there are so many columns and I'm the only one down here, so I didn't name every one, but just those that are landmarks for me." She continued forward, her steps sure, as if she'd walked in and out a dozen times a day.

Despite her dirty appearance and finding her in the cave, he was still having a difficult time connecting her to the young, proper woman he'd known. It appeared Joanna's influence had been substantial. His cousin's letters were full with news, not the least of which was about her latest students and instructors at the Belinda School for Curious Ladies. So he was well aware that Lady Elsbeth and Lady Astor, her mother, were two of the very first to join as student and instructor. "Why is your mother not with you in the cave?" As he remembered it, Lady Astor was quite protective.

Lady Elsbeth stopped suddenly and faced him. "Do you really think my mother would be interested in any of this? She teaches literature and astronomy, not geology. She wouldn't know where to look for irregularities or hypothesize why they may have occurred." She turned around and continued toward the entrance. "Did you know that some of the irregularities are caused by changes in our weather? After last year, I find these of the most interest."

He'd known she'd had a penchant for rocks but had not realized the depth of her curiosity. It perplexed him. "Why are you so interested in all of this?"

She didn't turn around, her voice easy to hear in the cavernous space. "Why is Lady Dorothea interested in philosophy? Why is Lord Sommerset interested in art? Why are you interested in…?" She stopped again and faced him. "What *are* you interested in, Teddy?" For the first time since finding her, she frowned. "Can it truly only be carnal pleasure that makes your heart race?"

At her question, he stiffened. Perhaps he deserved it, but it was so far removed from his life now that he couldn't keep the disdain from his voice. "Hardly." What would she know of pleasure? Though he imagined she thought crawling around in caves was pleasure.

Her eyes widened and she opened her mouth before quickly closing it. Turning around, she continued forward in silence.

He was pleased about the quiet but not happy with her assumptions or the feelings that seemed to be roiling in his stomach like a storm at sea. His surprise and shock had quickly changed to anger and irritation, having not expected or wanted to see her. But that part of his heart that carried an ugly scar still yearned for old memories. However, they were just memories and nothing more. Part of his misspent youth. He had people in his life now far more important than the lovely, though rather dirty, Lady Elsbeth.

As the mouth of the cave came into view, relief filled him. He wished to put as much distance between himself and Lady Elsbeth as possible.

Finally, they stepped out into the sunlight, the warm rays directly overhead. He looked about but saw no one. "Where did you say your mother was?"

She pointed to the ledge he'd originally seen, but like then, there was nothing but plants on it. "She's up there. The path from Porto Cristo comes to the top. It's this way."

"Wait. Are you sure your mother is there?"

"Of course." She looked up toward the ledge. "Mother, I'm coming up."

"Elsbeth? Already?"

She gave him a frown before answering. "Yes, I found something quite astounding."

He raised his brows but didn't comment.

"This way." She headed up the path.

He remained where he was, having no interest in reacquainting himself with Lady Astor, who'd frowned on his pursuit of her daughter in the past. Instead, he listened to Lady Elsbeth ascending the slope until she stopped. He couldn't see her, but neither could she see him. When the movement continued, he was satisfied.

"You must show me what you found." As Lady Astor's voice carried through the bushes, he turned, satisfied that Lady Elsbeth was safe.

He strode toward the rock where he'd left Mateo and found the man sitting on the ground with his back against it.

"*Vamanos.*" He waved toward the way they'd come.

The man's eyes rounded. "So soon?"

"*Sí.*"

Mateo scrambled to his feet, excited. "You have the dragon teeth?"

"Bloody hell." He'd forgotten all about the dragon teeth. He shook his head. They'd have to come back. He wasn't staying in the vicinity with Lady Astor nearby. "We will return."

"*¿Mañana?*"

He waved the man forward. "*Sí, mañana.*" It was just as well. He needed to talk to the local people who might know exactly where in the caves he needed to look for dragon teeth. Señora Bello and Consuela were of little help. At least he'd found the Dragon Caves.

Señora Bello's words whispered through his mind. "*In the Dragon Caves, you must face your greatest fear before you can find the dragon teeth.*" His step faltered, a sense of foreboding filling him. Purposefully, he focused on the path's incline. He was English, not Spanish. He didn't believe in local myths and folktales. He believed that he needed the blasted dragon teeth to get his wet nurse to England.

And since he no longer had feelings for Lady Elsbeth, he certainly was not afraid of her.

CHAPTER THREE

ELSBETH PAUSED, LISTENING to the sounds of the cave. She'd been silly to think that Teddy would return. He had no interest in geology or caves or the magic of nature. His interests lay elsewhere. No doubt his arrival the day before was due to a dare of some sort.

Seeing him again had brought so many happy feelings to the fore. True, before he proposed, he'd become overly dramatic, maudlin, even telling her he couldn't live if she rejected him. But before she debuted for her season, he'd been fun, even interesting, and he treated her with far more respect for her intelligence than the other suitors she had after he left England.

He'd changed substantially since she'd last seen him, at least in appearance. He was definitely taller and broader, as if he'd trained as a pugilist, but she couldn't imagine him doing so. No doubt it was due to his nighttime activities with the ladies or the sprints he ran escaping angry husbands, if Joanna was to be believed.

Teddy had seemed more confident too. Even as they had stepped into the sunlight, she could see his face had tanned, his hair grown darker. Though his dark brows over his gray eyes were the same, there was a wisdom about life in those telling orbs that seemed to shine through his obvious annoyance. She could tell he'd been quite irritated because that straight nose of his had twitched. Obviously, he had not been as pleased to see her as she'd been to see him.

Though it might simply have been that she missed home more than she had anticipated. Enjoying the season with her fellow Curious Ladies had made her realize what an isolated life she'd led with her mother and cousin in Peterborough. She quite enjoyed having so many friends and sharing experiences. Since coming to Mallorca, she'd spent the evenings with her mother and the days alone in the caves. Having Teddy appear made her realize how much she missed her new life and the many people in it. Though she'd never admit it, she even missed her cousin James.

Scraping a tiny piece of calcite from the stalactite next to her, she added the slivers to a small packet marked with her identifier. Next, she needed to collect a drop of the water that had created it. Adding the packet to a small box, she rummaged in her box for her tiny containers, not larger than her thumb. Finding one, she wrote with her stub of a pencil, then held the container beneath the tip.

Patiently, she waited. In two days, she'd be leaving for England once again, which meant she would need to decide on which suitor to encourage, assuming any of them were still available. Her mother had received a letter from Viscount Rushing's mother, who mentioned that he missed her company. That surprised her, as he had been dancing attendance on a number of ladies besides herself. She was pleased he said so, as she quite enjoyed his company. Perhaps if she were the first to encourage him, he might be interested in marriage. He was heir to an earldom, which would be acceptable to her cousin James and her mother.

The problem with him was he would want heirs and after her biology class, she shuddered at the prospect of becoming pregnant. Though not part of the class, she'd done further research on how to avoid said condition. But whomever she married deserved an heir, so that wouldn't be fair. She'd prefer a widower with a son or two. That would be best and there was a lord who had lost his wife not a fortnight before she'd left, but it would be far too early for him to show interest in anyone, never mind marry by the end of the season. He was older, but she wouldn't mind that. For a lord to already have boys, he would have to be an older man, perhaps by ten years, but not a score. She shivered at the prospect of a truly older man.

Quickly, she checked her position below the point of the stalactite, not wanting to waver. It could take a very long time for a single drop to descend. She looked upward, but her lantern on the floor of the cave didn't produce enough light to reach the high ceiling. She'd thought Teddy the perfect age, being that he was five years older, ideal for a husband, but that had been before she'd learned all about childbirth. A man of his age would want heirs immediately. Besides, she'd already turned him down because he'd reverted to a petulant boy the closer she'd come to her debut. Now, it was quite clear he'd never consider asking her again. Not that she wanted him to.

A small bead of water flowed toward the tip of her stalactite, and she held her breath as it came closer to the end. Carefully, she kept her tiny container steady, watching the drop cling to the very end, elongate, and finally fall. A surge of joy flew through her as she immediately capped the container as if the drop wished to hop out. She'd missed far too many droplets in her fortnight in the caves to not be excited by a successful sample collected.

Sitting down next to her bag, she made a note on her piece of paper with the date on top. There were two more stalagmites she wanted to investigate and then tomorrow she would go back to a few anomalies she noticed in the last week. Nature was so well ordered, with many reasons for being so, that when there was an oddity, the reason for it could be pivotal. Though she often imagined herself speaking at the London Geological Society, she was not nearly enough of an expert.

Depositing her pencil and paper into her bag, she prepared to rise when the sound of footsteps came from the entrance. She was not far from there, but after Teddy's sudden appearance a day earlier, she did consider dousing her lantern. The footfalls halted, and she held her breath.

"Lady Elsbeth, are you in here?"

At the sound of Teddy's voice, she breathed a sigh of relief even as pleasure filled her. "I am if you have not come to lecture me. If you have, I am but a fairy you have imagined." She grinned. He had said his favorite play was *Twelfth Night*, which featured fairies in the primary roles.

A snort followed her comment, but nothing further as his footfalls drew closer. Quickly, she rose and shook out the skirts of her cornflower-blue day dress. At least she wasn't as dirty as she had been the day before. Teddy's lantern light filtered around the bend first as he made slow progress. Hopefully, he'd miss the stalagmite on his left that was the perfect height for tripping over.

"Hell and damnation!"

She smothered a laugh at his obvious collision with it from the sound of the curse and his sudden extra steps. He would no doubt be unable to appreciate her humor. While the day before's chance meeting had been awkward at best and she'd prattled on, which she never did, she'd been very much looking forward to seeing him again. His outward appearance had changed for the better. She was curious as to whether his outlook on life had changed as well. Of course, that didn't mean for the better. But his high-handedness and curtness had certainly been a significant change from the Teddy who'd been forever solicitous and accommodating.

He stepped around a large column with ease, once again casually dressed in a simple linen shirt, brown pantaloons, and black boots. He'd always been tall to her, but he was no longer thin. His broad shoulders and muscular thighs caused her pulse to race, though she'd never been one to make judgments upon a person's appearance. However, she couldn't ignore the fact that Lord Mabry had become quite attractive during his travels. Of course, that most likely meant any conquests he made had been quite easy for him. She found she didn't like thinking about that and instead focused on why he might have returned after his sudden departure the day before.

"There you are. I thought you stated you were working nearer to the entrance?" He strode closer until he was no more than a few feet away.

She grinned. "I am closer than I have been. Good afternoon." At her pointed reminder of the niceties of civilized life, he grimaced.

"Good afternoon, though it is a bit difficult to tell the time of day down here."

"That is an acceptable explanation."

He raised his right eyebrow. "Acceptable?"

She chuckled. "Very well, it is not as if we are in a parlor, and I can offer you tea." In actuality, it was highly improper that they were in the cave together, alone. Then again, they were like old friends. Though in truth, they were distantly related now that his older cousin had married her older cousin, though the connection was a bit too complicated to contemplate at the moment.

"It is just as well, as I'm not in the mood for tea. I have come to ask for your expertise."

Her breath hitched that he would need her knowledge. "Of course. I am happy to share what I know." She smiled, thrilled that he had come to her.

"Have you heard anything about dragon teeth?"

"Dragon teeth?" The question caught her unprepared. "I have heard about myths with dragons, and we are in the supposed Dragon Caves." She wasn't sure she would be able to help and disappointment overshadowed her excitement at his request.

His lips quirked upward on one side. "I'm not surprised. It is a legend of only those here in Mallorca. From what I understand, if one wishes upon a dragon tooth, the wish will be granted. My guess is that they are very rare and so the legend was spawned. That is why I'm here. To find dragon teeth. I'm told they can only be found in this cave."

At his explanation, she could understand. She had heard that some locals thought dragons used to live in the caves and refused to enter. She rested her hand on her hip. "So are you looking for the teeth of an animal who lives here? I have to admit, I have seen no evidence of any creatures. Not even bats." Encountering those flying mammals had been her fear upon her arrival.

Teddy shook his head before pulling a small, folded piece of paper from his fob pocket. He unfolded it. "I had thought so at first, but from what I've come to understand, they are not real teeth but some kind of rock." He handed her the paper.

A rock? She lifted her lantern to study the drawing and excitement filled her. "Are they yellow?"

He stepped closer, his particular earthy scent wafting over her. "Yes. Have you seen any?"

The memory of Teddy teaching her to waltz before she'd come out had her warming with pleasure.

"Lady Elsbeth?"

At his question, she refocused her gaze on the paper before looking up into his gray eyes, which seemed to glitter with eagerness. "I think I have."

"Show me." Though he didn't touch her, his gaze was so intense, it was as if he'd taken her by the shoulders and squeezed.

She pulled her head back. "I'm not absolutely sure what I saw is your dragon teeth, so I suggest a little patience."

He gave her a curt nod and didn't say a word.

Was he gritting his teeth? She found humor in his need to control himself but didn't prolong his anxiousness. Lifting her lantern from the floor of the cave, she turned away from him. "It was back this way, on the wall not far from Bashful." She started forward briskly.

"Another column?"

His question coming from behind her made her smile. "Yes. Near that column, I was studying a stalagmite when I noticed something odd in the wall of the cave behind it."

"What was it?"

"There were what appeared to be yellow spots. I didn't investigate at the time because I planned to return to the spot tomorrow." She turned her head to speak over her shoulder. "I do have a method I follow."

Because her head was turned, her foot hit a baby stalagmite and she lost her balance. "Oh!" Fear shot through her as she tried to catch herself.

Strong hands grasped her by her waist, pulling her back hard. One hand released and an arm anchored her around her middle. Air left her lungs in a *whoosh* as her back hit the hard breadth of Teddy's chest. In that moment her heart, already beating rapidly, seemed to stop altogether as the heat and solidness of his body permeated her dress, causing ripples of pleasure to flow through her. Breathless, she remained still, more overcome by his nearness than her near fall.

She tried to take a deep breath, but at the realization that one of her hands gripped his wrist and the other his thigh, she barely pulled any air into her lungs, tingles skittering over her bare skin. That minimal air filled her nostrils with his scent. Teddy hadn't affected her in such a way over a year ago. He'd even kissed her on the lips once or twice, which had been pleasant, but not like this.

Behind her, his chest expanded as he took a deep breath, letting it out slowly. "That was far too close." His voice came out in barely a whisper.

It appeared he was as rattled as she, especially as she felt his heartbeat against the back of her shoulder.

"You still wear lily of the valley." The whispered statement sent a breath of air past her ear, giving her goose-flesh.

She needed to extricate herself, but she felt so lightheaded, she daren't move.

"Lady Elsbeth?" He loosened his hold but didn't let her go, instead turning her to face him. "Are you well? You weren't hurt, were you?"

His gaze studied her, forcing her to say something. "I feel a bit faint."

He looked over her then bent his knees and scooped her into his arms.

The move was so unexpected, she grabbed him about the neck, not a little afraid of them both falling, but he showed no signs of weakening as he moved back up the path to where he'd left his lantern before grabbing her. How had he thought so quickly? Hers had gone out, rolling somewhere after she dropped it.

He sat her down on a flat surface, which was a rarity in the cave. "I want you to bend forward and lower your head to your knees."

She blinked at the odd request. "Why?"

"It will help to keep you from fainting."

She frowned. Could he be making fun of her? "How do you know that?"

He gave her a humble smile. "From experience. I've had to do it myself a couple of times since arriving on the Continent."

"A couple of times?" She arched her brows, not sure if he was teasing or truly meant he'd almost fainted. What would cause a man to feel like that?

"Come now." He placed his hand on the back of her head and gently pushed her forward. "All the way, so your head is between your knees."

She would have argued if she weren't so short of breath. Instead, she did as instructed.

His hand left the back of her head, but he didn't move. "You won't be surprised to know that I almost fainted after running a long distance, digging in the heat of the day, and once when a man was sliced open by a sword. Though in that case, I had the indecency to lose the contents of my stomach before almost fainting."

She swallowed at the picture he painted. "That's not helpful." Though she could put no real effort into her voice and spoke to the ground, he heard her, based on the sound of his chuckle.

"I suppose you're right. Just focus on breathing."

She agreed that would be for the best and counted each breath until they became longer and easier. Feeling better, she started to lift her head, but his hand came back.

"Do you feel more yourself?"

"I do. I want to sit up."

"Do so slowly or you'll feel lightheaded."

Since she had already felt like that, she lifted herself slowly, not in a hurry to repeat the experience. After sitting straight, she noticed she felt fine. "I apologize. I don't know why I felt so poorly. I'm sure if you hadn't caught me, I would have been in much worse circumstances. Thank you for your assistance."

He held his hand out to her, and she took it. "I'm glad I was with you. I do not treasure the thought of you lying in the depths of those caves with no one about to aid you."

She grimaced, recognizing that he had a legitimate point. "I hadn't thought about it until just now." She shrugged. "I guess it's just as well that tomorrow is my last day to explore. We leave for home the following day. Even now, our maid is packing." She looked about the lit area. "I know it may seem quite strange, but I will miss my days spent here."

He lifted his lantern and held his arm out for her to proceed him. "That would sound odd coming from anyone but you."

Since his tone wasn't sarcastic, she appreciated his sentiment. "We best get my lantern lit and see about your dragon teeth."

"Only if you feel well enough to continue."

"I do, but perhaps you can lead the way to my light. I do not wish to trip again." Though if she were honest with herself, being held in Teddy's arms had been far more exciting than anything else she'd done in her life. Even the crossing from England to Spain had been uneventful compared to that.

He gave her an abbreviated bow, which hardly fit their environment, and led the way. Now *that* was the old Teddy. He had often found humor in the smallest of things. Now he was far more serious. She couldn't help wondering if something had happened to cause such a change. Perhaps the gutting he mentioned. She shivered at the thought and was quite happy that he found her lantern and lit it.

"There you are. Now, shall we find the elusive dragon teeth?"

She smiled, pleased to be of help. "Yes, we shall." Or at least she hoped they did. Holding her lantern before her, she moved farther into the cave, watching the columns for the one she called Bashful. It was a bit farther back than she'd thought, but she recognized it at once. Lifting her hand, she pointed. "There it is. Bashful. We'll have to go slowly, as it's important we don't break any of the stalagmites."

"And why is that? They'll just grow back, won't they?"

She halted and turned to face him to speak. "Yes, but it will take thousands of years."

His eyes widened. "Are you telling me that this here"—he touched a stalagmite that came up to his waist—"is a thousand years old."

"No, that one is over *ten* thousand years old."

He studied the calcified rock. "I do not remember learning that at Oxford."

"If you didn't focus on geology, then you wouldn't have been exposed to such knowledge." She paused, hesitant to ask her question but unable to resist. "What was your focus at Oxford? You never said."

Though his lips didn't even twitch, his gray eyes, which appeared silver in the lantern light, twinkled. "I thought you knew. I focused on enjoyment."

Rolling her eyes, she waved off his response. "Yes, I should have known." Turning back, she continued toward Bashful and the stalactite nearby. When they reached it, she held her lantern closer to the wall. "It was here, down near the floor of the—there!"

Excited, she knelt holding the light so Teddy could see what she saw. "There are eight of them. Do you see them?"

He crouched down next to her. "I do. That's them. You

found them!" He looked at her. "I would have never found these. They're smaller than a farthing each." He pulled her against him in a one-armed-hug. "Thank you." The next moment, he'd set her back, removing his hands from her to touch the small, yellow rocks in the wall.

She stared at him, stunned, and flushed at his embrace. He'd obviously adopted some other country's way of expressing gratitude. She tried to ignore the warm tingles still fading from having her breasts crushed against his mounded chest. Obviously, he wasn't giving it a second thought.

"But how am I to extract these?" He rose, turning slowly around, as if looking for something to use.

She remained where she was, not ready to stand yet, trying to refocus her thoughts. When his lantern fell on the yellow rocks again, she pressed her two fingers over one, testing the earth around it. Rocks were steady, safe, unchanging. Focusing on them helped her find her equilibrium again. "We'll need tools. I have a small pick that will work well to take these out, but I didn't bring it with me today. As I said, I planned to look at these tomorrow." Her tone came out a bit more irritated than she'd wished, so she smiled up at him. "You didn't happen to bring any tools, did you?"

The old Teddy would have flushed with embarrassment, but that wasn't what he did. "As I did not expect to find the dragon teeth embedded in a wall, I failed to bring anything with me." He looked about once again as if thinking about what he could do. "I suppose tomorrow will be acceptable."

Suppose? This time, she didn't hold back her irritation. She was usually more patient with people, but for some reason, her emotions were playing with her intellect. "Then I *suppose* it's a happy circumstance that I have one more day here."

That got his attention. "I apologize." He offered his hand to her.

Taking it, she rose, but at the heat of his bare hand against hers, she quickly let go and brushed out her skirts.

Teddy ran his hand through his hair, an old habit of his that warmed her heart. "It has taken me so long to find these da— elusive dragon teeth that I forgot how much help you have been. I had hoped to sail for England by now, but I need one of these teeth in order to leave."

Pleased by his apology, she started back the way they had come, careful to watch her step, despite her curiosity. She waited until there was a spot where two people could stand abreast and paused there. "Is the captain of the ship requiring a dragon tooth in payment? If so, I can assure you that there are many others who will gladly take you on board without one. The captain of the *SeaSprite* didn't request such an item. In fact, before you arrived today, I didn't know the local people thought yellow calcite stones were dragon teeth."

He grimaced. "No, I haven't booked my passage as of yet. I promised Consuela a dragon tooth, so I must fulfill that before I can leave."

Consuela? No doubt another lover of his. Oddly disappointed and not a little irritated, she turned. "Then I guess Consuela will have to wait one more day." Without another word, she continued down the path until they came to her bag of samples. Anxious to continue her own work, she scooped up the bag and headed for the next stalagmite she wanted to study. When she reached it, she set her bag down and turned to point the way to the entrance.

Teddy was no longer behind her. She hadn't heard swearing, so he hadn't tripped. Studying the darkness, her heart squeezed. Where was his lantern light? In her pique, had she missed him falling? Quickly, she retraced her steps until she saw his light. Relief swept through her. Hurrying forward, she found him not far from the path she used, studying something on the cave floor. "Did you find more dragon teeth?"

He shook his head. "No, but I did find a miniature dragon. Look." He pointed to a spot directly in front of him.

Squeezing around him, she held up her lantern to see the

light reflected off a tiny insect. "Oh." She really didn't care for bugs at all and had been pleasantly surprised at how absent they were in the caves. "I didn't think anything lived down here. It's so dark."

"Nor did I, which is why I needed to investigate. I imagine since it's not a rock, you are less than curious about it."

His comment brought heat to her cheeks, not because it was true, but because *he* knew it to be so. She shrugged. "We all have our interests."

He studied her. "Yes, we do."

Not comfortable with his focused attention, she gestured toward the insect. "I'm sure someone more interested than I will study that creature. Now I best return to gathering my samples and I imagine you will want to tell Miss Consuela of your success."

She'd tried to keep her irritation out of her voice, but from the way he raised his right brow, she was sure she'd failed. Not wanting to know why she was irritated or anything more about the lovely Consuela, she turned on her heel and strode back to her work spot. They were close enough to the entrance that he would be able to find his own way outside.

Once back at her bag, she sunk down and started scraping at the second-to-last stalagmite she wished to study. Though she attempted to concentrate, she listened avidly for Teddy's approach. A few minutes went by and there was still no sound, so she gathered her shavings and then stood to collect water from the matching stalactite, the two formations no more than three feet away from forming a column. Of course, that would take another thousand years to accomplish.

As she waited for a drop of water, she continued to listen, finally hearing cautious footsteps approaching. Would Teddy be bringing Consuela back to England with him or was the dragon tooth a farewell gift? Suddenly, the realization that he would be returning during the season while she searched for a husband had her tensing and she missed the water droplet she hoped to capture. "Dash it all."

"Do you need help?"

As Teddy came into sight, she stiffened. "No. This requires a lot of patience, and I doubt you would find it enjoyable."

"You are perhaps correct. Though I'm more patient than I used to be, I'm not sure studying whatever it is you're bent on learning in here would be of immediate interest to me. But I do hope that you're successful today."

At his kind words, her irritation abated. "Thank you. I've almost finished for the day."

He gave her a short bow. "Then I shall leave you to your exploring and return to Cala Magrana to tell Consuela to start packing. I cannot verbalize how grateful I am that you were here. I shall see you on the morrow."

She bit down on the retort she was about to issue and gave him a smile.

As he left, she watched him, confused by her temper and disappointed that he couldn't stay, even knowing he wouldn't enjoy the cave as she did. None of it made sense. One moment, she felt a thrill at his presence and the next, she wanted to rail at him for wasting his life on women who meant nothing to him. Then again, if he was having the Señorita Consuela pack, he must be planning to bring her to England. The thought did not sit well with her, and she turned back in time to miss another water droplet. "Well, damn."

As TEDDY WALKED the path once again to the Dragon Caves, he found himself jubilant at the prospect of going home. That he had one more day to spend with Lady Elsbeth also contributed to it, probably because being with her reminded him of home. As he had told Señora Bello at dinner yesterday, he had indeed faced his greatest fear in reacquainting himself with Lady Elsbeth and had conquered it. In fact, it was the lady's sudden fall the day before that had confirmed for him his feelings. He hadn't realized it when he'd wooed her, but he was simply attracted to her, just as he'd been to a number of other women since. He had mistaken attraction for love and that was all. A year of life had definitely brought much knowledge.

He hadn't loved Marianna's mother, either, but when Francesca had begged him to marry her for the sake of his baby, he did so for honor's sake. He never expected her to die just a few weeks after Marianna was born. His loss at her death had been greater than he expected, but it had been overshadowed by his sheer terror in raising their daughter without her mother. If it hadn't been for Consuela and Señora Bello, Francesca's aunt, he would have made far more mistakes than his daughter could have survived. But he had learned, and now he felt confident in bringing Marianna home to meet everyone.

He left Mateo to settle against his rock for a siesta and entered the caves. He expected to see Lady Elsbeth scraping somewhere near the entrance, but there was no light once he entered. Maybe she was already busy extricating the dragon teeth. He didn't know where they were exactly, but he would see her lantern light. Confident in his sense of direction, he started down the path she always took between the spear-like formations. It truly did look like the mouth of a dragon or some other mythical creature with thousands of teeth. That may have been why it had been named so.

After going farther than where he'd found her the day before, he stopped to listen. There was no scraping or swearing to be heard. Had she fallen? Fear squeezed his heart, and he moved forward quickly, holding his lantern high, searching the hundreds of shadows for her. "Lady Elsbeth, are you here?"

He stopped to listen for a reply, but silence greeted him, emphasized by the faint sound of dripping water. Truly concerned now, he continued down, the decline gradual but no less treacherous. When he reached the place where she'd fallen, he halted again. "Lady Elsbeth!"

Had she been delayed in arriving? It was midday, just as it had been the last two times he found her hard at work. Shaking his head, he continued toward what he felt was the direction of the dragon teeth. His lantern shone on the column she called "Bashful" and he moved toward it faster, constantly checking for any signs that she was about or in distress.

Maneuvering around the stone feature, he found the stalactite she'd pointed out, but she was nowhere near. Moving forward, he lowered his lantern to shine on the wall and froze.

Where the yellow stones had been were only holes. The cave floor had no additional dirt crumbles below, as if the dragon teeth had been pulled out with no disturbance of the surrounding area. There was only one person who would do such precise work.

"Elsbeth." He gritted his teeth. She'd already come and gone.

Confusion and anger warred inside him as he turned about and headed for the cave entrance. Why would she have taken all the stones? If she'd needed to leave, she could have left at least one behind for him to find. Her actions didn't make sense.

As he exited the cave, he moved toward the incline she'd ascended the first day he'd seen her and found the path to be easily discernable. He half-expected to see Lady Elsbeth, Lady Astor, and their guide on top, but when he reached the area, which was quite obvious by the many footprints and patted-down plants, neither Lady Astor nor Lady Elsbeth were to be found.

Not happy, he strode back down to wake Mateo. He needed a dragon tooth, which meant he *had* to find Lady Elsbeth before she left the island on the morning tide.

Shaking his unsuspecting guide, he stepped back as Mateo jumped to his feet.

"*Dios mío, señor!* I thought you were a goat." Mateo grabbed his hat, which had fallen off and brushed it against his leg.

"A goat? Hardly. *Vamanos.*"

"Now?"

"Yes, now."

As his guide stepped around him to head back to Cala Magrana, where he lived, Teddy stopped him. "Not this way."

Mateo halted, clearly baffled. "*Señor?*"

Where did Elsbeth say she was staying or did she? She said the path led to… a port? Her words filtered back through his mind. *"The path from Porto Cristo comes to the top. It's this way."* Relief filled him. "Porto Cristo. I need to go there."

Mateo frowned then shrugged his shoulders. "Porto Cristo is in that direction." He pointed toward the area Lady Elsbeth had gone that first day.

"Sí, vamanos." He nodded to encourage the man, hoping he knew the way.

Mateo started walking toward the path to the top of the cave but muttered under his breath *"Los ingleses son extraños."*

If Mateo thought Englishmen were strange, he obviously had yet to meet many Englishwomen.

Once on top of the cave, they continued on, mostly downhill with wide, sweeping views of the port below every few hundred feet. He was surprised to find the caves so close to the town. He and Mateo could have ridden on horseback from Cala Magrana as far as they could and then walked in. Obviously, his guide preferred to appear more needed than perhaps he had been.

He wasn't about to question the man. He needed Mateo's help to find Lady Elsbeth. It shouldn't be difficult. He'd been to the town before and there was only one inn where an Englishwoman would feel comfortable.

Mateo led him to the inn, and he inquired for Lady Astor, Lady Elsbeth's mother. But no one from England was currently staying there. Walking back outside into the warm sunshine, he clenched his hands to fists in frustration. Where was she?

Taking in the view below him, his gaze landed on three ships in port. "That's it." Quickly, he started down the road, Mateo following him this time. She said they were leaving on the *SeaSprite*. All he had to do was find the ship's captain and ask where Lady Astor and Lady Elsbeth were lodging.

In very little time, he and Mateo were on the wharf, and he strode toward the ship farthest east, no doubt the next to depart. As he walked, he couldn't help noticing a young woman with a toddler on her hip standing next to a crate begging. Would that have been Francesca's and Marianna's fates if her letter hadn't reached him? True, Francesca had most likely been of higher standing than the beggar woman, but the thought still sent a chill up his spine.

Reaching the ship, he strode up on deck and waited as the captain sent a man to bring Lady Elsbeth above deck. Looking over the side, he motioned to Mateo, who pointed to a dockside pub. Nodding, he watched as his guide went inside. He hoped the pubs in this port weren't as dangerous as the ones along the Thames.

Even at the thought, a blurry memory of drinking in one of those very pubs came back to him. He'd gone there to drink himself into oblivion after Lady Elsbeth had turned down his proposal, not caring if he lived or not. He shook his head. No wonder she refused to be his wife. He'd hardly been in a stable state. He'd like to have blamed it on his friends, but he was the master of his own fate and he'd simply been too lazy to put forth any effort to truly look for a woman who would one day be the Marchioness of Wakefield. Since his uncle and father were both healthy, he had time now to find an appropriate woman.

"Lord Mabry?"

At the feminine voice behind him, he turned. "Lady Astor." Elsbeth's mother appeared no different than she had last he'd been in her company. Like her daughter when he'd known her back in England, Lady Astor was dressed impeccably, her paler-blonde hair pulled back neatly and her brown eyes as shrewd as always. Her face appeared a bit plumper, but it in no way took away from her mature beauty.

"It seems Elsbeth was correct. You have greatly changed in appearance." She gave him a kind smile.

He was not unaware of the fact that she mentioned his appearance only as if she doubted he could be much changed as a man. But as he no longer needed to impress her since he did not seek her daughter's hand, he felt a civil but pointed reply was in order. "And you have barely changed at all."

Her smile froze and she gave a truncated nod, a habit of all in the duke's family. "Why is it that you seek my daughter?"

It appeared, as he had expected, that she had not changed in her ever-vigilant protection of her daughter's reputation. She need not worry about him. "Your daughter has taken something of mine, and I wish to have it back."

"What?" Lady Astor's eyes widened. "That is a harsh accusation, my lord."

"Is she coming forthwith? I have other people waiting upon me."

The woman's brown gaze took on a calculating gleam, no doubt thinking he had another paramour he must satisfy. He didn't respond nor look away as they stood in silence.

"Lord Mabry. I did not expect to see you here." Lady Elsbeth's approach had him turning toward her.

"You took the dragon teeth."

She didn't look surprised at all. "Yes, I did."

He needed to keep his patience. He was not the man he used to be, not even for her. "Why?"

"I could no longer wait for your arrival. So I dug them out and brought them with me. You said you'd be in England soon, so I assumed you would simply call on me to retrieve one."

"Call on you?" He forced his irritation away. "I had not thought on that, as I need a dragon tooth for Consuela to get her to board a ship. I cannot attempt to return home with her unless I have one in my possession."

Her eyes narrowed. "I know you to be quite smitten with women, but it surprises me that you would allow a woman to control whether you return home or not."

"*She* is not a woman. She's an infant."

Lady Elsbeth blinked. "An infant? What infant?"

"The Lady Marianna, my infant daughter. She has need of Consuela, her wet nurse, in order to journey home. Said wet nurse will not board a ship without having a dragon tooth upon which to wish for a safe voyage. Hence, I need a dragon tooth for Consuela, so my daughter and I can return home." He bit back the next thought, which was that it was not for her to be concerned about why he needed the stone.

Lady Elsbeth's eyes rounded and her entire face turned a rosy red. "I'll...I'll get them for you." She spun on her heel and walked so briskly, she almost bumped into a seaman readying the ship.

"Congratulations." Lady Astor studied him as if she could read his life story in his face, but he'd learned over the last year that showing one's emotions at inconvenient times could cause unintended consequences.

"Thank you." Refusing to reveal any more, he waited.

It did not take Lady Elsbeth long to reemerge, her skin back to its usual pale color. She stopped before him and handed him a small bag. "Here are four. Since I didn't know they had value here in Mallorca, it is only fitting that you have half."

He took the bag from her gloved hand and opened it. Four yellow stones with white wisps through them were inside. He pulled the drawstring tight. "Thank you. I hope you both have a safe journey." Turning on his heel, he strode down the gangway, his anger over Lady Elsbeth's assumption overshadowing the pleasure of knowing he could now book passage on a ship bound for home. He started for the pub Mateo had entered then halted.

He could book passage home. Today.

The realization had him perusing the wharf for a shipping office. Seeing one, he strode toward it. He was almost there when swearing to his right caught his attention. At the scream that followed, he spun to find the young woman with the toddler on the ground covering her child with her body as a brawny seaman lifted a loose stave from a barrel to strike her.

"Stop!" He ran forward, his shout, whether understood or not, distracting the man.

The man turned toward him and took a menacing step forward before lowering the stave to point it toward the woman. "*¿Ella te peternece?*"

Did she belong to him? The question caught him off guard until he remembered that in his boots, pantaloons, and shirt only, he looked like a merchant. "*Sí, déjamela a mi.*"

The next string of words was said so quickly and angrily that he didn't quite grasp them. But he did understand enough that the woman had been in the man's way.

He pointed at the woman. "*Vamanos.*" He waved her toward him.

Hoping she would obey and not force him into fisticuffs with the burly seaman, he released his breath as she rose, lifting the child into her arms and walking toward him, her head down. As if he knew she would follow him, he continued toward the dock office but halted well before it to address her. Her dark hair was mirrored in the boy's, as were her dark-brown eyes, though she was much thinner than the chubby-cheeked child.

She stopped immediately and looked at him. "Thank you."

He raised his brows, not expecting his own language from someone who was obviously a native of the country. "You speak English."

"Some. Thank you. I not take your time."

"Wait." He ran his hand through his hair. He couldn't just let her go back to begging. Now he felt responsible for her. "Can you work?"

She nodded then shook her head, looking to her child, frowning. "Not in bed."

Of course she would think that. He too looked at her son, who held fear in his dark eyes. To be afraid so young made his stomach tense. "No. Wash and cook."

Her face relaxed. "*Sí,* very much."

Señora Bello had been bemoaning the loss of her second servant to marriage all week. "Do you know Cala Magrana?"

"*Sí.*"

"I have a friend, Señora Bello, who wishes for someone to help in her home."

The woman's face lit with excitement then just as quickly, she frowned and sighed. "My *hijo*. She will not take me."

Her son? She thought her son would keep her from a position? He had little knowledge of what it was like for servants in England, never mind in Spain, but he had learned that his daughter's great-aunt had a soft heart, especially for children. "You need not worry on that account. The *señora* will welcome you." He gave her a reassuring smile.

"True?"

He nodded. "*Sí*. Here." He had no way to write a note, so he rummaged in his fob pocket and pulled out his pocket watch, the only thing on him that Señora Bello would recognize. "Take this to Señora Bello in the village. Tell her Señor Mabry said to hire you."

"Señor Mabry." The woman pronounced his name with an accent, but it was clear. "I go now. Thank you, Señor Mabry." With that, she headed for the end of the wharf, her stride confident despite the little boy waving to him from over her shoulder.

He'd probably arrive before she did, as it would take her at least an hour. If he could get passage booked and Mateo from the pub to find them a cart or horses, they would be there long before she was.

Continuing to the office, he stopped just before entering to survey the three ships and take note of the names of the other two. Glancing at the *SeaSprite*, he noticed two familiar ladies standing at the railing talking to each other. The last ship he wanted to be on was that one.

Once making his wishes known, he was shown into the Capitán de Puerto's office. It didn't take long to discover his choices were few, actually two. He could leave on the *SeaSprite* with the morrow's morning tide or wait two months. If he waited, Marianna would be six months old by time they set foot on English soil. Though he'd learned patience while on the Continent, he did not relish remaining for two more months. With no other choice, he booked the last available cabin of the four passenger cabins for Consuela and Marianna and consented to sharing one with a Mr. Silverton.

Exiting the offices, he knew Consuela would be angry with him for causing them to have to leave so abruptly, but he had her dragon tooth in hand. If he must, he'd bribe her with two. She'd been packing for the last two days, so it shouldn't take long to load what they had and transport it to the ship. Looking up at the *SeaSprite*, he was pleased to see that Lady Astor and Lady Elsbeth had returned to their cabin. If he was lucky, that was where they would stay.

Striding toward the pub to find Mateo, he determined that even if the women took air during the day, he could easily avoid them by going on deck at night. The trip would be about two weeks, depending on the weather. It was certainly a sacrifice he could make for Marianna.

Even as he thought of his daughter grasping his finger in her hand, his mood lightened.

They were going home.

CHAPTER FOUR

ELSBETH STOOD AT the railing with her mother watching Porto Cristo become smaller and smaller. She came to Mallorca to study the Dragon Caves, a dream she'd had for years. She should feel content or at the very least pleased with her accomplishment, but instead, she felt unsettled.

Though all her samples were carefully packed for the journey back to England, she wasn't pleased with how she acted her final day in Spain. She had been spiteful toward Teddy and for no reason. She'd never been so with anyone, but to have done so with him was inexcusable. It only made it worse that her motives had been poor at best and based on incorrect assumptions.

Her breath hitched as once again, she remembered his look as he told her he needed the dragon teeth for his daughter. Lord Theodore Mabry had a daughter. Even though she repeated that information to herself at least hourly, she still had difficulty accepting it. That meant he had a wife, and it was that which had kept her up most of the night before sailing.

Teddy was married and had started a family. The shock wouldn't go away, and her emotions were thoroughly jumbled. Part of her was happy for him, but she also couldn't help thinking that for him to have married so soon after leaving England meant that he really hadn't loved her. She had cared very much for him, but his melodramatic behavior had extinguished that feeling by the time he'd asked her to marry him. It had been the right decision, so why was she hurt he had found someone else? Could she be jealous that he had when she hadn't?

She shook her head even as a seabird swooped past riding the air currents. What truly baffled her was her own behavior on learning he wanted the dragon tooth for Consuela. She hadn't known she could be jealous of another woman, but she had been. She'd even left for the Dragon Caves early so she could take all the dragon teeth with her. To discover the woman was a wet nurse for his daughter just made her more disappointed in herself. She hoped she could come to some kind of understanding before she saw him again in England…with his wife.

"Elsbeth, now that you have accomplished your dream, will you plan a visit to another faraway geological site to explore?" Her mother looked at her hopefully. "Have you thought about what your next studious foray will be?"

She had, but that had all changed. Though her mother was in no hurry for her to marry, the Curious Ladies were counting on her. "I have had many ideas, but I thought perhaps I should start looking for a husband who would be willing to travel." She laid her hand on her mother's arm. "I can't keep forcing you to accompany me on my various expeditions."

"A husband?" Her mother's eyes widened. "Truly, I enjoy the adventure. No need for a husband on my account. I had not thought you ready for that step yet. I mean, after what happened with Lord Mabry." Her mother didn't continue, no doubt knowing how difficult it had been.

"To be honest, it is a relatively new idea. It could well take years to find a man willing to travel and indulge my odd interests." She held her breath, hoping her mother would reassure her there were plenty of men who would fit her requirements, maybe even suggest someone.

"Well, this is quite a development. You are smart to begin looking now, as it may take time to find such a lord." Her mother turned her head to look out at the shrinking sight of Porto Cristo.

"I had hoped you would continue your studies for a couple more years, but since I'm sure it will take that long to find the right man, I can be content that you can continue to thrive."

Though disappointed that her mother hadn't suggested someone immediately, she did wonder at her completely opposite goals. Most mothers were anxious to marry their daughters in a good match. She was grateful, of course, but now she wished her parent a bit more forthcoming with possible suitors.

Her mother turned, a smirk on her face. "At least we don't need to feel awkward around Lord Mabry when he returns to London. I had worried about that and the strain it might put on the duchess and ourselves, but since he's married and has a daughter, I feel all will be well." Her mother's smile disappeared. "I do wonder, though, what all that fuss was on the wharf yesterday. Do you think he knew that woman?"

She shrugged, having no particular insight. What appeared to have happened was the woman had been about to be harmed and Teddy stepped in. That wasn't the Teddy she had known. The Teddy she'd known in London had thrown a single coin among a dozen urchins to get them to leave his group alone. Had he helped the woman to be kind or because he had a relationship with her? It was difficult to tell from on board the ship, and she certainly wouldn't ask him when next she saw him…with his wife.

"Whatever it was about, at least the poor woman and her child were spared." Her mother leaned in to whisper. "I am quite glad this is an English ship, and the men here seem to respect Captain Gentry."

She silently agreed. The seamen onboard seemed well-behaved, but she would still obey the captain's orders that they not venture out at night. He said the men needed time at night to engage in their own activities. The good captain had obviously not wanted her or her mother to know what those activities were, and she was happy to remain ignorant.

At the sound of someone emptying the contents of their stomach on the other side of the ship, her mother grabbed her arm and held tightly. Neither of them suffered from seasickness, but her mother tended to become sick if someone else was.

Her mother's welfare took precedence.

"Would you like to go inside?"

"No." Her mother swallowed hard. "Maybe we could move farther down toward the stern."

Happy to stay in the sunshine, she gave a short nod, and they moved in that direction.

A voice floated across the deck on the breeze. "Here, wipe your mouth. Now keep your gaze on the horizon."

She grabbed on to the railing at the sound. It couldn't be.

Her mother continued along, oblivious to everything but getting away from the noises of the sick man.

She turned to look back and across the deck, but a mast was in her way. Slowly, she continued after her mother, farther along the railing, until she could see two men standing on the starboard side. One was shorter and larger, the other was tall, broad-shouldered, and most definitely Teddy!

Panic stole her breath for a moment before her mind came to her rescue. She had no reason to fear Teddy. They were friends. She could simply apologize if he should be so uncouth as to bring up her poor behavior. Of course, she didn't treasure the idea of meeting his wife...simply because it was such small quarters. With only four passenger cabins, one being used by the captain's brother and his wife, it would mean they would converse more often than not.

"I think this is far enough." Her mother halted but kept her gaze on the sea. "The weather is so pleasant and the seas gentle right now. It's hard to believe that in a couple days' time, we will once again be through the Strait of Gibraltar. I wonder if it will be easier sailing eastward through them?"

"I don't know, but it's best that we stay in our cabin this time." On their trip to Mallorca, while going through the straits, her mother's skirts had flown up to cover her face, causing her to lose her balance and she'd almost toppled overboard. By chance, Captain Gentry had been on deck shouting orders to his men about the sails and had seen her mother's predicament. He'd quickly assisted her before escorting them both off the deck with strict orders for them to stay in their cabin.

Their experiences on board were to be treasured, both the good and the bad, as they provided knowledge, or so Joanna was fond of saying. She glanced back toward where Teddy was but found the railing empty. "I do believe I saw Lord Mabry on board."

"Where?" Her mother looked about, but except for seamen, there were no other passengers in their immediate vicinity.

She waved, as if it mattered little, when she truly felt it mattered quite a bit. "Oh, he was helping that sick passenger. I imagine they have both gone inside."

"If it is Lord Mabry, that will make this voyage much more pleasant. I'm anxious to meet his wife."

She studied her mother. No, it wasn't Teddy's wife her mother looked forward to seeing. "Mother, why are you truly pleased that Lord Mabry may be on board?"

Her mother turned back to the sea. "I have a feeling that marriage has changed him. I'm very curious if it is for the better or the worse."

In other words, her mother planned to study Teddy and most likely take notes on his character. What had started as a fun pastime for her and her mother, to discuss the various people with whom they'd interacted after every outing, had become a bit more. Her mother had begun drawing up charts and had enough to constitute a full book. Unfortunately, she tended to focus on the negative aspects of each person, which had become rather tedious. In fact, every eligible bachelor in London had quite a few negative comments in their entries. It made her wonder, not for the first time, what kind of man her father had been to have passed her mother's high standards.

She opened her mouth to ask when movement to her left caught her eye. Teddy appeared next to her.

"Lady Astor. Lady Elsbeth. I see you are enjoying the pleasant weather."

Since his tone was polite, even if he didn't smile, she replied in kind. "We are. It seems the weather in Spain is always so pleasant compared to our seasons at home."

Since she had turned at his approach, her mother stepped around to flank her. "It is quite a surprise to see you on board, Lord Mabry. How lovely that we will have your company on our return journey."

Teddy, who wore his shirt buttoned, a white cravat, and a deep-blue waistcoat above his tan pantaloons, appeared much more formal than he had while on the island. He raised his right eyebrow. "Indeed. I will be sure to introduce you to Mr. Silverton as well so that you may enjoy his company."

Though he was polite, her instinct told her he hadn't forgiven her for her assumptions the day before. The fact that he mentioned they would enjoy Mr. Silverton's company insinuated that they wouldn't enjoy his. But before she could add that she was also pleased he was aboard, her mother responded.

"Tell us, my lord, is your wife about yet? I would so enjoy meeting her."

An odd look passed over his face that she didn't understand. That in and of itself, after knowing him in the past, made her feel that even now he was more stranger than an old friend.

"It is good of you to ask after my wife. Unfortunately, she is not with me." He paused, as if not sure how to continue. "She has gone the way of my own mother and your husband."

Her heart ached, suddenly understanding his facial features. "I'm so very sorry that she is no longer with you and your daughter." Her eyes itched with unshed tears, knowing how Teddy reacted to loss. He had to have been heartbroken. No wonder he'd been anxious to find the dragon teeth and bring his daughter home. It proved her to be even more a fool. How could she have behaved so, as she had with the dragon teeth? Though she'd been just a toddler when her father died in a carriage accident, she always had images of him to cling to. Teddy's daughter wouldn't even have that of her mother. How awful for him to have lost his wife so soon.

Her mother clicked her tongue. "That truly saddens me. I imagine it was childbirth?"

An icy shiver ran up her spine despite the warmth of the day. She'd read much about childbirth at school and feared it for that very reason.

"Not specifically. The physician said it was a fever she contracted in her weakened state. She simply had no time to recover her health." He looked over their heads, as if he could see his wife behind them. "I am sorry that she will not see Marianna grow to be as beautiful as she was."

She swallowed the lump in her throat, aching to reach out and comfort him but knowing it would not be proper. Instead, she blinked back her tears. "When Lady Marianna is old enough, you can tell her all about her mother." She looked at her own mother, thankful once again that she had her. "Though I had a few memories of my father, Mother told me more as I grew old enough."

Teddy's gaze came to rest on her. "I will. My father didn't need to tell me about my mother, as I was nine years old when she left us, and I remembered everything about her."

His reminder that he'd lost his mother, something she had momentarily forgotten, just made her want to cry more. "Memories are our only comfort, then."

"I have something more, my daughter." The way he said it, with so much pride and pleasure, made her heart ease.

"The duchess will be thrilled." Her mother's smile was genuine, as it always was when discussing Teddy's cousin Joanna. "Have you written her to let her know?"

"I have not. I thought it best to surprise everyone."

Her mother's eyebrows rose. "Oh, my. That *will* be a surprise. Last we had heard, you were still traveling and enjoying all that the Continent offered."

She forced herself not to react to her mother's veiled suggestion that Teddy had been wasting his year on pleasures when there was so much such travel could do for one's character, a complaint they'd heard many a time when the duchess had shared the latest news of him.

"It would be remiss of me not to experience the many cultures here, and so I have. However, now it's time to return home. I did not wish to wait another two months for the next ship to leave for England. If not for your daughter's help in finding the dragon teeth, I would still be searching."

Heat filled her cheeks. "I do apologize for taking them all. I didn't understand that you truly needed them to leave. I must assume since you're on board that Consuela was happy with the teeth?"

For the first time since approaching them, he gave her a true smile, the mischievous one he used to give. "I only gave her the one she requested. I've hidden away the others in case we need to make port for an unexpected reason, and I must coax her on board again with another."

She returned his smile, pleased that he seemed to have forgiven her. "That is a fine strategy. If you find you need more during sailing, I would be pleased to be of assistance."

"I appreciate the offer."

Feeling more comfortable, she opened her mouth to ask about his plans once home when something hit her on the shoulder. "Ow." Looking upward, she could see nothing but a seaman high in the rigging.

Teddy bent and retrieved an item from the deck. He held it out on his hand. "I believe this is what struck you."

She took the small object from him. "It's a rock." She examined it more carefully. "Actually, I believe it's a piece of granite. I'm not aware of a bird species that carry stones out to sea, but I admit I haven't studied ornithology like one of my other classmates has." She looked up to see if any birds continued to keep them company this far from shore. But there were none.

However, the seaman she noticed above was descending the rigging quite rapidly. Maybe something was amiss, and the rock was part of a piece of the ship, though how it could be, she couldn't fathom. The only purpose for rock on a ship that she was aware of was the ballast and from what the captain had said at dinner the evening before, they were loaded with cargo, so very little had been needed. Besides, ballast was used in the hull, not topside.

The seaman jumped down and started looking about frantically. It wasn't difficult to surmise he was searching for the rock. "Are you looking for this?" She held the stone out on the palm of her hand, its color and shape easy to distinguish against her white glove.

The man swept off his cap and held it in his two hands. "Yes, my lady. Mighten' I have it back?"

Her mother frowned at the man. "That rock hit my daughter. It could have severely hurt her."

She appreciated her mother's protective instinct most of the time, but right now, it was far from needed. "Truly, Mother? I doubt this could have done much damage. At the very most, if dropped from the height of the crow's nest and picking up speed as it descended, hitting me in a very particular spot on my head would have caused me to faint. I do not think this man aimed it at me."

The man, not taller than her, but much bulkier in muscle, shook his head. "I didn't drop it, my lady. It fell from me chain." He reached up with his pudgy hand to completely encircle something on a heavy and tarnished silver chain about his neck.

"You had this on you, then?" She continued to hold the stone out, but the man did not approach.

"I did, m'lady. Me son gave it to me when I left him and told me it would keep me safe."

Another stone that had magical powers? "How old is your

son?"

"He be five. A strapping young lad. Smart too." He pointed at her hand. "He found that there rock and brought it to the vicar to be blessed then said an ancient spell over it for good measure." The man beamed as he talked about his son, his eyes almost disappearing in his cheeks as he smiled, and her heart melted.

Closing her hand over the stone, she held out her other hand. "As it occurs, I am an expert with rocks, and I can see this one is very special. If you would like to give me your chain, I can see about affixing your rock back into it."

The man lost his smile, and his hands began to worry his cap. "I dinna know. I needs to take over the watch." He glanced upward, making it clear it was his turn to sit in the crow's nest.

Teddy held his hand out for the rock. "Then you had best have it with you until you are done. After your watch, you may find me, and I will be sure that Lady Elsbeth receives it so she can make the needed repairs."

She dropped the granite in Teddy's hand, but she could see the man was still nervous. "What is your name?"

"I'm Wiley Dodd, m'lady."

"Then, Mr. Dodd, I will be sure to have the stone repaired in time for your next watch above." She smiled confidently, happy to have a project for an afternoon at least.

The man's face lit with a grin. "That would be mighty good of you, m'lady." His smile disappeared. "I don't have no money to pay you until I get me portion."

"Pay?" Her mother frowned. "Absolutely not. My daughter is of the highest peerage. She will do it as a kindness or not at all."

The man had frozen at her mother's strident tone and quickly looked to Teddy. When Teddy nodded, the man finally moved his head to look at her. "I'd be most honored for you to fix it."

She clapped her gloved hands together. "Lovely. I'll be sure to have your lucky stone back to you in no time."

Finally, seemingly satisfied with the arrangements, Wiley Dodd took the rock from Teddy and stuffed it in a pocket in his breeches. "I'd best be aloft before me mate tells the captain I be dawdling." With that pronouncement, he turned and started up the ropes like a crab scurrying across the sand.

She turned her head to address Teddy. "Dawdling?"

He grinned. "Yes, it's another word for 'dallying.' I've heard it used along the docks before." His right eyebrow lifted. "Can you indeed fix the man's chain in an evening?"

"I'm fairly sure, though I was unable to see where it broke. I have many tools in our cabin, so I will do my best. If I can't complete it, I'll return it as it is, and he'll be no worse off than he is now."

"That's very generous of you."

She shrugged, not entirely comfortable under his close scrutiny. "It will give me something different to do. There are only so many books one can read on a voyage of this length."

He widened his eyes. "Don't let my cousin Joanna hear you say that."

She smirked. "Nor my cousin James. I certainly wouldn't let on that such a phrase ever passed my lips."

He straightened his shoulders and placed his hand over his heart. "And I pledge never to repeat that you uttered such nonsense."

She chuckled, happy that they were in accord again and not simply about what she'd said.

"Well, I make so such pledge to keep James and Joanna from knowing what you have said about books."

At her mother's words, she frowned.

"Lady Astor, will you not keep such an important secret?" That Teddy treated the silly words so seriously had her stifling a chuckle.

Her mother's eyes suddenly lit with triumph, as if she'd orchestrated the entire conversation, something she could well see her mother managing.

"I suppose I can be persuaded if you would agree to escort us on our evening walks about the deck. We do so enjoy sunsets at sea."

Elsbeth wasn't sure how she knew, but the moment her mother stopped speaking, Teddy's mood shifted.

"As much as I would enjoy making such a promise, I cannot. My daughter has yet to accommodate her schedule to mine, and so I must cater to her whims a bit longer."

Hearing his reasoning, she felt her throat close. He would be a wonderful father. His daughter had no idea how fortunate she was.

Her mother, however, was taken aback. "I thought you have a wet nurse."

"I do." He stiffened, seeming to grow an inch taller in the process. "But I am Marianna's parent, and her only parent. I intend to raise her as my cousins were raised, with a parent who is a part of her life from the day she is born, not only when she is old enough to be groomed for the marriage mart."

Feeling the tension between the two, Elsbeth quickly stepped in. "Wouldn't it be wonderful if Lady Marianna could attend the duchess' school? She would so enjoy it. I know I have. It is far more than a school. It's like having a large family, with many, many sisters." She raised her brows just thinking about all the women she could call friends now.

Teddy's shoulders relaxed. "I hadn't thought that far into the future, but that is something I will consider. It could be quite lonely for a little girl in a house with just her father for company."

Wanting to lighten his worry over his daughter, she quickly shared news he may not have received yet. "To that point, we did hear that Lady Beaumont—no, I should say *Lady Blackmore* is due to have a child in the new year."

"She is?" Teddy's smile was pure joy. "Then Marianna will have a cousin to play with. This is excellent news!" He stepped forward, as if he would hug her but recalled himself in time. "Thank you for sharing that. Do you know if Joanna or Amelia are in the family way as well?"

Her mother shook her head. "No. Only Lady Blackmore. We

are all so happy for them."

Teddy's smile softened. "Yes, Mariel deserves the family she always wanted. When I first heard Blackmore had turned up, I had hoped, but it wasn't until Joanna's last letter about their wedding that I could finally be content for her."

She'd always known the Mabry family was close, but seeing the happiness shining in Teddy's eyes, she felt a wistfulness come over her. As an only child with a much older male cousin, she'd always felt like a child among adults. It hadn't been until the Curious Ladies that she truly felt a part of something larger. And to that end, she would need to show her appreciation by fulfilling her promise. How odd that the school had given her friends a place of growth while for her, it had given her a family.

Teddy pulled out his pocket watch and checked the time. "I must take my leave of you, ladies, and check on my ill cabinmate, before I see if my daughter is awake. I trust I will see you at dinner?"

"You can be assured of that." Her mother gave an elegant nod and Teddy turned toward the cabins, his long-legged stride taking him out of sight beyond the mast in little time.

She swallowed a sigh. Teddy seemed to have kept his good qualities, discharged his poor ones, and grown much in his year away. She couldn't help wondering if it would have been so if she'd accepted his proposal. Even as the question formed in her mind, the answer was clear. No. Teddy was who he was because he'd run away to the Continent and as much as she didn't like how he'd spent much of his time, it had changed him for the better. Had she contributed to his poor character when first they had met? She definitely didn't like the answer that came to mind.

CHAPTER FIVE

TEDDY SAT IN his daughter's cabin, holding the sleeping bundle in his arms. She was so small, and so dependent upon him, that sometimes he didn't think himself worthy of the responsibility. Then there were times, like now, when he knew a love so strong that he felt he could fly like a bird if she needed him to.

Her curly, black hair framed her chubby face, and one little hand lay on her tummy, while the other held his finger even in her sleep. If her eyelids opened, he would be spellbound by her pretty, blue gaze. Señora Bello had warned him Marianna's eyes would probably change to dark brown like her mother's, but he liked to think that she would have her own color.

Though it was purely selfish, he was elated that Mariel had conceived. He wanted his daughter to know the warmth and love of all the Mabrys, and to have a cousin close to her age would make her feel like part of the family. He was well aware that he must marry again and produce an heir, but for now, he wished to enjoy his growing relationship with his daughter. Even at only three months old, her eyes lit with happiness when he walked into a room, and he couldn't wait for her to begin walking and talking and to share everything she learned. Yes, it was highly improper, and he didn't care. If Lord and Lady Wakefield could raise the Mabry ladies the way they had, he could raise his daughter the way he wished.

The light from the tiny porthole window cast a rosy hue, bathing Marianna in its soft light. Sunset. If he so wished, he could go out upon the deck and walk with Lady Astor and Lady Elsbeth. Though such an excursion was tempting, he'd spoken true when he'd stated his daughter's schedule was his own. This was where he wished to be. He had been keenly aware that Lady Elsbeth's face had changed the moment he explained he must dance attendance on his daughter, and it had looked as if Lady Elsbeth would cry. He found her reaction odd and still wasn't sure what it meant. Did she wish to have a child of her own? Had she been sad because he would not attend upon her?

Even at that thought, he shook his head. She'd rejected him. Still, he was happy for her company. In retrospect, discovering her in the Dragon Caves had been quite beneficial. Not only had he obtained the dragon teeth, but they had come to what appeared to be a warm friendship. He just needed to guard his heart. Despite his momentary anger with her, he was not so immune to her as to be unaware of how she had blossomed in the last fourteen months. She had always had a quiet confidence about her, but the Lady Elsbeth he'd held in his arms as he taught her to dance had been far more slender and wraith-like. Now, her curvy stature would cause any man to take a second look, and he had, more than once. But he needed to ignore her beauty and simply think of her as an old friend.

The door to the cabin opened and Consuela stepped in. She didn't need to duck through the door like he did because she was fairly short. The dark-haired woman was very curvy, and he was quite sure Marianna enjoyed her cuddles.

Before he could release his hand from his daughter's grasp to signal her to be quiet, the woman spoke. "*Ay, de mio. El cocinero no entiende lo que necesito.*" Her frown turned sly in an instant. "*Pero tiene muchos músculos y un buen mentón.*"

How the woman could complain about the cook in one sentence and admire his physique, and if he wasn't mistaken, the man's chin in the next, was far beyond him. Unfortunately, her loud voice also had his daughter complaining as she began to wail. Lifting Marianna up beneath her arms, he held her on his lap and smiled. "What is it, Marianna? Were you enjoying your nap?"

Her eyes grew wide as she stared at him, her little lip quivering, her tiny brows lowered in concentration.

"Would you like me to sing you to sleep again?"

Her hands flailed before she let out an earsplitting sound.

He winced as he sat her on his lap again.

"*Ella tiene hambre. Dámela.*" Consuela didn't wait for him to agree, convinced Marianna was hungry. She wrapped her hands around his daughter and pulled her onto her lap. "*Anda tu.*"

Though he had been adamant at learning to fulfill his daughter's needs, from changing her to playing with her to rocking her to sleep, there was one need he couldn't fulfill. Grudgingly, he rose and left the small cabin so his daughter could nurse. When had he become so possessive that he resented her needing anyone but him? Was that a good trait? He definitely needed to return home and seek his aunt's counsel.

As he walked through the open area between the cabins where they would all have dinner with the captain, men set about laying the plates down. It was not nearly as formal on board a ship as in a peer's dining room, but a merchant ship like this one that often catered to aristocratic passengers as well as others of means, tried to keep things as civilized as possible.

He grimaced as he remembered his crossing from France to Portugal. He'd had a rather angry husband on his heels and had bought passage under a different name, claiming to be a fellow merchant. He'd been fortunate in that the husband didn't catch up to him in time and that the captain of the merchant vessel accepted his ignorance about trade. He smirked. Of course, being tutored by a seasoned captain meant that he not only learned much about being a merchant but had been taught more than he had ever claimed to want to know about a ship.

Stepping out onto the deck, his gaze immediately alighted on

Lady Elsbeth dressed in a lilac dress and white bonnet. At first, she appeared to be alone, which immediately had him checking the area for seamen or other passengers. There were very few women on board, and they had only the captain's command to protect them. Starting toward her, he soon discovered that Lady Astor was not so far away and in deep conversation with that very captain.

Happy to play escort, he halted by Lady Elsbeth's side, just as she turned toward him.

"Lord Mabry." She smiled, her pleasure at seeing him obvious. "I wasn't sure if Lady Marianna would allow you to enjoy the lovely sunset."

Still not happy that his daughter needed Consuela, he shrugged. "It appears that I am neither wanted nor needed when my daughter is hungry."

She covered her mouth, hiding a chuckle, but he was well aware of her humor.

"Wait until you have a child." He'd thought to continue, but at how pale Lady Elsbeth's face suddenly turned, he stopped. "Are you ill?"

She shook her head but did open her fan and apply it. "I apologize. I fear I have learned far too much about childbirth to think upon it as anything but torture."

He opened his mouth to argue the point, but at the memory of Francesca's screams the night Marianna was born, he closed it. He could not in good faith refute her fear. Francesca had been exhausted for days and never regained her strength, which the physician had said was why she succumbed to an illness so quickly. Placating Lady Elsbeth wouldn't be successful, anyway. She was far too intelligent and well-read to be dissuaded from her views.

Curious about how her knowledge affected her future plans, instead he asked what to him was a critical question. "Do you then not wish to be a mother?" That would definitely hamper her marriage prospects.

She closed her fan but met his gaze. "I do. I would love to have children. I think I simply need a few years to overcome my fear, find an excellent midwife, and read more about how to mitigate the pain and the odds of dying."

His chest tightened at the thought of her dying like Francesca. The feeling was far stronger than the potential loss of a friend, and he silently cursed. Still, he needed to both allay some of her fear and his own. "I'm sure my cousin Joanna would also be happy to assist. From her letters, I understand she saved Lord Blackmore's friend."

As if she were as relieved as he to leave the other subject behind, she gave him a pleasing smile at the change in subject. "Oh, yes, she did. Mr. Taylour had lost vast amounts of blood, and she refused leeches." She sighed, clearly in awe of his cousin. "Joanna is truly the most learned woman I know."

"Is she quite involved in the lessons at the Belinda School for Curious Ladies, then?" He couldn't imagine Joanna being any other way, but it was clear that Lady Elsbeth thoroughly enjoyed the school. It was also typical of Joanna to name the school after her late sister Belinda, the angel of the family.

"Joanna involved? Yes. But she doesn't teach everything. She has hired some wonderful teachers in addition to herself, James, and my mother. Do you know we've even had classes in estate management and physical defense?"

He grinned, a warm feeling of home filling him. Only Joanna would think of such subjects. "Surely, there is also embroidery, letter writing, and practicing the pianoforte." He held a serious face as her eyes rounded.

"Absolutely not. It is not a finishing school. It is a school for the mind. To allow us to exercise our own intelligence before we... You're teasing."

He chuckled. "Yes, I am. Remember, I grew up with the duchess. I know her well."

"I do believe the only criticism I would level at the school is there is no dancing."

He raised his right brow. "Do you mean, you've had no chance to teach anyone how to waltz?"

Her gaze turned soft. "No one has floated me across the floor like you did."

For a moment, he was lost in her blue gaze as memories of them twirling around her cousin's ballroom filled him with warmth.

She blinked then grimaced. "I admit to attempting to teach Dory how to waltz when a renowned dance instructor refused, but I couldn't seem to explain the tempo correctly."

A spike of jealousy ran up his spine. "'Dory'?" Was this her latest beau?

"Actually, her name is Lady Dorothea Ansley. She's very intelligent, but she thinks too much. She kept trying to make the waltz a four-beat dance." She touched his arm with her gloved hand. "Truly, it was an awful sight, and we must never speak of it within her hearing."

He tried to resist the warmth of her personality, but nothing his mind did kept his heart from racing at her touch. He needed to keep his distance. She was his Achilles' heel.

"Lord Mabry, I see you were able to join us for this evening's sunset." Lady Astor approached him on the arm of their bearded captain.

"Indeed. I may not always be able to, but I certainly find it a most pleasing view."

"If you all will excuse me." The captain inclined his head. "I have a few duties to attend to before dinner. My lord. Ladies." He made a quick exit.

No doubt, the inquisitive Lady Astor had beleaguered the man with a hundred questions from how the rigging was set to who his ancestors were.

"What a lovely man." Lady Astor watched the captain until he disappeared below. "He is far more knowledgeable than I expected."

"Mother." Lady Elsbeth's critical tone caught his attention.

"*Anyone* who knows more than their particular trade is more knowledgeable than you expect. But most people need to know a variety of subjects in order to go about their daily lives. Unlike we two, who simply indulge in learning as a pastime with no real use for it."

"Elsbeth. Why so cynical?"

Her mother's question was on the tip of his tongue.

Lady Elsbeth shrugged. "Just an observation." She suddenly pointed. "Look. The sun is about to sink beneath the waters."

Her mother was quickly distracted and moved to the side of the ship, but he remained studying Lady Elsbeth. There had been almost an envy in her tone as she spoke of those who worked to survive and a clear bitterness about herself. Did she not enjoy learning or was there something more to it? She'd always seemed so inquisitive. Had that changed?

Though she gazed at the sea, he could almost see her mind working, constantly moving like the water beneath them. And he found himself wanting to know every thought. Chastising himself, he took the opportunity to slip away. Though his cabinmate was no doubt resting, he headed toward the relative safety of said cabin.

Entering quietly, in case Mr. Silverton had finally found restful oblivion, he was surprised to see the man, not only awake, but sitting on the side of the small bed built against the wall. Despite his stocky frame, he appeared weak. His blond hair lay limp, and his face was ghostly pale.

"I fear I may have a more miserable trip back to England than the one that brought me to Mallorca."

Obviously, the man was not much better. Moving the lone chair from beneath the window to the opposite side of the small space, he sat. "Why would returning be any worse than arriving?"

Mr. Silverton grimaced. "It was a short trip from Spain to Mallorca. But since I got sick on every crossing, I thought to get it all done at once. Now, I am not so sure."

Not only did he not enjoy the thought of sharing the cabin

with a sick person, but he also felt a bit of sympathy for the man. He'd seen a new sailor on his voyage from France who had been violently ill yet was expected to fulfill his duties. At least Mr. Silverton, as a paying guest, could rest.

"I have asked the captain if he has any white hellebore on board. I had meant to search for some before embarking but was distracted by a particularly lovely señorita." Mr. Silverton managed a tight smile.

At the mention of hellebore, he stiffened. His cousin Joanna called it a poison and berated physicians for using it. "If the captain has it, don't take it. It will leave you worse than you began."

"Truly?" The man frowned. "Then what should I take? I don't think I'll live until we make port if I feel as I do now for the rest of the trip."

It was an appropriate question. If he had been in similar circumstances, he might be anxious to attempt anything. Searching his memory for any remedy Joanna had mentioned about treating sickness, he berated himself for not paying attention to at least half of what she'd said. At least he had sent a letter of apology last month. His own selfishness during their last few conversations even now made him uncomfortable.

"Lord Mabry, I'm afraid if you have no better option, then I must search out whatever the captain may have on board."

"No." Suddenly, a memory from when he'd come home from Oxford and been terribly sick resurfaced. "Bread."

Mr. Silverton's eyebrows lowered. "Bread?"

He grinned, more confident now. "Yes, bread. Not too much at first." The man still looked doubtful. Not sure why the bread had worked, he made up his reasoning. "Yes, bread absorbs the fluids in your stomach, so they don't lurch so much. It settles it like a cloth wiping up a spill." He didn't move a muscle as he waited for the man's reaction.

Finally, Mr. Silverton gave a nod. "That does sound logical. I'm no physician, but it did help when I looked at the horizon as you instructed me, so I will take your advice once again."

"Then may I offer you additional counsel?" A loud noise like a plate dropping onto the table outside the cabin punctuated his offer.

"Please."

"As dinner is about to commence momentarily, you may wish to take some air on deck. I would be willing to procure bread for you during the meal."

The man's eyes rounded as he took in a deep breath and no doubt, smelled the aromas even now seeping beneath their cabin door. Scrambling off his bed, he grabbed the doorlatch. "I would be ever so grateful. Please excuse me." In the next moment, Mr. Silverton yanked the door open and then slammed it shut.

If Mr. Silverton expected to reach the deck without taking another breath, he'd best run. Shaking his head at the unfortunate circumstances of his cabinmate, he wished him well before opening his own chest and pulling forth his tailcoat. He was about to don it when a knock at his door stopped him. It must be Consuela. Taking the two steps toward the door, he opened it to find the seaman from earlier in the day looking far from comfortable.

"My lord. I brought me stone and chain."

Having already forgotten the incident, he didn't respond at first.

"Do you truly think m'lady can fix it?"

Realizing the trust the man was putting in Lady Elsbeth, he nodded. "I know she will do her best to repair it. She is well versed in rocks." He held back his smile at the idea of how she'd react to his statement.

Mr. Dodd shifted his weight from one leg to the other while clutching the chain in his fist. "And I can come back tomorrow by midday to retrieve it?"

Though he laughed at such superstitions, Consuela had taught him to take them very seriously. "Yes. You can have it back then, even if she fails in her attempt to secure the stone to your chain." The man still hesitated. Realizing Wiley needed something akin to an oath, he laid his hand on his chest. "I swear upon my life that you will have your stone before you alight upon the rigging once more."

Wiley visibly relaxed. "Thank you for that, m'lord. I knowed you were good for it." Smiling now, the seaman held out his jewelry.

Taking it, he gave Wiley a serious nod before the man turned about and exited back onto deck, probably to descend below for his own victuals.

Retreating inside his cabin, he slipped the items into his waistcoat pocket and shrugged on his tailcoat. Though he had grown used to the more casual life of living with a merchant family in Spain, it was time to remember who he was and dress and act accordingly. He had a new reputation to establish for his daughter and who better to impress than Lady Astor? That he looked forward to dinner conversation with Lady Elsbeth was not something he would dwell upon.

His daughter was now his priority and always would be.

CHAPTER SIX

ELSBETH BIT ON her lower lip as she bent the small, metal cage tong back into place. Holding the chain off the table where they'd eaten the night before, she scrutinized the design. To make sure the stone didn't fall out again, she would need to fire the connections. Two of them were broken. However, she doubted the captain would allow her to use an open flame on his ship. They'd been given strict instructions on that topic upon boarding.

She studied the setting for the rock. If one were to look at it about the seaman's neck, they'd never know it was broken, but she wasn't comfortable with returning it as it was. If only there were a way to secure the stone inside the little cage. A little leather bag would do, but then the rock wouldn't be seen. If the bag were clear...

With an idea forming, she rose and walked to her cabin door, quietly opening it. Her mother remained asleep, claiming the rocking of the ship induced the best rest.

Kneeling, she opened her chest of clothing. On top of her day dresses were two bonnets. She grinned, pleased that she had decided on them for the voyage. Lifting the white one, she started to close the lid and stopped. She would need needle and thread. Lifting her day dresses from the top, she found what she needed along with scissors, then returned the dresses and closed the lid carefully before stealing from the room.

Back at the large dining table, she carefully peeled the white tulle from around the crown of the bonnet. Laying out the material, she set the metal cage with the stone upon it then cut a square that would encircle it. She had thought to cover the whole cage, but the material might wear away. Seeing no other way, she used her tools again to carefully bend the prongs of the cage back to release the stone.

The door to the ship's deck opened, and she looked up to see Teddy entering the dining area. He wore a dark-brown waistcoat over a white shirt, cravat, and black pantaloons. His hair was slightly tousled from the wind and his gray eyes seemed to twinkle with pleasure. "I see that you have risen early as well." He reviewed the room with his gaze before taking a seat opposite her.

"Oh, yes. That's why I'm awake. I fell asleep much too early."

He ran his hand through his hair. "I, unfortunately, cannot say the same. Marianna awoke in the middle of the night with no use for Consuela, so it took me much time to get her to understand that it was not yet daylight." He gave her a crooked grin. "My ability to communicate with her is still rudimentary at best."

She smiled at the thought of Teddy having a conversation with a baby. "I'm sure in a few years, your communication skills will greatly improve."

"My communication skills?" He folded his arms as if affronted, but his eyes danced with humor. "I'll have you know, I'm considered quite the conversationalist by my peers."

She cocked her head. "Truly? I had heard that you were more suited to the stage."

He sighed, his demeanor no longer teasing. "Yes, I was. But that is in the past. My days of frivolity and pleasure are no more." He paused, his gaze looking beyond her to another time. "And I am happier for it."

Her heart squeezed. Something in his gaze told her the lessons he'd learned while abroad had not been always easy, and losing his wife must have been truly heartbreaking. That he'd found contentment now impressed her. "I'm pleased for you."

His gaze returned to her then dipped toward the table. "What are you about?"

"I'm fixing Mr. Dodd's chain. I was able to enclose it, but it needs to be fired and I don't think the captain will allow that."

"No, he won't."

"As I thought. So, I'm going to sew a drawstring bag for the stone, set it inside, tie the strings to the chain and sew them together before I bend back the prongs."

"Are you also making a repair on your bonnet?"

She chuckled. "Quite the opposite. I removed the tulle from my bonnet to make the bag. I wanted Mr. Dodd to still be able to *see* his son's stone."

Teddy stared at her in silence.

Her confidence in her repair wavered. "Do you not think my plan will work?"

He picked up the bonnet and examined where the tulle had been. "I not only think it will work, I think it inspired." He set the bonnet down. "And very, very generous."

Her cheeks heated at his praise, which was odd, as he used to praise her consistently and she'd not felt half as pleased. "I still have to achieve it, but I believe I can."

"What will you use for a drawstring?"

She hadn't thought upon that. "I might be able to take some length from one of my dresses."

"No. I believe I have something else you could use."

Before she could respond, he was walking into his cabin. Hoping his suggestion would accomplish the goal, she threaded the needle and started on the small bag. She was half done when he reappeared.

He strode forward and pulled out the chair next to her. Sitting, he held out his closed hand. "I believe this will secure it better." He unfolded his fingers to reveal a small amount of leather tie.

"Oh, that's perfect." Pleased, she reached out to take it from him and his hand closed around her bare one. A shock of pleasure went through her, catching her breath. She raised her gaze to his in surprise.

"Why do you go to so much trouble to help a simple seaman?" His eyes appeared to have darkened.

His question baffled her, and she shrugged. "He needed help that I had the ability to provide."

"Yes, but he is a seaman, not one of your friends. He's not even of the same class."

This time, the heat that infused her body stemmed from embarrassment and she looked away.

"Lady Elsbeth, can you not tell me?"

His question brought her gaze back to his. There was a sincerity there and a promise that had her trusting him. She leaned forward and kept her voice low. "Have you read Thomas Paine's *Rights of Man?*"

His eyes rounded, but he didn't back away in shock. "I have."

She glanced toward her cabin door just to be sure her mother remained within, then looked at him. "I have greatly pondered his idea that all men are created equal, and that social standing is only predicated upon the public good. In regards to Mr. Dodd, I wonder if perhaps while on this ship if he is not of higher importance since it is his skills that will contribute to us returning to England safely."

"That is an interesting application of the man's ideas. I would need to reread that treatise to have a valuable opinion." His lips quirked up. "I must point out you sound practically American."

"Oh. No. Not at all." Or rather she hoped she didn't. "I simply see no harm in helping one of the crew who will take us home." She glanced at her cabin door again. "Please don't let on to my mother that I have such ideas. She is very intelligent and well-read but firmly believes social order is ordained and inherited."

He lay his hand upon his chest. "You honor me with your confidence, and I will not betray it."

Relief filled her and she relaxed. "Thank you, Teddy."

He squeezed her hand within his then let go and sat back. "As it happens, you and I share similar views, though I admit I had not thought upon how I developed them. My life on the Continent has brought me in contact with all classes in many countries. In fact, after a while, I forgot to remark upon them."

She looked up from her task. "So then you did not hesitate to marry your wife despite her being from Spain?"

"No, I did not. But I admit it was because I was far more concerned for my child."

"And what of the lady on the dock before we set sail?"

He frowned, as if trying to remember, then his brow raised. "The lady with the boy, who I gave my pocket watch to?" He grinned, reaching into his pocket and pulling out said watch. He studied it for a moment. "I haven't given her much thought, but yes. She now has a position with Francesca's aunt. I simply saw no reason for her to be beaten for standing in the wrong place. Since she was willing to work, I directed her to a better position." He dropped the watch back into his pocket.

She studied him, in awe that he could have found such humility in a year of travels. Did he not see how heroic he'd truly been for the poor woman? Afraid he might see her own admiration, she quickly directed her attention to her task.

Taking the leather tie, she checked to be sure it would fit within the fold she'd sewn. Pleased that it would, she set it aside and picked up the small bag to finish. "My sewing skills are merely adequate. Some of the ladies at school do exquisite needlework."

He raised his right brow. "I'm surprised my cousin allows such a time waste. I'd expect Joanna to have you—" A high-pitched wail came from the cabin behind them, and Teddy grimaced. "That would be my daughter requesting my presence."

She'd dropped her sewing and covered her ears at the sound, but as he rose, she put her hands down, pleased the sound had stopped. "Is that normal?" She'd never heard a baby wail so loudly—not that she'd been in close proximity to many babies.

"So, I'm told. It's considered *healthy*." He shook his head as if he didn't understand the concept at all. "Would you like to meet—" Another wail interrupted him.

She clapped her hands over her ears. How did one become used to such a sound?

Teddy rose quickly and pointed to the cabin door next to his.

Nodding, she kept her hands over her ears as he disappeared into the cabin. She lifted one hand and at the eventual silence, resumed her sewing. She glanced toward the cabin Teddy had entered a few times as she finished the small bag and tied the knot. What had he done to keep his daughter from crying?

She had just finished threading the leather tie through the bag top when she heard an odd sound. Putting down the bag, she listened. It sounded like a laugh. It had to be the baby. She smiled in response, listening carefully, wishing to hear more. After a few moments, she was rewarded with the sound again.

Her heart melted and a part of her almost wished for such a sound. Happiness for Teddy filled her and an odd sadness for herself. Shaking her head at her thoughts, she picked up the stone and dropped it into the tulle bag. Then drawing the leather tight, she fitted the bag into the setting. The stone seemed to shimmer with the tulle pulled tight around it. Guiding the leather ties between the prongs that remained steadfast, she tied them in a knot and sewed it to add further strength. As she bent the two tongs of the small cage back into place, her cabin door opened.

Her mother stepped out and stared hard at her. "What was that terrible sound that woke me from such a pleasant sleep?"

She bit back a smile. "That was Teddy's daughter."

"Oh, that is quite a shock to one's body to be jolted awake by such a high-pitched noise. I don't remember you being so loud. I'm very grateful it has stopped. I imagine the wet nurse did her duty."

"No, it was Teddy."

Her mother waved off her comment. "Elsbeth, you know

very well a man cannot feed a baby, not even porridge."

"I don't believe it was food that Lady Marianna wanted."

Her mother gave her a skeptical look. "It's morning and the baby screeched. That means it wants food."

She had to wonder if she'd done that when she was small. "Actually, she just wanted her father. Once Teddy went inside, she stopped and then she began laughing."

Her mother's gaze softened. "There is nothing quite like a baby's laughter. It is so free and innocent."

She lowered her voice. "If we keep quiet, we might hear it again."

Nodding, her mother quietly pulled out a chair and sat.

They both remained silent. Creaks from the ship seemed louder. Even the lapping of the waves against the hull could be heard in a dull rhythm. Then it came. The tiniest of sounds, a giggle before a small squeak and a childish laugh.

Her mother's face broke into a wide smile and her hand came up over her chest. "Truly, the most wonderful sound on Earth."

She'd never heard her mother speak so. "Did I do that?"

Her mother's eyes misted as she nodded. "You did. Your father would ask me to make you do it again."

Suddenly curious, as she always was when her mother talked about her father, she had to ask. "How did you make me laugh?"

"I would run my fingertips over your belly. You would giggle and laugh. But look at you now." Her mother's gaze turned wistful. "I wish your father could see what an intelligent and proper young woman you have become."

Her mother's praise was never given lightly, which made her heart warm. "I am as I am because of you."

"True." Her mother grinned. "Though when you were but five years, I wasn't sure you'd ever be a young woman. You would go outside just to spite James, who would watch you from the window as you dug in the garden, the planters, anywhere you could."

She did remember digging and finding pretty rocks. When

she grew a little older, she would bring them in to James and he'd help her identify them. "My cousin was a good fellow about it. Though I couldn't imagine him being a parent alone, like Teddy is."

Her mother's gaze shifted toward the cabin where the laughter had emanated from. "I think Lord Mabry has changed significantly since becoming a father and being widowed. I'm very curious who and when he will choose to marry again."

At the thought of Teddy marrying someone else, her mood soured. This time, she recognized the change for what it was. She was jealous of some future unknown woman who would be Teddy's wife. That was hardly appropriate. She should be happy for him. He was an old friend. Yet even that thought felt wrong.

To her, Teddy was pyromorphite. Some said the stone could relight old relationships. It also stimulated new ideas and supported change. It was said to bring abundance as well. That was Teddy. He had brought to the fore new feelings she hadn't realized she had for him. Not only had he changed, but her perception of him had too. That he could bring an abundance of laughter, love, and understanding was all true. Whoever married him would never want for attention or happiness.

Her mother rose. "I suggest we take a turn about the deck before breaking our fast."

"Of course. As soon as I put this all away." Pondering her new status as friend to Teddy would have to wait. She slipped Mr. Dodd's chain and stone into her pocket then gathered her tools, bonnet, scissors, and sewing thread.

"What did you do to your bonnet?" Her mother's sudden question had her halting.

"I'm going to change the decoration. It was far too plain."

"You mean it didn't have pink or lavender on it?"

Grinning, she shrugged her shoulders before entering their cabin. Setting everything back whence it came, she returned to the dining area. Her mother was no longer there, no doubt awaiting her on deck. Quickly, she stepped over to the cabin

Teddy had entered and tapped on the door.

It opened and a dark-haired woman with eyes that matched looked at her in surprise. "*¿Quién eres?*"

Teddy spoke from behind the woman. "Lady Elsbeth, this is Señorita Consuela Castilla. Señorita, this is Lady Elsbeth Rawley of Astor. Consuela was asking who you are."

"Yes, I understand. I've brought something for Lord Mabry."

The woman's brows rose, then she turned her head to look behind her. "*Necesito hablar con el cocinero.*" Then she stepped out and walked by.

Elsbeth watched the woman, who seemed to be a bit older than her, but far less refined. Were all wet nurses so?

"You have something for me?"

At Teddy's voice, she turned back toward the open door and stared. He relaxed on a chair, smiling at his daughter, who sat on his lap facing him. One large hand completely covered the baby's back. It took her a moment to reconcile the scene. Teddy had often made excuses not to be around children who'd been paraded in parlors for friends to see. This man, a very different man, seemed completely enchanted by the child on his lap.

Her heart fluttered and she took a steadying breath. "Yes, I've completed the repairs on Mr. Todd's chain. He should still have it fired once we make port, but I do believe it will remain intact for the rest of the voyage.

Teddy glanced at her. "He'll be very grateful. The power of superstition is strong and his belief in that rock's ability to protect him will give him his confidence back."

She looked about to set down the chain, not wanting to interrupt Lady Marianna's play time. Spotting a chest, she took a single step into the room and bent to set it on the lid.

"Here. We best not lose it." He held his hand out, though he kept his gaze on his daughter.

It was highly improper for her to enter his cabin. Lady Marianna hardly qualified as a chaperone, and even then, it would be improper. Looking over her shoulder to ensure no one was about, she quickly took the three steps across the small room and dropped the chain in his hand. She stepped back, her intent to leave at once.

"Would you like to meet Marianna?"

Once again, she looked over her shoulder. "I very much wish to, but I cannot tarry in this cabin. Mother is waiting." Turning, she almost ran into the dining table before heading toward the door that led to the deck.

"Lady Elsbeth."

Teddy's voice demanded she stop, and she did. "Yes."

"I'm sorry. I have been out of society too long." He stepped from his cabin and placed his hand on the back of a chair. "Come, I will sit here. I would very much like for you to meet my daughter."

Her heart started to pound in her chest. She didn't want to know why, but she couldn't be rude, so she turned back to find Teddy sitting at the dining table, Lady Marianna once again on his lap, but with the infant facing her, Teddy's large hand holding his baby girl across her tummy.

Lady Marianna gave her a toothless grin, her hands held out before her as she bounced, as if she would jump from her father's lap.

Enchanted, she found herself walking forward.

"Lady Elsbeth, this is my daughter, Lady Marianna. Daughter, this is my very good friend, Lady Elsbeth Rawley of Astor." Teddy grinned proudly.

"Good day, Lady Marianna. It is lovely to make your acquaintance."

The little girl squealed, bouncing harder.

Teddy laughed. It was a sound she'd never heard from him before, despite having heard him laugh many times while he'd courted her. It was deeper, relaxed, and happy.

He rose, holding his daughter against his chest. "I believe she'd like to join you on deck."

"She can walk?"

He laughed again. "Despite the strength she's showing you, she cannot. She can hold her head quite well now, though. I'm told she'll be crawling across rooms very soon."

At his words, she flushed. How ignorant she was about babies!

"Would you like to hold her?"

Completely unprepared and not a little worried she would drop the chubby child, she fell back on etiquette. "I would, but I would need a lesson on how to do it properly, and I've already kept mother waiting."

"I understand. I'm sure there'll be plenty of time on this voyage for you to get better acquainted with Marianna."

She liked the way he phrased it, as if he wished her to know more about his child. "I would enjoy that very much."

At his searching gaze, she blushed and quickly turned away. Even as she opened the door to the deck, she wished she could stay. But the thought of her mother coming down to find her and making a scene had her slipping out and closing the door behind her. Still, she leaned against the door, trying to understand the strange emotions that were running through her. With no one to talk to about it, she gave up and looked about for her mother.

She frowned to find her mother talking to the captain near the main mast. Her mother was usually the ever-vigilant parent. Perplexed, she strolled forward, curious as to what had changed her mother's constant watch.

CHAPTER SEVEN

TEDDY FOLLOWED CAPTAIN Gentry to the helm. The man had a stern face, but on the rare occasions when he smiled, it made the deep wrinkles around his eyes crease, and he appeared quite jovial. He wore a full but trimmed beard of dark brown with a few wisps of white, though the dark, curly hair on his head showed no sign of age. His nose was a bit large, but his brown eyes were sharp. He was also rather lean, and his hands showed much wear. He was a truly seasoned sailor.

The man had survived the Battle of Grand Port in the Indian Ocean despite his frigate going down. He was knowledgeable on both navigation and defense. He had lived to aid in the island being taken and with the fall of its sister island as well. Those facts alone gave Teddy a sense of comfort that he and his daughter would arrive safely in England.

They passed by two seamen repairing rope and one looked up at him. It was Wiley. He stopped what he was doing and lifted the chain about his neck to dangle the stone set inside. The Mediterranean sun made it shimmer in its small confines. The man grinned before dropping it under his shirt and going back to work.

It reminded him that he had yet to give Lady Elsbeth the man's gratitude. She had not been on deck the day before when he'd been out. Was she ill? Or was she avoiding him? He didn't like either possibility.

"The *SeaSprite* is well built and but two years old."

The captain's continuation of their conversation brought him back to his inquiry. "So you say your artillery men have all seen battle?"

Captain Gentry ascended the steps to the aft deck and slowed. "Yes, though not all on board have naval experience." He pointed to the row of canons. "I have fifty-eight on board. Your passage will be a safe one." The man looked to the sky and pointed. "Mother Nature is my trickiest enemy. She can bring up a wind that would rip the topsail asunder or she can put the ocean to sleep, leaving us to drift aimlessly. While I can usually count on the winds at the Gibraltar Strait, anything else she conjures up is always unexpected."

"Do you run into many storms on this route?"

"Sometimes." The captain conferred with the officer at the helm then turned back to him. "But no more or less than anywhere else. Though my cargo is my livelihood and important to my investors, I do not take chances."

He liked the man's practical approach to his profession, which was slightly different than how it'd been on the last merchant ship he'd traveled on. Then again, the last one's captain had thought him a merchant as well and slyly confided ways in which he made profits on the side. "How long will you stay in port when we arrive in England?"

The man opened his mouth to respond, but before he could speak, he was interrupted.

"Oh, there you are, Captain Gentry. Would it be convenient for you to come down?"

At the sound of Lady Astor's voice, the captain pulled down on his coat before stepping to the railing. "My lady, you have indeed come upon me at just the right moment. I'm sure that Lord Mabry will be happy to relinquish me to such lovely company."

Lovely? Yes, he supposed for her advanced years, Lady Astor

was still beautiful, but he hadn't expected the captain to voice that opinion.

"Shall we, Lord Mabry?" The man lowered his voice. "Perhaps you could take a turn about the ship with the lady's daughter?"

Surprised by the captain's obvious interest in Lady Elsbeth's mother, he silently nodded, forgetting for a moment that he was anxious to inquire into Lady Elsbeth's welfare. Had the captain's interest been the reason why the dinner table seating had changed, making it impossible for him to talk to Lady Elsbeth?

As the steps were too steep to go down facing forward, he waited while the captain descended. It gave him the opportunity to make two observations. The first was that Lady Astor seemed to be as pleased as the captain by the man's availability to spend time with her and the second was that Lady Elsbeth looked particularly lovely in a lavender dress, even if she did not look up to see that he was about to descend.

It wasn't until he started down the stairs that anyone recalled his presence.

"Oh, Lord Mabry. I did not see you above there. I trust you are well?"

As he stepped onto the deck, he answered Lady Astor. "I am. And does this morning find you and Lady Elsbeth in good health?"

Lady Astor waved her hand aside. "We are quite fine, indeed. Perhaps you could keep my daughter occupied while I have a few words with the captain?"

He lowered his head to acknowledge his acceptance. "Of course." He held his arm out to Elsbeth. "Would you walk with me, Lady Elsbeth? The captain assures me the rest of the morning will remain pleasant."

She didn't respond beyond a short nod before taking his arm.

Curious about her behavior, he kept silent, the breeze keeping the sails taut and their movement over the water fairly smooth. He waited until half the ship lay between themselves and her mother before questioning her. "I have been wishing to speak to you, but this is the first I've seen you out on deck. Are you well?"

Instead of answering, she stopped. "I apologize." She looked past his shoulder before finally meeting his gaze. "My mother has been rising much earlier in order to have time to talk with the captain. At first, I thought she was gleaning as much information about the ship from him as she could, but now, I'm not sure."

Pleased to discover she had not been avoiding his personage, he relaxed. "I do believe that the captain and your mother enjoy being in each other's company."

Her eyes widened, the violet specks in them more obvious in the bright sunlight. "Surely, you do not mean in an amorous way."

Catching the nearly panicked sound in her voice, understanding dawned.

"Though they may enjoy conversing while on this voyage, I don't believe you need to worry about a continued relationship. The captain made it clear to me just the other day that he is married to the sea, but I'm sure he finds your mother's conversation a pleasant change. They are each of an age and your mother is very intelligent."

"I suppose." She moved to the railing and rested her hands on it as she stared at the open sea.

The water lapped at the ship as it moved through each small swell and the wisps of white clouds did little to distract from the warmth of the day. He moved next to her, leaning his elbow on the railing. "Do you worry that your mother may one day marry again?"

She didn't answer for a long time. Finally, she spoke. "I'm not sure how I feel. I shudder at the thought of losing yet another parent, even if it is to marriage, but I know that I will one day move on to have my own family." She turned her head to look at him. "It seems that everything is changing. Before we arrived in London for my first season, there were people and events I could depend upon. But ever since then…"

She turned back to gaze once more at the sea, her mouth firmly closed.

He understood how she felt. Since she'd turned down his proposal, his life had changed on a daily basis—from new activities to new friends to new women to even new countries. But for him, home, England, was a place he could go back to and resume his old life. Even as he contemplated that, he saw the multiple flaws in his thinking. Unable to offer any comforting words, he set his hand upon her gloved one on the railing.

At his touch, she looked at him. "I think that's why I love rocks so much."

The switch in topic had him fumbling. "I'm not sure I follow your reasoning."

She winked, her lips quirking up. "No, I don't suppose you would."

"Please explain, as I would like to."

"I can try." Turning away from the view, she faced him, her hand slipping from beneath his as she did so. "I lost my father as a toddler. Even then, mother says I would go into the gardens and dig out rocks, keeping them in my room. I'm afraid that didn't change as I grew older. I just prepared better."

He tried to imagine her as a child, but instead, he saw her as she had been in the Dragon Caves, down on the ground, a smudge of dirt on her cheek. "Is crawling around a cave considered better prepared?"

She chuckled. "I did have tools. But to be fair, no one was supposed to see me."

"Point accepted." He grinned back, pleased he'd made her smile again.

"Having my father pass while I was so young, I think it made me yearn for stability. Though I study 'geology,' it truly is rocks that call to me. They're always there, rarely changing unless over long periods of time that we as people can't even see. They're dependable."

He couldn't help thinking how he must have looked to her. After her rejection, he'd gone down to the wharf and drank until he lost consciousness. Then he'd left for Europe without taking leave of anyone and gallivanted around for a year. If she knew even a few of the scrapes he'd managed to extricate himself from, she'd be appalled. He could hardly be considered dependable.

"I imagine that sounds quite boring to you." She sighed, turning back to the railing.

"No, it sounds peaceful. I never thought about rocks to be truthful. But your points are well made, and you are hardly boring. Here you are travelling back from Spain, and the Dragon Caves no less. That is hardly the typical journey for a young lady of the *ton*."

She smiled widely and lifted her face to the sun. "No, it isn't. I have enjoyed every minute." She lowered her head. "I'm very glad to have been able to study the caves, but I admit to being ready to be home."

Her face became pensive, and it made him wonder what it was she thought of. He wanted to ask, but something held him back, whether it was the fear that she thought of another man or that he didn't deserve her thoughts, he wasn't sure. Still, he wanted to know why she was anxious to be home. "Do you miss home so much? Your mother travels with you. Is it your cousin the duke's company you miss, or someone else?"

Damn, he hadn't meant to ask that.

She laughed. "Even if I did miss my cousin James, I would not admit to it. He is far too sure of himself as it is. No, I refuse to say I miss him." She gave a quick shake of her head for emphasis. "I do, however, miss Dory and Ellie. And Georgina and Sophie."

"They are others at school?"

"Yes. I spoke of Lady Dorothea before. Lady Eleanor Dulac is the daughter of your aunt's good friend."

He vaguely remembered the young lady but nodded politely.

"She has a heart as large as London but is perhaps not the most graceful." She set her hand on his arm. "Please don't ever tell her I said so."

He shook his head, not being able to imagine having a conversation with the woman during which he would be tempted to mention it.

"Then there's Lady Sophie Howard. I don't know that she'll ever wed. She is painfully shy. Why, I've never seen her hold a conversation with anyone beyond those of us at school."

"Could that be perhaps because you are not with her at other times to observe?"

She stuck her tongue out at him, and he sucked in a breath. "No, it's not because I haven't been there. Even with her own mother, she speaks less than with us."

He couldn't help teasing her. "I can think of any number of men who would enjoy that trait in their wife."

Lady Elsbeth rounded on him, one hand on her hip and fire in her eyes. "Are you saying you think women speak more than they should? I can tell you that having a wife who has more on her mind than the latest gossip and who can contribute to the well-being of the family should be lauded."

He stifled a grin and held both his hands up. "I agree. I agree. I've been tutored well by my cousin Joanna on the intelligent minds of womanhood. I was simply stating what I know to be true among *some* men of the *ton*." Since she still looked skeptical, he decided that had not been the best teasing remark, even if it was true. "And what of the other ladies? Do you truly miss them all?"

Her face softened and he could see in her eyes, she cared much for her classmates.

"I do miss Georgina too, but I only just met Lissette before I left, so I don't know her well. She is from France and from what Joanna said, she helped her grandmother nurse Lord Blackmore back to health."

"Did she? I have not heard the entire story on Lord Blackmore's resurrection from the dead."

"Then you should definitely have my mother explain. It is

rather complicated. I would—"

"Señor Mabry!"

At the sound of Consuela's voice, he immediately strode for the cabins, surprised to find the wet nurse out on deck with Marianna. Concern filled him. "What's wrong?" At her frown, he repeated himself in Spanish. "*¿Lo que está mal?*"

Consuela spoke so fast, he barely understood, but it seemed not to matter as she handed Marianna to him. Then muttering and cursing, she turned on her heel and stomped back inside.

He soothed Marianna's back as she looked over his shoulder, piecing together the tirade he'd just listened to.

"Is something amiss?"

At Lady Elsbeth's voice, he turned, having forgotten her in his haste to care for his daughter. "If I'm not mistaken, my charming child just urinated all over Consuela's favorite shawl as she was changing her." At least it was something close to that.

"Oh, dear." Lady Elsbeth looked askance at his daughter, her nose scrunched. "Is she wet?"

He checked to be sure then shook his head. "No, it appears that Consuela completed the task before removing Marianna from the scene of her faux pas."

"I wonder how that could have happened?"

At Elsbeth's remark, he studied her. Did she really have no idea? He could imagine at least three scenarios in which such an event could occur. "Have you not had the pleasure of knowing any infants?"

She backed up a step. "No. I am an only child and with no other cousins beyond James, I've had no reason to make them a particular study."

"Then I think now is a perfect time to further your education." He grinned, happy to share such a pleasure with her.

She put her hand to her chest and stepped back again. "But I don't know anything about them. What if I do something wrong? Truly, Teddy, I couldn't bear it if I hurt your daughter."

Damn if his heart didn't slam hard in his chest at her admission. He softened his tone. "You do hope to have children of your own, do you not?"

"I imagine I will have to."

Her odd answer surprised him. "Do you plan to leave them in the care of servants, then, like your cousin James had been?"

"No! I mean, I wouldn't abandon my children like that. I just wasn't expecting… I mean, I hadn't thought…"

Her hesitancy reminded him of himself just three months past. "Come. I'll show you how to hold her."

When she didn't respond, he raised his right brow. "Certainly, you don't mind making mistakes in front of me, do you?"

Her back straightened. "No, of course not." She lifted her hand palm up. "Show me what to do."

"Let's start as I did. Come." He led her to a short barrel near the main mast. "Please sit here."

She took an inordinate amount of time arranging her skirts.

"This isn't a ball. It's just a three-month-old."

"Of course." She finally looked at him. "Now what should I do?"

"Now I'll put her in your lap facing me and you hold on to her around her belly. Let her head rest against you to support it. Her neck muscles are not strong yet."

Lady Elsbeth's eyes grew wide, her uncertainty evident. Still, she gave him a short nod. Pulling his daughter from his shoulder with one hand supporting her head and shoulders and the other under her bottom, he sat her on Elsbeth's lap so Marianna could still see him.

Marianna's eyes widened and her forehead puckered.

Not wanting Elsbeth to have an unpleasant first experience with a baby, he knelt down before his daughter. "I'm right here, Mari."

Her forehead wrinkles relaxed, and she made a squeak before flapping her arms.

He chuckled. "She wants to bounce." Moving his gaze to Lady Elsbeth, he found her frozen in place, one hand firmly around his daughter, the other clutching the barrel upon which she sat. It appeared she was in more need of reassurance than his daughter.

"Elsbeth, I'm right here. You can relax."

"I am."

He choked down a laugh. "Take your other hand and let her hold your finger. She likes to grip things."

It took a moment, but Elsbeth's hand finally moved, and she touched Marianna's hand. His daughter immediately grabbed her.

"Oh." Elsbeth's eyes rounded. "She's strong."

"Yes, for a baby." He gave Marianna his other finger and she held it as she bounced, little noises issuing from her, proving she enjoyed the attention. Of that, he had no doubt. He fairly spoiled her with attention. "You can gently bounce her if you like. Just raise your knees a little and bring them down."

"Like this?"

At her movement, he nodded, and Marianna let out an ear-splitting squeal.

"I hope that was a happy sound." Lady Elsbeth grimaced.

He grinned, quite pleased that his daughter could be so loud. "It was."

"Can I see her?"

Happy that she was more interested now, he removed his finger from his daughter's grasp. "Are you ready to see who holds you?"

As Marianna's blue gaze focused on him even as she pumped Lady Elsbeth's finger, he wondered if he'd ever tire of seeing her react to him. To turn his daughter around, he would have to insert his hand between her and Lady Elsbeth's chest. That was hardly an acceptable action, no matter how enjoyable it might be, so instead he instructed Elsbeth on turning Marianna to face her. Though the feat was accomplished rather awkwardly, his daughter finally looked upon Elsbeth.

"My, you are very pretty, Lady Marianna. You're a very fortunate little girl to have such a caring father."

As Elsbeth smiled kindly at his daughter, his heart lurched. One day, she would be a loving mother with children of her own who would fairly worship her. If he hadn't been such a buffoon, she could have been his. Regret made bile rise in his throat until his daughter started bouncing again, clearly not caring that Elsbeth was a stranger.

At the reminder that he would not have Marianna if he'd acted any differently, even if he hadn't been the most chivalrous to Francesca, he found his moral footing in time. He was content.

"You like to bounce. You are a bouncy baby. Very well, then." Elsbeth started moving her knees up and down again gently.

"She's quite energetic when she's awake, but that isn't for very long."

At the sound of his voice behind her, Marianna tried to turn her head.

Quickly, he rose and sat next to Elsbeth. Marianna's gaze rested on him and then switched to Elsbeth. She stopped bouncing and her hand made a fist and then opened, only to close again. He lifted his finger for her to grasp and she held on tightly, the touch seeming to relieve her.

Lady Elsbeth spoke to him, though she didn't take her eyes off Marianna. "I didn't know that babies could tell who their parents were."

"This is a relatively new movement for her. She's always been aware of my voice, but it is only recently that she looks for me and reaches out with any accuracy. There is so much to learn, which is why I'm anxious to return to England. I am sure my aunt, Lady Wakefield, will be able to explain what I can expect in each stage of Marianna's growth."

Elsbeth chuckled, pulling Marianna's attention from him to her. "And if Lady Wakefield doesn't know, I'm quite sure her husband has read something about it somewhere."

That was very true. Lord Wakefield was the most-read person he knew, after his cousin Joanna and her husband. "As much as Francesca's aunt was knowledgeable, her lifestyle is quite different from what Marianna will know." He grinned at his daughter as her gaze came back to rest on him when he spoke.

"In what way?"

At Elsbeth's question, he wished he hadn't mentioned it. It would be hard finding a wife who would accept his daughter. If the *ton* found out her mother had not been equal in social status to him, it could greatly affect her. He was just too comfortable talking with Elsbeth that he'd forgotten to keep silent. Seeing no help for it, he would have to take her into his confidence. "I first must have your promise to never tell anyone, not even your mother."

Elsbeth frowned at him, obviously insulted by his hesitancy. "Teddy, you can trust me." She returned her attention to Marianna. "I could never do anything that would harm your beautiful little girl."

She may believe that now, but he worried what she would do when she found out he didn't intend to tell his future wife.

CHAPTER EIGHT

A T TEDDY'S SILENCE, Elsbeth looked at him again. "You hesitate. Can it truly be that terrible?"

He ran his hand through his hair, a telltale sign he was in a quandary.

"Lady Marianna, please tell your father that I would keep his secret until my very last breath, which I hope will be many, many years from now. He is a dear friend. You are a very fortunate little girl." She received a big smile for her words as well as a bit of drool.

Teddy perused the area, obviously making sure that no one overheard, then he leaned in anyway, his earthy scent almost distracting her from his words...almost. "Her mother was not quite gentry level. I do not want the *ton* to ever know this. They can be far too cruel."

Not a little surprised by his revelation, her mind spun with questions that she wished answered. "Then I must assume you were very much in love with her." Even as she voiced her thought, her belly tightened. To know he had loved another so much as to marry out of his class pained her, though it shouldn't.

"I wish that were the truth, but I admit we married for Marianna and honor. I could not allow a child of mine to be considered illegitimate. Her existence has changed so much in me. Now, I truly understand what it is to love and to put another before myself."

Forcing down the joy that erupted inside her at his admission, she focused on his commitment to his daughter. "She has definitely changed you for the better." She offered him a gentle smile. "I will never betray your confidence."

"Thank you." Though he said the words, she could sense he still worried.

She would simply have to prove to him that she wouldn't betray his trust. "Lady Marianna, you have no idea what miracles you've wrought."

Teddy lifted his chin and looked down his nose at her in feigned arrogance, his eyes full of laughter. "Now, wait a moment. Surely, I wasn't so irredeemable."

She looked askance at him. "You most assuredly were, and if you doubt me, you can ask your cousin Joanna. In fact—oh." Lady Marianna burped, and from the appearance, some of her milk came up. "I think she needs to be cleaned."

"So she does. Here." He held out a white, linen handkerchief.

"You best do it. I'm not sure I can with my gloves on."

Instead of doing as she suggested, he took her hand and removed the glove. "There."

At the touch of his fingers, a tingle of warmth ran up her arm, catching her by surprise. Quickly, she took the handkerchief and gently wiped away the spittle. Her finger brushed against the baby's cheek, and she halted. Dropping the cloth, she brushed back the little curls from Marianna's forehead. "Her skin is so soft." She loved the feel of little Lady Marianna, her heart warming at their connection.

The infant's little brows lowered, and her nose crinkled just before she started to wail.

It broke her heart that the baby was so undone. "Did I do something wrong?"

Teddy pulled his daughter from her lap. "Not at all. She is simply unhappy about something, but it could be anything, from being hungry to wanting me to having messed her napkin." He cradled his crying daughter in his arms. "I believe it is the latter reason. Would you like to learn how to change her?"

She rose, donning her glove once again, not in a hurry to handle a baby's mess. "I think I've learned quite a bit for today. I do thank you for your instruction."

He smirked as if daring her to reconsider, but she had no intention of doing so.

"Then allow me to escort you to your cabin, and I will take care of my daughter."

Not a little surprised that he had thought of her after the way he had practically run to Lady Marianna when Consuela had come on deck, she acquiesced. She was also surprised he planned to clean his daughter himself. Didn't a wet nurse do that? She'd have to ask her mother.

He held out his free arm while cradling his daughter in the other. Lady Marianna continued to whimper, but the crying was not quite as loud.

At her cabin door, he left her and proceeded to his daughter's. She stood there for a moment staring at the closed door, listening to Teddy talking to Lady Marianna, or "Mari," as he called her. A strange despondency settled in her belly, and she examined the feeling. It wasn't difficult to understand whence it came. It was her heart, reawakened to Lord Theodore Mabry and all the qualities she'd loved about him before she'd come out in society, without all the melodrama of his youth. Of the qualities she was discovering now, his love for his daughter outshone them all. If only—she shook herself. Regret was a waste of good intellectual resources, or so her cousin James always said. It was best to look toward the future and what could be rather than the past and what had already been set in stone.

She placed her hand on the cabin door. Her future was looming closer, and she had decisions to make to fulfill her promise. She would start with a list of the men who'd been available before she left London and the characteristics she liked in each. She turned and lifted the latch then paused. Maybe she should first make a list of the qualities she wished in her husband. She had done so before she'd come out in society, but that was practically two seasons ago. It was time for a new list. About to step into her cabin, the sound of a man clearing his throat had her looking over her shoulder.

"Lady Elsbeth, is that you?"

"Mr. Silverton, how are you feeling today?" The man, of an age with her, seemed to be a likeable person, but his constant bouts of seasickness had made it difficult to assess him in terms of rocks yet. Still, he was passably handsome and appeared to be quite civil.

"Remarkably, much better. The captain says I am getting my sea legs."

Though social rules were a bit more relaxed within the confines of a ship at sea, she did not feel comfortable speaking to an unwed man without a chaperone. Teddy was different, as they were distantly related. "That's wonderful news. I hope you will be able to enjoy the rest of the voyage. Good day."

Quickly, she slipped inside her cabin. Once inside, she immediately went to work finding her writing materials and one of the few pieces of paper she had packed between the pages of a book. Slipping a page out, she sat on her narrow bed, setting the ink on a beam next to the porthole. Letting her thoughts spew forth, she jotted down the many characteristics that she wished for in husband. In little time, she had twenty-two.

She grinned. She was not so naïve as to believe any one man could indeed have all of them. In fact, she found opposing characteristics. She'd written down that he must be dedicated to his family, but she'd also written that he must be willing to have new experiences. Perhaps she should prioritize the top three most important characteristics. That was far much more difficult, but eventually, she checked three.

Now to the unwed gentlemen she'd met so far in the season. There was Mr. Bingham and Lord Avondale. She categorized them as rhyolite and fluorite, her top tiers of stones. Both had shown much interest in her and were very attentive, well-mannered, intelligent, and handsome. Though she hadn't listed "handsome" as a priority, the first man who came to mind with that quality was Mr. Sonning. She wrinkled her nose. He always smelled of liquor and though he didn't slur his words, he seemed to be forever in his cups. Immediately, she drew a line and started on characteristics that would knock a man from her list. "In his cups" was quickly followed by "gambler" and "lightskirt," though she wasn't sure what a man would be called in that position, nor did she know how she could surmise that. Next, she added "flirt." She needed a man who was ready to marry, not simply enjoying the season. He couldn't be deep in debt, though she could see overlooking a little debt if she truly enjoyed his company.

He couldn't be cruel. Next to that she wrote, "Lord Gasford." There had been whispers, but nothing concrete. Still, just looking at his face, she could easily believe—

The door to the cabin opened, startling her.

"Elsbeth?"

"Mother. I didn't hear you approaching the cabin."

Her mother frowned as she closed the door. "I was talking to Mr. Silverton just outside our door. How could you not hear me?"

She shrugged, carefully putting the quill into the ink bottle. "I was concentrating."

Her mother took off her gloves and set them on her chest before sitting on her bed, the space between them not more than two paces. "What is it there that has you so focused?"

Not a little proud at how quickly she was able to determine her preferred characteristics for a husband, she handed her mother the sheet of paper. "Since we may only have five or six weeks of the season left, I thought it prudent to come up with a list of traits I would like in a husband."

Her mother's brows rose. "You are serious about this so soon. This is only your second season. You can certainly wait until next year."

She didn't meet her mother's gaze, instead pointing to the sheet. "Oh, I'm aware of that, but there is still time this season to see if there is anyone of interest."

Her mother finally looked down at the list and read it silently.

She studied her mother as she did so, trying to imagine how she appeared to the captain. That her mother was just over two score with golden hair and intelligent, whiskey-colored eyes must be of great appeal to the man. If she were to guess, based on appearances and what history she knew from being seated nearby at dinner, he must be at least two score and five if not older.

"Oh, Elsbeth." Her mother looked up with tears in her eyes. "These were all your father's traits."

Her heart thudded hard in her chest. "They were?"

Her mother nodded even as she handed back the sheet. "Most definitely. If you were to find a man such as he, you would be very happy."

She rose and crossed to her mother. Sitting next to her, she took her hand in hers. "Were there any traits about father that you did not care for?"

"Of course not." Her mother chuckled. "I'm lying. Your father had a few traits that were not especially my favorites."

"Truly?" She'd never heard her mother make a single state-ment of censure about her father. "Do tell me."

Her mother gazed at her for a moment then, squeezing her hand, sighed. "I suppose you are old enough to know. I certainly don't want you thinking Edward was perfect. He was hardly that, until I had him to myself. Even then, he rarely spoke about his feelings. Except for the day he asked me to marry him, he never told me he loved me, but I knew he did."

Beyond curious now, she remained silent as her mother's gaze seemed to move off to another time and place.

"When I met Edward, he was far too arrogant about his looks and had spent too little time about his studies. Half the unwed women were in love with him, and I'm quite sure half the ladies of ill repute."

"Mother! How can you say that?"

"I told you. Your father was not perfect. He was a young man about town, and I heard whispers, finally paying my footmen to follow him. My worst fears were confirmed, at which point I determined to cross him from my husband list."

She caught her breath. "You didn't."

Her mother nodded, but she must be teasing.

She'd been under the impression her parents had fallen madly in love on the dance floor or some other usual place. There'd never been talk of other possible men. Though it happened before she was born, she shivered at the idea that her father had almost not been her mother's husband, but her curiosity was piqued. "You had a husband list?"

"Of course. You must remember that marrying for love was not quite the norm when I came out, and so I made a logical list of prospects."

She grinned at the fact she had begun just such a project. "Did you come up with traits such as mine? Were many men on it?"

Her mother's cheeks heated, a highly unusual occurrence. "I must admit my list was far more extensive than yours. I was also much less willing to compromise. I noticed you had three traits checked. I had similar checkmarks about those characteristics my future husband *must* have, but mine numbered over twelve."

"Oh, dear. How many men did that allow for?"

Her mother grinned, releasing her hand to hold up two fingers.

"Was my father one of them?"

"Hardly." Her mother's chin lifted, and she looked down her nose. "He wasn't even under consideration. As I said, I had eliminated him quite early. So at my next ball, which took place outside of London, though it would be within the city now, I searched out the two men who had appeared to fulfill my every requirement."

"And…"

"One I sat next to at dinner and the other I spent time getting to know while in a walk in the garden, chaperoned, of course. Both men had attended university, had estates of their own, were in line to inherit the family title, and were the epitome of gentlemen. In other words, they were both duller than a doorknob."

She laughed, unable to help herself. "Were they, truly?"

"Quite. And I must tell you, I was at a complete loss as to how to proceed. The ball ended and I had no prospects and no plan. That was when it happened."

"What happened?" She had never heard this story. She'd heard of her parents' first meeting and their courtship, but not about the time in between.

"Our family coach broke down on the road back to Town. There we were in the middle of the night when Edward came riding down the road on horseback with two friends. From what I learned later, it was to attend a house party."

"That late at night?"

Her mother looked askance at her. "It was a different type of house party."

"Oh." She wasn't sure what type it was, but she was not ignorant of some of the things young men did before marriage, and even *after* marriage for many.

"Anyway, your father and his friends stopped to help. They insisted that they could aid us, so we all exited the coach. When he saw my mother and I were there, he rolled up his sleeves and he and his friends were able to fix the wheel temporarily. When they finished, he and my father came over to where my mother and I stood to escort us back into the coach. He took advantage of the unusual circumstances and loitered behind my parents. Whispering in my ear that he thought it was fate that we have a chance meeting, he kissed me on the cheek. When he helped me into the coach, he squeezed my hand and winked."

"I didn't know father was so forward. Did you?"

Her mother waved off her comment. "Of course. That was why he was not on my list. But the fact was, that light kiss on my cheek and his words had been more exciting than my entire season. He then escorted us back to Town to make sure the wheel held while his friends continued on their way. When we arrived at our townhome, he requested my father's permission to court me and so began our life."

"You accepted his courtship after he had taken such liberties?"

"Yes." Her mother chuckled, her gaze far from the tiny cabin they shared. "What I discovered was that all the planning, all the intellectual exercise, could not provide that special spark between two people who are meant for each other." Her mother's eyes twinkled as she met her gaze. "That, my dear, comes from your heart, not your head. Yes, your father had an illustrious past and many adventures, but that was what made him interesting and exciting because he was so very imperfect."

She contemplated her mother's words. Did she dare go back into the season with no list and simply base her decision on feelings? Could they even develop in so short a time to give her the confidence to accept an offer? "So maybe I need to make a list of men that I know I have no feelings for and then see who is left."

"That's a good start." Her mother patted her hand. "Just remember, you don't have to make a decision this year. I wouldn't mind having you at the School for Curious Ladies a couple more years."

Her stomach tightened as she rose from the bed. If only she had two more years instead of six weeks once they arrived home.

As her mother lay back on the bed to rest, Elsbeth picked up her paper and turned it over, prepared to write down names of men she had no interest in, but she barely remembered any of them. The ones who stood out to her were those she'd already listed as unacceptable. Hopefully, the winds would be with them, and she would have the full six weeks to reacquaint herself with those not yet promised to others.

Turning the paper back, she read through the traits she'd listed once again, the ones her father had. As she reached the bottom, she froze. There was one man who had them all. Teddy. She'd described him exactly.

CHAPTER NINE

TEDDY LAID HIS sleeping daughter back into the box he'd secured to the bed across from Consuela. The woman smiled and kept her voice down as she spoke. "Gracias."

He nodded. For the last three nights, as they navigated the Mediterranean, Marianna had woken in the middle of the night, refusing to go back to sleep after being fed. He hoped once they crossed into the Atlantic, where the seas might be a bit rougher, that the significant rocking of the ship would help her fall asleep after her feedings. Quietly, he slipped from the cabin and into the dining area. At the sound of the latch on the door to the deck, he turned in that direction to find Lady Elsbeth opening it, intending to go out.

"I suggest you refrain from going any further."

At his words, she jumped, closing the door in the process. Turning around, she scowled. "Teddy. You gave me a fright."

He strode forward. "Good. What were you thinking to go out on deck at night? You know the captain gave strict orders that no women are allowed out there after the sun sets."

She glanced at the door then moved forward, setting her lantern on the table. "But it's important."

He strode around the table to move closer to enable him to keep his voice low and not wake Marianna. "I don't think you understand. The captain's orders on a ship are law. They cannot be ignored, and that is for the safety of everyone. He could lock you in your cabin or worse, put you ashore."

Her eyes widened before she pulled out a chair and slumped into it. "I meant no disrespect. I'm just worried about my mother."

Confused, he pulled out the chair next to her and sat. "Are you saying that Lady Astor is on deck?" He couldn't quite believe that.

Elsbeth didn't look at him. Instead, she worried the silken belt of her dressing gown. At her state of undress and her obvious intention to go about on deck, his protective instincts rose like a wild bear defying capture. "Why do you think your mother is on deck when she knows as well as you that she is not allowed out there at night?"

When she didn't answer, the few facts he knew fell into place. "She's not in your cabin, is she?"

She shook her head once.

There were limited places the woman could be. She may have gone in search of something to eat, or off with someone. He doubted she was with the captain's sister-in-law. However, Lady Astor had been in the company of the captain quite often while on deck. "It's the middle of the night and she's gone."

This time, she gave a single nod.

Though it was difficult to believe, his instinct told him Lady Astor was sharing the captain's bed. But Elsbeth likely didn't see that as a possibility, hence the intent to venture onto the deck in the middle of the night in her dressing gown. He frowned just thinking about it, his whole body stiffening. She obviously refused to acknowledge what he suspected. Using his hand, he lifted her chin. "Elsbeth?"

Her eyes shimmered with unshed tears. His heart ached for her. Her life had been far more sheltered than his. He stroked her cheek with his thumb, marveling that it could be as soft as Marianna's. "I think you know where she is."

She pulled away. "I cannot believe it. My mother is a lady."

"Your mother is a beautiful lady for her age and also a widow."

She rounded on him. "She's forty-two!" Her eyes were wide, the color high in her cheeks.

He held his finger to his lips, both to signal that she be quiet and to keep from chuckling. Obviously, he couldn't tell her that he'd enjoyed the pleasure of the bedroom with more than one woman of that age. "Marianna just went back to sleep."

She crossed her arms and pouted before murmuring under her breath, "It's not right."

He disagreed, but she was hardly in the mood to hear that. "Why is it not right?"

"She is a mother. She also loved my father very much. How can she...be with another man? How can she have such strong feelings for him already?"

Though he regretted many of the escapades he had while on the Continent, at this moment he was happy he'd experienced every one. He'd learned much he'd been naïve about, especially from women. "Which upsets you more, that she is with the captain or that she may have deep feelings for him?"

She frowned at his question, but she took a moment to ponder it. "My father was a wonderful man. He was nothing like Captain Gentry. She hasn't even known him a sennight yet."

"I don't think your mother feels strong affection for Captain Gentry."

Her brow furrowed. "My mother is not a lightskirt. If she is truly spending time with the man, then of course she does."

He sighed, not sure how to help her understand. Though she may think the worst of him, the only option was to tell her the truth. "It is not that simple. When I was in Bayonne, I met a French widow at an inn where I was staying. She had lost her husband years earlier and was traveling to visit her sister. We conversed into the night. Upon saying good night, she asked if I was staying in that small town. I had no intention of doing so, but I knew that she was not leaving for two more days. After learning so much about her, I told her I was. The next two days, we spent touring the limited sights of the area. On the last night, I invited her to my room."

She looked away. "You do not need to tell me this. I am upset about my mother, not you."

This was going to be more difficult than he'd first expected. "I understand that, but you need to hear this. I am not proud of all that I have done while living abroad, but this was one part of my journey when I was. You see, this widow had been alone for years, and while at home, she had to conduct herself as was expected by her acquaintances, yet she yearned for human touch, more particularly, a man's. Since she was traveling, and quite sure that no one in Bayonne knew of her, she felt secure in keeping her reputation at home while still experiencing the joys of the bedroom."

"Teddy, truly, I do not wish to hear about your many conquests."

Obviously, she wasn't listening. He took her hand in his. "Elsbeth, listen to my story without judgment until the end. Please."

Her eyes in the limited lantern light seemed as blue as the darkest depths of the ocean and just as turbulent. Finally, she gave a short nod.

"Thank you." He kept his voice gentle, as if coaxing Marianna to smile. "This widow and I spent the night together. Though her husband was dead, *she* wasn't and she yearned for that part of her marriage that another man could give her. While we enjoyed it, neither of us expected anything more in our relationship. She continued on her way to her sister's, and I resumed my travels in the opposite direction. I gave her what she needed without anyone she knew the wiser."

"Are you saying my mother feels nothing for the captain? Is that not worse?" Her gaze turned glassy with unshed tears.

Why did he have to be the one to explain and take away her innocence? "What I'm saying is that as a widow, your mother is allowed certain freedoms, but she is restricted by the society in which she lives. Being on board this ship with a man she enjoys a friendship with means she can indulge, when usually she can't."

Elsbeth put her hand on her hip and gave a short, emphatic shake of her head. "I don't believe it. I know how a man and a woman create a child. We read about it at school. Right along with how a child is born." She shivered before continuing, her nose crinkling. "I cannot believe that my mother, who has no wish for a child at her age, would wish to act in such a way simply because she hasn't in a score of years."

He sat back, confounded by her knowledge about some things, yet her lack of knowledge about others. A small part of him celebrated her innocence, but it did make helping her accept her mother's need for the captain more difficult. Based on Lady Astor's behavior, he had little doubt that this was not the first time she had taken advantage of being away from home. If he were to do what was best for him, he'd simply agree with Elsbeth and return to his cabin, but he'd never been very good at doing that, especially with her.

Cocking his head, he studied her. "Have you ever been kissed?"

She winked at him, a soft smile tilting her lips. "Of course. Don't you remember? You kissed me in the garden at the Dulacs' butterfly ball."

He coughed to keep her from seeing his surprise. That kiss had been nothing but a brush of their lips. Could it be true that no other besotted swain had seen the beauty of the passion inside her? "Is that the only time?"

She huffed, and he mentally berated himself for asking while at the same time reasoning it was important if he was to make his point.

"Surely, you remember the kiss you gave me before you proposed."

Actually, he didn't, but if it had been made of any great passion, he was confident he would have. Brushing off that reminder, he pressed further. "I mean, has anyone *else* kissed you?"

Even in the limited light, he could see her cheeks flush, and he kicked himself for prying. That's what he deserved for asking. A strong wave of jealousy threatened to make itself known, but he forced it down, swallowing hard.

She didn't look at him as she answered. "It's hardly appropriate for me to be kissing every man I meet. Truly, Teddy, I see no reason why this is relevant to the current dilemma with my mother."

He'd thought to have her remember a time when a kiss had excited her, but now at the thought that someone else may have provided that moment for her, his intentions took a completely different direction. "May I kiss you?"

"What?" Her blush, which had been fading, returned. "Why would you wish to do that?"

He shrugged, pretending a nonchalance he was far from feeling. "I wish to demonstrate a feeling."

Though her cheeks remained rosy, he could tell she was giving his request serious contemplation.

What if she said *no*? What, then? Then he'd wish her a pleasant sleep and return to his cabin, which he should have done earlier. But he'd be disappointed, not just because he wished to help her understand, but because he wished very much to kiss her.

She sighed. "Very well. You may kiss me."

At her acceptance, albeit not overly enthusiastic, relief flooded him. Not daring to say anything more that might have her changing her mind, he cupped her face with one hand.

She closed her eyes and lifted her chin.

He smirked. It wasn't exactly what he had in mind. He wanted her to feel passion...hopefully for the first time. At that thought, his humor disappeared. "Open your eyes, Elsbeth."

She did as told, blinking, her eyes filled with curiosity.

He leaned forward, his head just a foot from hers. "Now wrap your hand around my neck."

Hesitantly, she did as he requested, her gaze having moved to his lips. Her tongue came out to lick her own, and his body reacted.

Keeping his body under control, he lowered his lips to hers and brushed a light kiss across them.

As expected, she relaxed at such a light and familiar touch.

He'd forgotten how soft they were. He needed no more encouragement to press his lips more firmly against hers. At his pressure, her hand on his neck grasped him tighter.

Pleased with her reactions, he licked at her lips, encouraging her to open them. Finally, she seemed to understand, and he quickly slipped inside to taste her.

Her sudden gasp of surprise gave him pause, but since the pressure on his neck held him to her, she evidently did not dislike it.

He wrapped his other arm around her as his tongue explored her mouth. Hesitantly, she tangled her own with his and that gentle touch had his body reacting far faster than expected. Unable to help himself, he deepened the kiss, letting her feel some of his own passion.

She didn't hesitate. Instead, she tilted her head and accepted his invasion, causing a spear of excitement to race through his chest.

Eventually, she tired of accepting and she pushed her way into his mouth. Her boldness had him growing hard, but he forced himself to hold back, even as old dreams of her tried to force their way into his mind. Moving his hand behind her head, he adjusted her angle to better taste her, even as he pulled her closer.

At his embrace, her other hand came down on his thigh, holding tightly as a soft moan filled his mouth.

His hand moved from her head to her collarbone of its own accord. Just as it started toward her breast, he caught himself.

He wanted her too much.

Gently, he pulled back, finally leaving her lips, but her grasp around his neck let him go no farther.

"Elsbeth."

"Hmmm."

"You can release me now."

Her eyelids fluttered open. "Oh." She dropped her hand, which slid down his chest before coming to rest on his other thigh.

Stiffening in more than one place, he took both her hands and set them on her lap. "Tell me. Did you feel anything?"

She blinked. "I did. I've never felt so much in so many places."

Triumph surged through him even as his body reacted to the knowledge of what places she spoke of. Sitting back, he put the space he needed between them to regain his composure. "Was it pleasant?"

"No, not *pleasant*. It was exhilarating, exciting, and..." She paused, as if searching for the right word to explain what she felt. Her brow furrowed. "It was odd, too. The longer you kissed me, the more I wanted you to." She studied his face. "What is that phenomenon?"

"It's passion." That was perhaps a simple word for it, but the only one she might understand with her lack of experience. And he was confident now that she'd never been truly kissed before. That knowledge soothed his soul.

"Passion." She cocked her head. "I've always thought of that in the context of someone pursuing something they love, like Lady Sommerset's passion for painting or even my cousin's passion for books."

She'd just defined exactly how he felt, but at the mention of her cousin, the Duke of Northwick, his ardor cooled considerably, which was just as well since the whole experiment was to help her understand her mother. Though it had allowed him to do what he'd wanted to do since the day he'd first met her almost two years ago, it was not his purpose now. Even if his conscience tried to tell him otherwise. "It is similar, only it is considered a passion for another person. What you felt is just the beginnings, the preamble, shall we say, of what your mother feels."

"My mother?" Her brows furrowed for a moment. "Oh, yes." She cocked her head. "My mother feels that?"

He gave her a nod. "But much more."

She remained silent, giving him time to cool his own desires for her. In hindsight, it may have not been the best way to go about helping her understand, but he'd never claimed to know the best route to every solution.

Rising, he held out his hand. "I suggest you return to your cabin."

She took it and rose, reaching for her lantern. As she did so, the outline of her breast was clear against the silk of her dressing gown, and he swallowed a groan.

"I know not what to do. You have given me much to think about. Should I wait up for my mother?"

"I cannot advise you on this, as it is beyond my experience. I would, however, suggest you understand your own feelings before speaking to her."

"Yes, that does make sense." She squeezed his hand then let go. "Thank you, Teddy."

He wanted to tell her he was pleased to be able to help her as a friend, but the words became stuck in his throat. Instead, he gave her a nod and opened his arm for her to precede him to her cabin.

He waited until she was safely inside, then turned on his heel and headed for the deck. Stepping outside, the cool evening air hit him, and he breathed it in, needing it to clear his mind and the floral scent of the woman he'd always loved.

He was quickly on his way to Dante's second circle of hell. The circle for those who lusted, though it didn't quite fit, for he loved as well, which just made his craving that much worse.

He strode toward the front of the ship where the breeze was the strongest. The crewmen watched him but didn't say anything. Since the captain was likely below deck otherwise occupied and the officer at the helm wouldn't leave his post, he was assured some solitude. He'd taken a fair amount of sea voyages since coming to the Continent and had no problems navigating the relatively quiet deck as the ship raised and lowered over the growing swells. When he could go no farther, he stopped before the railing, the air cold so far forward on the ship at night. Laying a hand on the railing, he stared out at the darkened sea, the only lights the stars above and an occasional whitecap below reflected in the moonlight.

His emotions were raw. He should have never touched Elsbeth, but he couldn't regret it. All the love for her he thought buried and gone had risen up from the depths of his soul like a kraken of old rising from the sea and just as deadly. How was he to ever find a mother for Marianna if his heart remained with Elsbeth? And how was he supposed to guard himself against her when she traveled in the cabin next to his daughter? Though he'd not behaved well all the time while traveling, at least he'd been able to stifle his feelings for her, but now, having come upon her again, having talked to her, held her, and now kissed her, she was all he could think about when not caring for his daughter.

But he would not ask for her hand again. She'd made it clear he was not the right man for her. He was no fool. Yes, she looked at him as a good friend and distant relative, someone on board who was familiar and comfortable. Someone safe.

He gripped the rail with both hands in frustration. He had to remove himself from her presence, but there was nowhere for him to go on board the ship, except to stay in his cabin as much as possible. But even that wouldn't be helpful, since he'd still see her at dinner, hear her outside his door, smell her scent as she walked by. He took a deep breath, filling his lungs with salty air, a far rougher concoction than Elsbeth.

Running his hand through his hair, he could see the rest of the journey being torture. Perhaps he deserved it after the women he'd bedded, both unwed and married. For the drunken carousing through the streets of Paris and Barcelona. And especially for the thefts and midnight escapades with passing friends. This was his payment for his transgressions.

Now he had a choice. Enjoy Elsbeth's company, making the pain of parting that much more painful. Or avoid her as much as possible to become used to her not being in his life…again. It was a pitiful choice, but the only way he could take some control of the situation and the damage to his heart.

CHAPTER TEN

Elsbeth sat beside her mother, covertly watching her. Seated as they were next to the captain, it was easy to do. The two conducted themselves as if there was nothing special between them, talking to others at the table and conversing normally. It would have made her doubt herself, but for the last two nights, she'd woken in the middle of the night to once more find her mother gone.

Glancing down the table toward Teddy, she tried to catch his attention, but he conversed with the captain's sister-in-law. Not being able to talk to him all day had made it more difficult to sort out her feelings. Not only was she confused about her mother, but also her own reaction to him. She could only guess that Lady Marianna had been demanding much of his time. She hoped he wasn't avoiding her after their kiss. It had been a true revelation, not only about passion, but also about her reaction to him. She wanted to know if that was how it always was. Would she feel that way with her future husband? It wasn't exactly something she could ask her mother.

"Lady Elsbeth, I did not see you on deck today. I hope you are still enjoying the travel." At Captain Gentry's direct address, she smiled.

"I am. I did enjoy the afternoon breeze, but I have been so engrossed in a book I am studying that the time quite slipped away."

The captain's brows rose. "A book. Was it a novel, by chance?"

"Oh, no. It's actually a map in book form. It was recently published. The map is quite beautiful with thirty-four colors. It's by William Smith and is called *A Delineation of the Strata of England and Wales, with part of Scotland.* He used his study of fossils to study the layers of rock, clay, and sand throughout those countries."

Captain Gentry stared at her for a moment, obviously perplexed.

She braced herself for a condescending remark at worst or a mundane change in subject at best. "My mother has actually done some mapping herself after studying cartography."

Finally, the captain looked to her mother and his brother next to him. "If only we could have a scientist study the seas in such detail. It could greatly benefit us captains at sea. Sometimes we still discover land that has yet to be added to a map."

She appreciated his comment being related at least to her book. "Where have you encountered unmapped land? Here in the Mediterranean?"

"No. This body of water has been well-charted for hundreds of years. But navigating to India can be quite an adventure."

As Captain Gentry went on to regale the table with his adventures of anchoring off an unknown island, she studied him. He was quite knowledgeable in his field and a war hero, from what she'd heard. He was handsome but a bit weathered. His skin was quite tanned and almost leathery, but his warm, brown eyes were the color of the Madeira wine served on his ship. His trimmed, dark beard showed very little white, his hair had none, and his forehead was high above thick eyebrows.

Was it his physical attributes that her mother found appealing or his mind? Maybe it was his ability to control his crew with a firm hand yet be comfortable among the aristocracy. That would definitely pique her mother's curiosity, but as far as she knew, the oceans and lands far away had never held great appeal for her. She truly wanted to know how her mother felt about the captain but was taking Teddy's advice and trying to decide how *she* felt first. It wasn't as easy as she'd thought.

Glancing down the table toward Teddy, she found him looking her way. He gave her half a smile before turning his attention to Mr. Silverton. How quickly she had come to depend upon him again. Before she'd debuted, he had always been there. Whatever event she attended, even if he did not escort her, he would appear. His admiration for her had been heady, and in hindsight, she hadn't truly appreciated it.

After she'd completed her first dance with her cousin at her coming out ball, request after request to dance had followed, until she found herself partnered for almost every dance. Her own popularity had led to her rash decision about Teddy. She hadn't known what to do about all the attention. Only after the newness of it wore off did she find herself rather bored, but by then, he'd been gone months. It wasn't until she became friends with the other Curious Ladies that she learned how truly fortunate she had been.

"Elsbeth, what are you thinking about? Is it that map?"

Her mother's question brought her back to the present quickly. She gave her a sheepish smile. "I spent the whole day with it. The strata of rock depending on the regions is truly fascinating."

Her mother studied her before shaking her head. "The captain asked you a question."

She moved her attention to Captain Gentry. "I apologize. Please allow me to answer."

"I asked if you've been to Stonehenge in our own country? Your mother tells me you were in Mallorca studying the Dragon Caves. So I was curious if there were formations in England that were of interest to one such as yourself."

"Oh, my, yes. There are quite a few places to examine in England, and I have been to Stonehenge. The rock itself is not from the surrounding area, the structure is hardly natural, so it is too far from the realm of my studies for me to draw any conclusions."

The man raised his brows. "I did not know this. Where is the rock from?"

"That, I'm not sure about, but I believe if I study the map in the book I've been reviewing, it may give me possible sites."

"And is there a study for the material beneath the ocean as well?"

"Captain Gentry, I'm sure no one else is quite so interested in this topic. Perhaps you and Elsbeth can discuss it further on the morrow?" Her mother used her hand to indicate the others at the table, specifically the captain's brother, who appeared as if he'd rather be anywhere else.

She bit down on a smile as the captain seemed to recall he was hosting dinner.

"You are correct, Lady Astor. I sometimes forget that not everyone is as fascinated by the sea as I am."

A bit guilty for leading the captain astray, she sought a topic that would interest the others. "Perhaps you could tell us why our sailing through the Strait of Gibraltar was so smooth. I'm sure that is something we are all quite curious about."

"Yes, Captain, I was bracing for a rough passage, yet yesterday as we sailed by, the ship made good progress." Mr. Silverton shrugged. "Or so I was told. I cannot say I have nearly as much knowledge about such things as Lord Mabry."

The captain's brow furrowed. "Going through the straits can be smooth or rough. Personally, I prefer it to be rough. Usually, when it's not, it means we may encounter rough seas farther north." He glanced over them all before continuing. "But the sea is a fickle lady, and there's no predicting how she will act. We may make good time getting back home or we may hit a calm that barely tightens the sails, or we may have winds so fierce that we must wrap the sails and hunker down. All I ask of you all is that if we do hit a storm, you remain in your cabins."

He held his hand up as Mr. Silverton opened his mouth to

speak.

"Even you, Mr. Silverton. I'm afraid any malady that may befall you due to rough seas is far better than what you would encounter on deck."

Mr. Silverton closed his mouth and nodded his acceptance of the captain's advice. Next to him, she found Teddy looking at her, this time one eyebrow raised.

Fortunately, the final course was served, and she was free to focus on her food. As everyone finished, the men rose and stepped outside onto the deck for a drink, and she was left with her mother as the captain's sister-in-law excused herself immediately, as was her custom.

"I fear you may have scared her away." Her mother's whispered words gained her attention.

"Mayhap, Mother, on the morrow, you could engage her in the latest fashion or a play she might have seen."

"Yes, I suppose I could. I do believe those would be her topics of choice. Though you could have easily discussed those as well. You appeared a bit distracted this evening. And I do not for a moment believe it was that map. This is hardly the first time you've studied it."

She rose, needing to move away from her mother's close scrutiny. "No, it's not. But every time I open it, I do find something new that's significant."

"Elsbeth, don't try to distract me. What were you thinking upon?"

She walked around the head of the rectangle table where the captain had sat and moved to stand across from her mother. "I was thinking of many things. About how young I was when I first debuted and how changed I feel now. I was thinking about my friends at school."

Her mother didn't look away for an instant. "And what else? Come, I'm your mother."

Yes, and that was the crux of her dilemma, but she couldn't bring herself to discuss it, at least not yet. However, there was something else that weighed on her mind. "I was also thinking about the fact we didn't see Teddy all day until dinner and that may be because his daughter needed him. He fairly dotes on her. He has changed so much."

"Ah, yes, Lord Mabry. He is an interesting study. I've been pondering him myself. Judging from what Joanna told us from his letters, he was wasting his life on silly pleasures. Yet here we find him much changed, either by his experiences or his fatherhood."

"I think it may be both." She shrugged. "I just became distracted by the thought of the changes the past sixteen months have wrought on all of us."

Her mother relaxed and waved her hand. "Hardly all of us, unless you are purposefully referring to those gray hairs that I recently showed you. I am exactly the same."

"I'd quite forgotten about those." But obviously, her mother was thinking about them. Because of the captain?

Her mother rose from the table. "I suggest we retire for the night. I wish to rise early to see the Atlantic again. I missed the passage into those familiar waters, never expecting it to occur while I rested."

She was well aware of why her mother wished to sleep now. She wished to leave in the middle of the night, only to return just as the rays of the sun began to light the sky before it even broke over the horizon. She pretended to sleep each morning when her mother returned after four hours of absence. She could only guess the regularity of her mother's visits were based upon the captain's routine. She still could not quite believe that her mother did anything more beyond kisses and perhaps sleeping side by side. Her actions while in his company were no more than polite conversation and a few more smiles than was her wont.

Standing, she pushed the chair back beneath the table then moved toward their cabin. "Since I spent most of the day in our cabin, I too am anxious to see the Atlantic."

Her mother stepped into their cabin just as the ship seemed to come down off a particularly high wave, jolting it, sending the lantern light swinging back and forth.

She grabbed the doorframe with each hand, but her mother lost her balance and fell into her as the ship creaked its displeasure. Holding tight, she was able to keep them both from toppling backward.

"My, that was quiet the welcome back." Her mother righted herself then stepped to her bed and sat. "I suppose we need to be ready to hold on. If I remember correctly, our journey to Gibraltar was a bit rougher than it was once in the Mediterranean."

"I remember that as well." She moved to her own bed and began to disrobe.

After helping each other with their clothes, they lay down to sleep. Lying in her bed, she relived Teddy's kiss. Maybe it would give her pleasant dreams because she had no doubt in just a few hours, she would awake again to find her mother gone.

But she was wrong.

After barely an hour, the ship shook so hard, it woke her from her sleep. She lay wide awake listening to the loud creaking of the wood, faint shouts coming from on deck, and rain pelting the small porthole.

The ship's rolls over the water were more pronounced until they seemed to float above the ocean before crashing into the water again. Dread filled her as the reality of the raging storm outside made itself known. Lightning lit the cabin for a quick moment before plunging them back into inky darkness.

Turning her head to look at her mother, she could see nothing, so she waited for the next flash. It came much too quickly, followed by a loud rumble of thunder that drowned out the noise of the ship. Her mother lay on her bed, also awake.

Throwing her legs over the side of the bed, she thought to dress, but upon the next roll of the ship, simply grabbed her dressing gown and donned it. "I don't think we'll be sleeping tonight."

Her mother's voice came from the darkness. "No, I suppose

we won't. Now if we can only light the damned lantern. Everything seems better in the light."

She'd only heard her mother curse once before and that had been at James, but she'd been mad then. Surely, she wasn't angry at the storm. "I'll light it."

Standing, she held on to the built-in bedframe and looked at the pitch-black space above her, waiting for another slash of light from Mother Nature.

Instead, what she received was a loud crack and multiple flashes. She jumped at the sound but quickly reached out to touch the lantern. As loud thunder filled the air around them, she worked in the dark to unhook it. "I have the lantern."

"Oh, thank the heavens."

At that response, she began to wonder if her mother was afraid but didn't dwell on it, instead carefully feeling her way toward the porthole, where the tinder box was kept for lighting the wick. Another burst of lightning filled the cabin at the same time thunder rolled directly overhead. Quickly, she opened the door of the lantern, steadying it on the cross beam. Balancing the lantern made striking the flint impossible, as that required two hands. "Mother, I'm going to need your help."

"Anything to get light in here."

"Make your way toward my voice but hold on as you come." The ship pitched and she grabbed the beam, almost losing her own balance. "I'm over here. Feel your way along the wall."

Her mother's hand touched the lantern next to hers. "I've got it."

She let go to open the tinder box. As soon as lightning struck again, she managed to light it.

Her mother sighed as she closed the glass.

Taking the lantern from her, Elsbeth set it on the hook in the ceiling. Though it swung to and fro, it did not jump off. "I would have never guessed that lighting a lantern could be so taxing." Though she teased, her mother's face relaxed. "Would you like help with your dressing gown? It is far cooler in here than normal.

I wonder if the door to the deck is open."

"I'm sure it is. William will have all his men out to manage the sails or whatever other tasks are needed."

Her mother's voice was calm, but as she helped her with her dressing gown, Elsbeth could feel her shaking. She also noticed the use of the captain's first name, proving her mother was rattled. She needed to give her a task. If her mother could focus on something, she'd feel much better. But what?

The ship suddenly tipped to the side, as if caught sideways by a wave. They both grabbed a beam to stay upright. "Maybe we should sit on our beds. I believe standing could be dangerous."

Her mother remained silent but did sit, her hand grasping the frame of the bed tightly.

Shouts were heard over the roar of the storm as the ship pitched and moaned. Doors banged and she was quite sure chairs in the dining area had fallen over. Another burst of lightning hit with its accompanying thunder, as if it followed the *SeaSprite*.

"Captain Gentry knows what to do. Everything will be fine." Her mother's words surprised her, but she imagined they were more to comfort herself.

"I'm sure he does. He's a war hero. Has he related any of his battle scenes to you? If not, I think you should ask him so you can tell everyone back at home."

Her mother shook her head. "No, he most likely believes them far too—"

A banging on their door made her jump. Frowning, she slid from her bed and opened it. "Teddy?"

He stepped in with Lady Marianna in one arm, closing the door behind him, filling what little space there was between the two beds. "I need your help." He was dressed in his boots, pantaloons, and shirt, much like he'd been when he first appeared in the Dragon Caves.

She held on to her bed with one hand. "Of course. What can we do?" She glanced at her mother, who nodded silently.

"Can you care for Marianna?"

Her heart thudded in her chest at why he might need her to do so. "I can. Is Consuela unable to?" She couldn't voice her fear that the woman had hit her head or worse.

Though frustration showed in the tightness of his jaw, there was no fear in his eyes. "No, she can't. I found her huddled in the corner of her cabin wailing." One corner of his lips quirked up. "She's louder than my daughter."

His daughter, who had her two fingers in her mouth, simply looked around curiously. Lady Marianna didn't seem in the least bit uncomfortable with the larger movements of the ship.

That explained Consuela, but why not him? "And are you unable to? I thought you rather skilled. Definitely more skilled than I."

All humor disappeared from his face as he stiffened. "The captain needs my help. One of his men has been knocked out. I need to assist. It's a bad storm. To get through this, he needs every man that's able. And there are a few tasks I know how to do."

Fear, sharp and strong, sliced through her heart, causing her to catch her breath. "But what if something happens to you? What about Marianna?" Even she heard the panic in her voice.

His gray gaze turned silver. "If anything happens to me, I ask that you ensure she is delivered to my family."

Her throat closed at the thought of losing him far more than the idea of the huge responsibility he asked of her. Tears pricked the back of her eyes and she swallowed hard. "Of course." She moved her gaze to the wide-eyed baby and felt a tug on her heart. "I promise to care for her as if she were my own."

His body appeared to relax. "Thank you."

She set her hand on his arm. "Be careful out there. Marianna needs you."

"I will." For the first time, he looked at her mother. "Thank you." Then he lifted Marianna and put his daughter in her arms. "I will return as soon as I'm able. Hopefully, by morning."

Then without a word, he turned and left, closing the door

firmly behind him.

She quickly moved back onto her bed, where she could protect the child in her arms. Looking down into Marianna's curious, blue eyes almost made her forget there was a storm wreaking havoc upon them. Almost.

Her mother rose and moved to her bed. "Here's my pillow. We should make a pile with the bed clothes to keep her safe."

Of course. Her mother's knowledge would help Marianna, and having someone to care for would help her mother. "You can use my pillow too. I don't believe anyone, except maybe Marianna, is going to sleep tonight."

As her mother went about preparing a nest in the corner of the bed, she held her finger out to Marianna, who immediately clasped it. Her heart warmed at the grasp. The little girl was adorable and a very important piece of Teddy. She yearned to be a part of Marianna's life. That was hardly possible. Maybe it was simply that Marianna was the first baby she ever held, but her instinct said otherwise.

A sudden lurch of the ship had her pulling her hand from the baby's grasp and grabbing the side wall to keep them from being thrown from the bed. Her mother, who had been gathering a blanket, was not as fortunate and fell against her own bed.

"Mother!"

"I'm fine. But I think we should move this makeshift baby bed to the center." Her mother stepped forward and grabbed on. "This way, we can sit on each side." She rolled the blanket and set it against the back wall, then moved the two pillows and other blanket until there was an oval space just big enough for Marianna. "You can set her down now."

She didn't really want to, but her mother was right. Gently, she laid the baby in the nest. Marianna looked at her, brows furrowing. Quickly, she held her finger out and the little girl grasped it before sticking the fingers of her other hand in her mouth.

"We're going to need napkins in order to change her."

Her mother's observation had her feeling more confident. At least *she* knew what to do. "I can go to Consuela's room and get some."

"No. I don't want you trying to traverse the ship while its movements are so unpredictable. I have an old shift we can use."

"And I have that white, linen shawl."

Her mother nodded before kneeling on the floor to go through their chests.

The ship moaned as it came down off a large wave, then the crash of water hitting the deck outside had her stiffening. With little Marianna safe inside their cabin, she couldn't help wondering what Teddy was doing and if he was safe.

Her mother pulled the garments from the chests then sat on the floor and used her scissors to cut and rip the material apart.

She watched Marianna, who seemed neither concerned by the crashes of items not secured in the cabins on either side of them and in the dining area, nor by the loud creaks and groans of the ship. Even as another crack of lightning struck above them and shouts came from the deck, Marianna simply released her hand and grabbed her own foot.

"That should be enough." Her mother closed the lid and rose to lay the strips of cloth on her own bed, then moved to sit next to Marianna as well.

A roll of thunder sounded above, continuing as the ship rose and fell at least three times. "It sounds as if the storm is following us, or we are following it."

Her mother's attention was on Marianna as she responded. "I don't know the strategy for ships in a storm, but as soon as we get back to Haven House, I plan to find out. James must have a book on that somewhere."

It was hard for her to think of Haven House, where she and her mother lived with James and Joanna during the season. In the middle of the night on a ship in a storm, it seemed like another life. Another large wave hit their side of the boat and crashed on the deck outside. She looked to the door and found water seeping underneath.

The fear she was attempting to keep at bay traveled up her spine to make itself comfortable in her head. The ship slammed down again, and her hair brushed the ceiling of the cabin as she was thrown upward. Immediately, she looked to Marianna, who gurgled with delight. Worry filled her for the baby, herself, her mother, and Teddy.

Pulling the sash from around her waist, she laid it across Marianna and underneath her mother's pillow. "Can you tuck this in beneath the mattress at the foot?"

Her mother immediately understood her plan to secure Marianna. "I think I can."

With one end secured, she grabbed a strip of linen her mother had cut and tied it to her sash then pulled it under her pillow and across the bed to tuck it beneath the mattress at the head of the bed.

With the baby secure, she breathed easier, but as the ship rocked and creaked while the angry ocean battered it, her thoughts kept straying to Teddy. Her mother focused her attention on Marianna, which left Elsbeth with her worry. She had no idea how long they sat there before her fear for him turned to panic. She had to know he was safe.

Jumping from the bed, she took a linen strip and tied it about her waist to hold her dressing gown closed against the cold.

"What are you doing, Elsbeth?"

"I'm going to check on Teddy. Keep Marianna safe until I get back."

Her mother's eyes widened before narrowing. "You most certainly are not."

She didn't plan to argue about it. Opening the door, she stepped onto the wet floor of the dining area.

"Elsbeth, you come back in here immediately!"

Closing the door on her mother, she held on to the wall, feeling her way forward toward the door to the deck. "Ow." Her shin connected with a chair that had fallen and she paused.

Lightning lit up the room, proving the door was indeed open, though at the next pitch of the ship, it slammed closed again.

As quickly as she dared, she crept closer. Another large wave caught the ship on the side and threw her from the wall. The dining table, which was anchored to the floor, caught her at her thighs and her breath *whooshed* from her. Fortunately, lightning struck again as the ship tilted back and the door opened to let the light in.

Stepping over a chair, she dashed forward, catching the door-frame as the ship's bow tilted upward, hanging in the air like a gannet before dipping downward as if spotting its prey. She grasped the other side of the doorframe as the sky lit up, showing her for a brief second the men scattered about, the pelting rain, and what she thought might be Teddy. He stood near the foremast, his shirt ripped and hanging over his backside, his muscular torso wet with rain as he handed a seaman a tool of some sort.

Holding on tightly as the ship continued down the giant wave, she kept her eyes trained on the area of the mast, breathlessly waiting for the next strike of lightning.

Finally, the sky lit up just as the ship hit the bottom trough and water crashed over the deck toward Teddy. Her breath filled in her lungs even as men shouted, and she screamed.

The giant wave washed across the deck and over the railing into the ocean.

Teddy! Darkness filled the night again as her heart threatened to break. She tried to move forward but couldn't seem to let go of the doorframe. Light flashed once more.

No one was at the mast and her gaze flew to the railing. He stood there against a cannon, a rope tied about his waist stretched across the deck, as he gripped the collar of a seaman whose legs dangled over the side.

Darkness descended once again and with it, her fear for Teddy. Tears of relief fell down her cheeks as she tried to suck in air, her breathing ragged after her scare, but before she could settle it, the door slammed closed again. She moved her hand to set the latch before leaning back against the wall, her heart racing faster than a fox before a pack of hounds.

Standing there in the darkness, braced against the wall, she admitted the truth if only to herself.

She loved Teddy Mabry down to the depths of her soul.

CHAPTER ELEVEN

As DAWN LIT the eastern sky, Teddy walked on tired legs to the door to the dining area. The ship still rolled and pitched, but the storm had passed, and the sea no longer washed over it. He was bruised, battered, and wet, but alive thanks to the captain's precautions, and now all he wanted was to hold his daughter.

Stopping before Lady Astor and Elsbeth's cabin, he tapped lightly. Hearing movement inside, he waited, unable to quell the need to see Marianna immediately. The door opened and Lady Astor in her dressing gown smiled at him, though her voice was just above a whisper. "Glad I am to see you, Lord Mabry. I trust the storm has left us?"

He nodded, even as he stepped inside, unable to wait another minute.

Lady Astor put her finger to her lips. "They fell asleep not an hour past."

It took a moment for his mind to understand what he saw. Lying on her bed, a sleeping Elsbeth cradled Marianna in the crook of her arm, his daughter's hand grasping a handful of blonde hair in her sleep. His heart thudded hard in his chest. Seeing them together filled a dream he hadn't known he had. Relief, love, and happiness swept through him, leaving him exhausted.

The ship moved suddenly, and he lost his balance, his legs far too tired to hold him. He pressed his hands against the wood ceiling to keep from falling.

"Might I suggest some rest?" Lady Astor's quiet words made sense. "We will care for Marianna a little longer."

As much as he wished to hold his daughter, he was soaked and tired, and she was well cared for. Seeing her thus calmed his anxiousness. He nodded, too tired to speak. Turning back to the doorway where Lady Astor stood, he forced his mouth to work. "Thank you."

He stepped out and made it to his cabin without further mishap. Stripping off his wet clothes, he left them on the floor before collapsing onto his bed, sleep taking over.

It was after noon when he woke, the sun throwing a shaft of light through the cabin. Pleased that Mr. Silverton was not present, he took the time to wash the sea salt from his body and hair before donning his clothes. The ones on the floor had hardened as they'd dried, and he had them thrown away. Though his muscles ached in places, he felt refreshed.

Anxious to see his daughter, he strode out of the cabin and knocked on Elsbeth's door. Hearing no response, he hoped she no longer slept and was out on deck enjoying the day. Just to be sure, he knocked on Consuela's cabin, but she was either still too scared to venture forth or she was below with the chef. Had she fed Marianna? Concern spurred him on.

The ship was back to a pleasant rocking, and he quickly made his way out on deck. It appeared as if everyone was enjoying the sun after the night of rain and wind. Studying the people, he noticed the first officer talking to a seaman, no doubt taking stock of anything lost or anything damaged. The captain also spoke to crewmen while his brother and wife strolled the port side.

Striding forward, he headed toward the bow, careful to stay out of the crew's way. He'd never shied away from storms, but last night on the deck of the *SeaSprite*, he'd discovered a new respect for them. Spotting his quarry near the bow by the starboard railing, he quickened his pace.

Elsbeth, who wore a pink day dress, had foregone her bonnet, her golden hair left long down her back. And in juxtaposition with her was Marianna's dark head of curls as she rested her cheek on Elsbeth's shoulder with a handful of Elsbeth's hair in her hand. His heart swelled with love for them both.

"Ah, and here comes our hero now."

At Lady Astor's words, he realized she was also present, as well as Mr. Silverton. He hadn't noticed them, so intent on Elsbeth holding his daughter was he. Elsbeth turned to face him and gave him a soft smile before turning her back so Marianna could see him.

His daughter's eyes lit with recognition and her hand reached out, opening to release Elsbeth's hair then closing her fingers. He stepped up to her. "Mari, did you miss me?"

She started to push up in Elsbeth's arms, anxious for him.

"You'd best take her, Lord Mabry, before she jumps out of my arms." Elsbeth lifted Marianna, and he held his daughter aloft before giving her a kiss on both cheeks. She squealed, making little noises, as if she wished to tell him all about last night. Holding her against him, he hugged her gently, feeling whole once more.

Elsbeth looked on, a wistful, half-smile on her face.

He settled Marianna against him with one arm then stopped himself from reaching out to hold Elsbeth's hand. In his happiness to have his daughter safe, it was easy to forget that Elsbeth was not his.

"Congratulations, Lord Mabry. The captain told us how much you helped us weather the storm, so to speak." Mr. Silverton raised his brows, as if he wasn't quite sure how that could be.

"I did what I could." It appeared the man, who'd claimed seasickness the night before, had suffered no lingering effects. "I was aware that being down a man is dangerous when on a ship at sea."

"Lord Mabry, you are being far too humble." Lady Astor waved off his comment. "Captain Gentry told us one of his men would have been lost at sea if not for your quick response."

So that was what they all referred to. While Mr. Silverton looked doubtful, Lady Astor seemed curious to hear the tale, but it was Elsbeth's gaze that gave him pause. She looked upon him with a knowing smile and a gleam in her eye. "It was only instinct. The captain had enough experience with storms to have me tied to the mast or otherwise, I would have gone over the side as well. It just happened that when a particularly large wave crashed onto the deck, it threw me toward starboard. The rope about my waist held, keeping me on deck. But just as it brought me up short of the railing, a man yelled as he passed me. I simply reached out and grabbed him. Caught him by the back of his shirt collar."

Lady Astor grinned, as if she had been the hero herself. "That man must be very grateful."

He nodded. "Wiley swears it was the rock his son gave him that swept him near me."

"It was Mr. Dodd you saved?" Elsbeth's eyes widened.

"Yes. He was just coming out of the rigging and had stepped on deck when the wave caught him."

Mr. Silverton frowned. "I noticed this morning that not all the sails are raised. Our progress is quite slow. Was there damage last night?"

Before he could answer, Lady Astor addressed them. "The captain said we're heading for the nearest Portugal port. Something about a boom hit by lightning and in need of repair before we can continue."

He looked up to see that indeed the top sets of sails were open, but the bottom were not. He hadn't been aware in the dark that anything had snapped. Between the crack of the lightning, the roar of the ocean, and the rumble of the thunder, it would have been difficult to notice. He had heard that two sails had ripped, but from what he knew, they could be repaired while underway. "Did the captain say which port we are close to?"

Lady Astor shook her head. "I didn't—"

Marianna suddenly squealed, and he looked down at her to find her reaching out with both hands. "I think I've been remiss in seeing to my daughter's needs. I'm sure she is very hungry."

"I don't think that's why she yelled." Elsbeth moved to stand in front of him so she could face his daughter. "She's had plenty to drink both this morning and this afternoon."

It was his turn to be surprised. "She has? How?" Consuela's terror was so great, she couldn't even stand last he'd seen her, never mind feed Marianna.

Elsbeth looked past him at Mr. Silverton before returning her gaze to him. "Perhaps I can explain at another time."

"Lord Mabry, my daughter can be quite demanding when the situation warrants it." Lady Astor nodded emphatically. "And this morning it definitely did."

He noticed Elsbeth blushing. He could not see her *demanding* that Consuela feed his daughter, but that must have been what she had done.

She spoke up. "Marianna's needs outweighed the fear of the wet nurse. I simply helped her to see the advantage of complying."

Now he was truly curious and would ask how she'd done it in private.

Mr. Silverton chuckled. "I, for one, am not surprised. I'm learning so much about Lady Elsbeth. Lord Mabry, did you know this is her second season and she took time away to investigate a cave? That is quite remarkable."

At Mr. Silverton's interest in Elsbeth, he felt his hackles rise. "Yes, she has always wished to study the Dragon Caves of Mallorca."

"That is what I understand." Mr. Silverton moved closer and spoke directly to Elsbeth. "I must say, Lady Elsbeth, I am quite impressed by your willingness to put knowledge above marriage."

Elsbeth's cheeks heated. "I do not believe one must over-shadow the other and my fellow classmates are of a like mind. Perhaps you have not traveled among the same people I have."

He held back a chuckle at her ability to correct Mr. Silverton's assumptions while remaining perfectly polite.

Mr. Silverton, rather than taking offense, seemed to interpret her remark as an invitation. "Then I must definitely change my venues once we return to England. In the meantime, perhaps you would walk with me and tell me more about your study in Mallorca."

Alert to the stiffening of Elsbeth's shoulders, he quickly inter-vened. "Mayhap, Mr. Silverton, the lady could enlighten you another time. She has promised to lend me a book of hers so that I might read it before we disembark."

"Oh, I almost forgot." Elsbeth gave the man a gracious smile. "Maybe another time, Mr. Silverton."

"Of course. Perhaps this evening then." The man smiled at her and gave a slight bow with his head.

She gave the man an equal nod. "I shall look forward to it."

And now his unease was back. It was ridiculous, of course, that he didn't want anyone to spend time with her. Mr. Silverton had shown nothing but good manners and came from a good family. There really was no objection to him.

Except that he still wanted Elsbeth for himself. It was illogical, but he wanted all her attention while on the ship.

"Yes, I believe we can be available for a stroll this evening." Lady Astor spoke up, her comment a relief. How could he have forgotten she protected her daughter's reputation always?

Mr. Silverton smiled, obviously not deterred. "My lady, it would be my pleasure."

Not wishing to remain with the man, he looked to Elsbeth. "Shall we?"

"Of course." She laid her hand on his forearm that supported Marianna and they walked toward the cabins.

He kept their pace slow as to enjoy the sunny weather. As

soon as they were far enough down the deck, he leaned in. "You must tell me how you were able to get Consuela to feed Marianna."

Elsbeth grinned, a twinkle in her eye. "I simply stated that if she were going to go overboard, she would be lighter without her milk."

"You did not say that."

"I most certainly did, though my Spanish is far from perfect as I understand it much better than I can speak it. I wasn't heartless. I sympathized with her and then mentioned that." She paused, obviously thinking of the encounter. "I understand why you needed the dragon teeth so much. She held that stone in her hand the whole time."

"I suppose if a token gives comfort, or as in Wiley's case, it answers the question of why he was saved, there really is no harm in it."

"Yes, I can see your point. But what happens when the lucky possession fails?"

He lifted Marianna to his shoulder and opened the door to the dining area for Elsbeth. "It never does. I believe they endow it with all the good that happens to them and reason away any bad."

She halted and turned to face him. "Then I may have to make a wish on one of the stones I have."

"And what would you wish for?" He held his breath, anxious to know what her dream would be.

She shrugged. "That's my dilemma. I don't know what I would wish for. Even though I'm not happy about my mother's situation, I would not wish her otherwise."

At the mention of her mother, he stilled, having thought he'd made his point with his kiss. It certainly had haunted him since the other night. "You are not pleased that your mother has found some small amount of happiness on this voyage that will not damage her reputation?"

"I cannot believe she *is* happy with her arrangement. She

leaves at midnight and returns just before dawn. How can such clandestine meetings bring joy?" She shook her head. "But I have decided not to say anything. Soon I will be married myself, and it is not my place as her daughter to either approve or criticize her actions."

With that pronouncement, she turned and headed for her cabin. He followed as his was past hers.

She stopped at her door. "Thank you for the excuse to leave the deck. I did not feel like entertaining after so little sleep. Did you wish to borrow a book, after all?"

"No. Marianna is all the entertainment I need."

Elsbeth's face softened, and she stroked Marianna's hair. "You are so fortunate, Teddy." With that, she disappeared into her cabin.

He stood there staring at the closed panel, the wistfulness in Elsbeth's voice haunting him. Did she wish to have a child, or did she wish to be Marianna's mother? His heart started to race, but he shook his head and stepped back. Now he was seeing things that weren't true.

Walking past Consuela's door, he opened his own and stepped inside. He should have continued to keep away from Elsbeth, but it was as if she were the sun and he Icarus, flying far too close, even knowing what would happen. At least this time, he knew she wouldn't accept a marriage proposal and that there was no hope for them. She looked at him as a friend, as she had in the past, but he'd been too wrapped up in his own feelings to recognize it. This time, he would simply enjoy their moments together and suffer the loss of her all over again when they stepped back onto English soil.

He lifted Marianna from his shoulder and set her on his bed. Her lips puckered and her eyes squinted before a loud fart filled the room. She giggled, obviously happy with herself. He bent over to kiss her before standing straight again. He would definitely need extra cloths for this change of her napkins.

CHAPTER TWELVE

ELSBETH SAT AT the dining table, her back to her cabin door, the only light the meager rays of the single lantern hanging from the ceiling that had been turned down. It wasn't appropriate for her to be sitting in her dressing gown in a public area in the middle of the night. Mr. Silverton could wake and exit the cabin he shared with Teddy, though she very much doubted such an occurrence. She'd already categorized Mr. Silverton as basalt, which she found more often than not uninteresting. The man hadn't been able to keep from yawning during their sunset stroll on deck. Then at dinner, Teddy elbowed him not once, but twice. So, appropriate or not, she was here because she'd spent far too much time in her cabin, having slept away the afternoon.

If she were honest with herself, it was her mother's empty bed that had her fleeing the cabin in the hopes that Teddy might be about. He always seemed to make her concerns fade. Part of her wished the trip would be over soon so she no longer needed to pretend her mother wasn't making nightly visits to the captain. But part of her wanted the trip to last longer so she could spend more time with Teddy. The problem with that was it would make her time during the rest of the season even shorter.

She wished she could simply marry Teddy and be done with it, but he would never propose a second time, and she couldn't very well say she'd reconsidered her rejection of almost two years ago. He certainly hadn't shown any of the lovesick tendencies he'd had last time he proposed, so she doubted he held any deeper regard for her than that of a friend. It was also obvious that he wasn't nearly as effected by their kiss as she had been. Though she shouldn't be surprised since he had so much experience in kissing. Most likely, he already had someone at home in mind to be Marianna's mother.

At the thought of the little girl, her heart melted. There was something about the baby that tugged at her heart. Maybe it was the tempestuous time they spent together during the storm. Or maybe she simply reacted toward babies that way, but since she'd never known any, she couldn't be sure.

She turned her head to look at Consuela's door. Did Marianna wake already tonight? Despite her better judgment, she rose and quietly crept toward the girl's door. She listened carefully, trying to hear beyond the small creaks and squeaks of the ship. Was that a whisper? She couldn't be sure. Maybe she simply hoped it was. Quickly, she returned to her seat, her back to the cabin. Had she imagined it?

At the scratch of a latch on a door lifting, she turned her head. *Teddy!*

He backed out of the cabin quietly, closing the door slowly, barely making a sound. Then he turned away from her to go to his cabin.

She didn't want him to leave. "Teddy?" She kept her voice soft.

Startled, he turned at his name. He shook his head, even as he grinned and walked toward her in bare feet.

She'd never seen his bare feet. He had nice feet.

"What are you doing out here at this hour?" He kept his voice low as he carefully pulled out a chair and sat next to her. He wore only his pantaloons and shirt, which was open almost to his waist.

Heat filled her at his state of undress, but she found her voice. "I couldn't sleep. I slept all afternoon."

He ran his hand through his hair, leaving it very disheveled. "I think the only person still on a regular sleep schedule is Marianna. Mr. Silverton is in our cabin snoring loud enough to wake the fish at the bottom of the ocean."

She chuckled but quickly covered her mouth. Removing her hand, she smiled. "I fear I bored him so much talking about stalagmites that he could barely stay awake at dinner."

"That was not you. He did not wish to sleep during the day, so I'm sure he won't wake until almost noon."

She didn't mind. The man was well-mannered and attentive, but he definitely was one of the *doorknobs* her mother had mentioned. "Did Marianna fall back to sleep, then?"

"Yes." He hesitated before asking. "Is your mother not in your cabin?"

And there was the crux of her restlessness. "No, she isn't. I thought I would sit here for a couple of hours in the hopes that you might be up and about."

"Me?" His eyes widened in fake surprise. "I thought surely you were hoping to converse with one Wiley Dodd about his rock."

She patted his arm at his silliness. "I do have other interests besides rocks."

He leaned back and crossed his arms, covering most of his chest. "Do you, now? Pray tell, what could they be? Perhaps subjects learned at the Belinda School for Curious Ladies?"

At his knowing look, she wanted to surprise him. Since his cousin ran the school, he might have heard what Joanna taught there. What *didn't* they teach? She smiled slyly. "I'm quite interested in this thing called passion."

His chest rose with a deep breath and his Adam's apple bobbed as he swallowed before speaking. "I'm surprised Joanna hasn't made that an independent study."

"Maybe I should suggest it."

"No." He uncrossed his arms and leaned forward, his body no more than two feet from hers. "Why do you wish to know about passion? Ladies are not taught about this until they marry." He paused, then murmured, "If even then."

She pounced on his remark. "Do you mean to say some women *never* learn about passion?"

He stiffened, obviously not happy with her question. Then, as if making a decision, he answered. "I won't ever lie to you. Yes, some women never know passion. Some marry and their husbands only need them for childbearing, enjoying themselves with their lovers." He looked away. "I met quite a few on the Continent, and there are plenty like them in England." His tone of voice made it clear he highly disapproved.

"Is passion something to be sought, then?" Despite the odd topic, she was truly curious.

His gray gaze met hers, his eyes seeming almost charcoal. "It is the ultimate joy of man."

"What of women?"

He smirked. "Women too. What is unique about passion is that both partners not only feel joy themselves, but also joy in bringing it to each other."

She raised her brows and looked askance at him. "That is a terrible amount of joy. If this is true, why would not everyone seek it?"

He sighed as he shook his head. "I should know better than to discuss such a subject with one so innocent. I suggest you ask your mother."

At the reminder of where her mother was, she stiffened. "Not only do I not trust her to tell me the truth, but I'd be skeptical as such a question pertains to her judgment."

He raised his right eyebrow. "And you trust me and my judgment?"

He had a point. Did she trust him? The answer came swiftly. "I do. You would not hide information from me because you don't want me to know. Which begs the question—if passion is so joyous, why is it hidden from us while you and other men are well-versed on the subject?"

"That's simple. Reputation. Passion leads to acts of intimacy.

If a young woman succumbs before she is married, she is ruined. But if she knows not what she is missing, there's no reason for her to fall prey to her own passion." He gave a satisfied nod, as if that made sense.

Becoming frustrated, she put her hand on her hip. "That's silly. 'Knowledge is power.' 'Forewarned is forearmed.'"

He chuckled softly. "Now you sound like my cousin, quoting some ancient philosopher."

"The first is from Sir Francis Bacon and the second is a proverb." She would not be distracted. He was attempting to change the subject. "It doesn't make them any less relevant."

His face lost his smile, and he leaned forward. "Elsbeth, passion is powerful. Once you know it, you may not be able to resist…like your mother."

"I don't believe my mother has fallen prey to passion. Maybe companionship, but nothing more." The former felt wrong to her.

Teddy's face softened as he cupped her cheek. "I wish I could show you, but that is for your future husband."

Tears stung the back of her eyes, her frustration growing. "And what if he won't enlighten me?"

His gaze wavered, looking away, then back to her, then away, as if he contemplated some weighty decision. Then with no warning, his hand moved behind her neck and he kissed her.

Something inside her sighed in relief, as if this was exactly what she had wanted. All she knew now was that his mouth on hers made her feel better.

Abruptly, he pulled away, his forehead resting against hers. "You make me forget myself. Your curiosity is too strong."

"Please. Show me what I need to know."

He sat straight, taking his hand from her. "I can't."

Irritation burned through her. "Can't or won't?"

"Both."

She wanted to hit something, storm about the room, go out on deck, anything to get rid of the strange need to know everything. She rose, thinking to stomp out when her gaze landed on Teddy's door, where Mr. Silverton slept.

A terrible idea occurred to her, and she pushed it away. It was manipulative, but she had nothing to lose and much to gain. She forced herself to shrug. "Very well. I will ask Mr. Silverton about this passion. I wonder if I would feel the same when he kisses me."

Teddy rose up so fast, she stumbled back.

"No. You will *not* ask Mr. Silverton."

"But—"

"No. If you are so bent on ruining yourself, then *I* will show you."

Part of her danced in triumph, but another part of her feared what was to come. "Does passion mean ruination, then?"

"Yes. No. It's—it depends." He ran his hand through his hair, clearly frustrated with her.

She didn't want him to think. She just wanted him to feel. *She* wanted to feel. With a bravery she didn't know she possessed, she laid her palm against his bared chest, something she'd wanted to do since he'd joined her.

"Elsbeth." He whispered her name as his hand covered hers.

He felt so warm yet hard. She couldn't stop staring at her hand on his flesh, the thrill of touching him making the air around her sizzle.

"Elsbeth?" He tilted her chin with his free hand, forcing her to look at him.

"Yes?" His gaze was on her lips, and she licked them, anxious to kiss him again.

He groaned softly before his head lowered and he did just that.

This time, she was ready and invited him in. He tasted of Spanish sherry and spices, his earthy scent overwhelming her. She wanted more and swept her tongue into his mouth. Excitement skittered up her spine as she ran her hand up his chest, his larger one still over hers. She liked the feel of the soft hair with muscles beneath.

He finally let her hand go, only to pull her close as his mouth moved from her lips to the side of her neck.

A rush of heat settled in her chest as he bent her backward, her robe falling to the side as his lips traveled across her bare skin along her shoulder. Anxiously, she wished her robe off, even as she wished his shirt gone. Then his teeth tugged at her shift, and she wanted nothing more than to rip it apart. "Teddy." The word was half entreaty, half moan.

He lifted his head from her, his eyes shards of silver in the lantern light. "Not here."

It took her a moment to understand him, but as he took her hand and pulled her toward her cabin, his meaning became clear.

Opening the cabin door, he brought her inside then reached behind her and closed it, flipping the lock.

Her heart thudded in her chest as a spark of excitement raced through her body at the sound. And then he was there, pushing her against the door with his body as his mouth took hers and his hands pushed the robe off her shoulders.

She pulled at the sash before slipping her arms from the dangling sleeves.

His hands ran up her arms then down her sides, brushing the sides of her breasts. A surge of *need* ricocheted through her before settling deep in her belly. Astoundingly, she wanted his hands on her breasts. Surprised by the thought, she stilled. Did he wish her hands on him as well?

His mouth left her lips and started its journey down her neck once more. Grasping his shirt, she pulled it from his pantaloons, anxious to feel him again. He pulled his hips back, allowing her free access, or so she thought until he brushed his fingers over her breasts still covered by her shift.

"Oh." The lightning that seemed to shoot from his touch to between her legs was as strong as what the storm brought the night before.

Teddy immediately stilled. "Do you wish me to stop?"

Stop? How could he ask such a thing when her body craved more? "No. Please. I need..." She didn't know what she needed, but Teddy must have understood because he untied the neck of her shift.

Anticipation filled her as the material hovered on the very edge of her shoulders. All it needed was a simple—she shrugged. The shift fell down her arms, brushing across her sensitive breasts to settle at her waist. She jerked her head up to see Teddy's reaction.

His nostrils flared as his gaze feasted upon her. There was no other word for the intense focus with which he stared.

"Beautiful." The word was whispered with reverence.

A strange relief flooded her, as if she'd expected rejection, but before she could contemplate that odd reaction, his hands cupped her bare breasts. The area between her legs seemed to heat, even though he did not touch her there.

"So soft, yet hard too." He ran his thumb over her taut peaks, causing such a spike of *need* that she grasped his waist to steady herself.

Immediately, he dropped his hands and moved her so her behind was against her bed. "Sit."

She didn't question him but hopped up on her mattress.

He took the opportunity to rid himself of his shirt, letting it fall to the floor.

She'd known in the caves that he was broader than he'd been the last time they'd been together, but now he revealed why. His shoulders had thickened with muscle, his chest now revealed large mounds, and his abdomen rippled down to his waistline. Something inside her wanted that strength against her. He was Teddy, yet far more.

Before she could reach out, his hands cupped her breasts once again and he bent over. As his mouth descended, she held her breath, both in excitement and surprise. His lips closed over her left nipple, and her whole body shivered with glee as air *whooshed* from her lips. His tongue played with her tightened peak, while his fingers played homage to her right one.

The warmth below began to feel moist and achy. She grasped on to him, and he laid her back, his mouth and fingers never leaving her breasts, making her crave more. When he did leave off his attentions, to loom over her and kiss her, disappointment filled her.

She broke the kiss. "Isn't there more? I want more."

He lifted his head to look at her, his eyes that hard, shiny gray, though his lips twitched. "Yes, there is more. If you truly want it."

Couldn't he see how much she wished to be with him? "Yes. Please. I need more."

All humor disappeared from his face. "Then I will give you all that you need."

Illogically worried he would stop their inappropriate activity, she grabbed his head between her hands. "Promise?"

His chest brushed her own as he took a deep breath. "I promise."

Searching his eyes and finding only the truth, she pulled him down for a kiss of gratefulness. It quickly turned demanding on her part, but he did not try to break away.

The feel of his hand upon her knee below her shift should have shocked her, but she welcomed it. It was Teddy. She was safe with him, even if he didn't love her, but he did care. She wanted this memory forever.

He broke the kiss to move his lips lower. When they reached her nipple, she almost sighed with relief, but the relief was short-lived when he nipped at her, making the *need* in her belly burn stronger. It was then that his hand slid up her thigh toward the very spot that had started to ache.

Instinctively, she spread her legs, not caring whether she should or not, just wanting whatever it was she needed from him.

His mouth paused while his fingers moved to the juncture of her thighs.

She stopped breathing, hoping he would continue. He'd

promised.

Finally, his mouth resumed, but instead of nipping at her flesh, he sucked on her breast.

She moaned, arching her chest, loving the feeling of being desired, pretending he felt as strongly for her as she did for him.

Then his hand moved over her mons and down between her legs. Before she could think to object, his fingers ran over a spot that had her hips moving upward of their own accord as pure pleasure shot through her. This was what she needed.

He moved his mouth to her other breast and sucked, even as his fingers played against her again.

She didn't know what was up and what was down. Pleasure flowed from that very spot to the core of her. She grasped his head, holding him to her even as she set her feet on the bed and lifted her hips, wanting the tantalizing end just beyond her reach.

Teddy obeyed her silent command and increased his touch, his fingers playing with her, winding her up then relaxing before winding her up further.

She moaned, and he left her breast to capture her sound. The touch of his body against her, his tongue in her mouth, his fingers exciting her below all converged. He played in circles, pressing more, longer, until her body spiraled into pure joy.

She grasped him, holding him, the only stability among the sparks of happiness shooting through her and melting into absolute satisfaction.

"Ells." His voice was soft.

She blinked as she opened her eyes. "Yes."

"*That's* passion."

She didn't comprehend at first. Her life having just opened to a whole new world with him. "Passion?"

His eyes smiled, even if he didn't. "Yes. You asked me to show you what it was. Now you know." Something in his voice was odd, strained.

"Thank you."

He rose from her, pulling the bottom of her shift down.

Suddenly realizing her state of undress, she pulled the top of her shift up to cover herself and sat up, not sure how she should feel about what had just occurred. What she felt was more connected to him than she ever had. Did he feel it too?

"I best leave before your mother returns."

She opened her mouth to tell him he still had time but thought better of it. "Thank you for showing me. I am indebted to you."

He stilled as he reached for the door. He shook his head but did not look at her. "No. It was a pleasure to assist you." Then, without another word, he slipped from her cabin.

Was Teddy suddenly uncomfortable? She'd have to check after his health in the morning. She wasn't sure what to think about passion now. But she was absolutely sure of one thing. Something had changed between them. Something good, or so she hoped.

CHAPTER THIRTEEN

TEDDY STOOD AT the rail as the men lowered the gangway that would bring people and supplies to the wharf. Fortunately, he had yet to see Elsbeth, as it was still quite early. He smirked, rather certain she slept well, probably not even waking when her mother had crept in.

He wished he could say the same for himself. After a brisk walk that had done little to calm his need for her, he'd given in and gone to bed, providing his own relief. Yet he'd been haunted by dreams of her, the images of her coming to her peak burned into his mind. Her flushed cheeks, arched body, soft moans, and the little shiver as she finished. It had been too much for the flimsy barriers he'd built around his heart. Now, not only did he want her love, but her body too. He could not return to England without telling her. It may have been selfish, but if she wanted him to stay away, she would have to reject him again.

As the crew were securing the gangway, Consuela arrived on deck with Marianna. He strode forward, happy to see his daughter had risen. It was early yet, but there was a certain contentment inside him at having made his decision regarding Elsbeth. He took Marianna out of Consuela's arms and lifted her high above his head.

His daughter laughed, sending a screech across the deck.

"Señor Mabry, you make her sick."

At the English words from his wet nurse, he brought Marianna down to look over his shoulder. "You can speak English?"

The woman didn't look at him. "A little. I hide it to see you true. I wrong. I have other chance be honest."

"Another chance? Oh, you mean the storm?"

She nodded.

If he wasn't mistaken, she thought the storm had been brought on by her hiding her knowledge of English from him. It would be far too complicated to explain why that wasn't so. "I am pleased you told me now." He smiled to show her he forgave her.

"*Gracias.*" She held her arms out. "She need her burp. Give me before she sick."

He would have preferred to hold Marianna a bit longer, but he didn't want Consuela to think he held a grudge. "Of course." He handed his daughter back to her. "I will take her when the captain says it's safe to leave the ship. I'm guessing you wish to stand on firm ground."

"*Si, por favor.*" The woman's relief was obvious.

He didn't know what it was like to be so frightened. He sincerely hoped that once back on firm ground, Consuela would return to the ship before they departed for England again. Marianna needed her. Luckily, he still had three dragon teeth if he needed to coax her aboard once more.

The door to the deck opened and Lady Astor exited, followed by Elsbeth dressed in her pink day dress and matching bonnet, which gave her skin a rosy hue. Surprised to see Elsbeth up so early, he studied her. Except for a slight blush in her cheeks, she appeared well.

"Lord Mabry, I see you have risen with the sun today." Lady Astor strode forward as Consuela moved toward the mizzenmast with Marianna.

"Not so early as that, Lady Astor. Did you have a pleasant night?"

At his question, Elsbeth's eyes rounded behind her mother's back.

"Why yes, I did. I slept quite well compared to the night before."

"I imagine we all did. And you, Lady Elsbeth? Did you sleep well?"

Her blush gave her away, but her mother's attention was on the gangway.

"I did, Lord Mabry. Thank you." She moved to her mother's side. "I admit that the delay here is rather exciting since I hadn't thought I'd ever journey to Portugal."

He would like to show her many sights in the country, but Port Selva would not have been his choice. It was a quaint area and one he'd visited before. But as far as having art, music, or sites of great geological interest, he only knew of one in the vicinity, and he had not seen it. "I'm not sure how long the captain expects to remain here, but if it's more than a day, I would be happy to show you the Caverna de Pedras Perdidas or 'Cave of Lost Rocks.' From what I've heard, it wouldn't be nearly so interesting, nor as large, as the Dragon Caves, but it is the only rock formation I know of in the area, and given your geological studies, you might find it of interest."

Her eyes lit with excitement. "I would very much enjoy seeing that."

"Yes, it sounds quite interesting." Her mother made it clear she'd be accompanying them, which was of little surprise. "The captain said we will be here for at least three days while repairs are made. He also said something about adding additional provisions since this area is known for its almonds, pears, and of course, fish."

"Three days. Then it appears we can all enjoy our time off ship." He didn't comment that the captain had been on deck all morning and the only way Lady Astor would have known that information would have been if she'd talked with him in the middle of the night. She obviously thought her visits to the captain were completely unknown. As long as his visit with Elsbeth was unknown as well, that was all that concerned him.

He loved her, but he wouldn't compromise her to keep her. He had too much respect for the woman he'd come to know so much better.

The captain approached them with a smile on his face, which was not a usual occurrence. "Ladies, Lord Mabry, you are all free to disembark if you wish. We will be here for a few days, so you may like to take advantage of the two lovely inns here for more robust and flavorful meals."

"Captain, your hospitality has been exceptional." Lady Astor's comment elicited a bow from the man.

"I thank you for your kind words, but I assure you the food on land far surpasses anything we are able to manage on board."

As Lady Astor continued to praise the captain, Teddy moved next to Elsbeth. "I will do some exploring today and find out exactly where that cave is. I know it's inland, so we'll need to ride there."

"I don't want to be a bother, but I do have a certain curiosity about it." She winked, her lips twitching.

He chuckled. "I have no doubt you have quite a bit of curiosity and won't be able to enjoy Port Selva until you've seen it."

"Very well, I admit you're quite correct." She smiled, her blue gaze dancing with laughter.

"*¿Señor?*"

He turned at Consuela's voice, immediately focusing on Marianna. "*¿Sí?*"

"We go?" She pointed to the gangway, seamen already disembarking to begin their duties.

"Yes." He turned to Elsbeth. "I promised Consuela she could leave the ship as soon as it was acceptable."

"Of course." She stepped around him to directly talk to Consuela. "I'm so glad the dragon tooth protected you."

The woman's shoulders relaxed as she grinned. "It did."

Elsbeth patted Consuela on the arm before looking to him. "May I hold Marianna?"

Pleased by her continued interest in his daughter, he nodded.

Elsbeth took Marianna in her arms, bestowing her with a kiss. "I do believe I missed you, little one."

Marianna immediately grabbed at the strands of hair Elsbeth had left loose about her face—not the best decision when carrying a baby, but she didn't appear to mind.

"Are you ready to disembark?" He held his arm out to Elsbeth.

She nodded. "Mother? Are you coming?"

Lady Astor was quick to end her conversation with a smile for the captain, and the four of them descended to the wharf. Though the land rose steeply from the rocky shore, the area closest to the sea was filled with homes and a few shops, as well as one of the inns the captain had spoken of.

If he remembered correctly, the other inn was a bit higher.

They strode down the wharf toward the opening to the dirt road.

"Theo! Is it truly you?" A young woman in a pale-green dress with black ringlets framing her face strode toward him, her booted heels striking a staccato on the wooden planks as her servant hurried behind her with their horses.

He groaned. How could he have forgotten why he knew the area so well? "Senhora Rocha." He pasted on a smile.

"*Senhora Rocha?* Come, come, Theo. Do you not remember your Cinnie?" She strode up to him and took his head in her hands as she kissed both his cheeks before adding a lingering kiss on his lips. Laughing, she let go. "If you need another kiss to remind you, I can make such arrangements." She winked at him, even as she took his free hand in hers, completely ignoring the ladies with him.

Elsbeth's hand on his arm tightened. He didn't relish explaining Cintia.

There was only one way to handle Cintia—flattery. "I could never forget such a lovely woman. I believe you have become more beautiful since the last time I saw you."

"It is the truth you speak. It is a curse." She laid her hand on her chest just above her ample bosom.

"You bear it well." He purposefully did not look at her chest. "May I introduce you to my daughter?"

The woman's eyes widened, as if he'd told her he had a tiger for her. "A *child*? Theo, tell me you did not marry."

"Indeed, I did." If he was lucky, the fact that he married and now had a daughter would keep her from wishing to renew their affair. At the time they had been lovers, she'd been exactly what he needed, a woman of great passion who cared more for the physical than anything else. Now, he wanted far more from someone far different.

"This is not she?" She waved toward Elsbeth.

The two women stared at each other as if they would like nothing better than for the other to drown. Inwardly, he tensed. This was not the optimal situation. At the obvious animosity, he made the introductions. "Lady Astor, Lady Elsbeth, may I present Senhora Cintia Rocha. Senhora Rocha, Lady Astor and Lady Elsbeth Rawley, very good friends I'm traveling with." He took Marianna from Elsbeth. "Lady Marianna Mabry, this is Senhora Rocha. Senhora Rocha, my daughter, Lady Marianna."

"You hold her?" Cintia stepped back. "Is that not what this woman is for?" She pointed to Consuela.

"Cintia, this is my daughter's wet nurse, Consuela de la Torre."

The two women studied each other, neither impressed with the other before Cintia turned back to Lady Astor and Elsbeth.

"'Friends'?" Cintia stepped forward, her gaze sweeping over Lady Astor quickly but returning to Elsbeth. It was to her she spoke. "You know Theo from back there in England?" She waved toward the ocean.

Lady Astor stepped closer to her daughter. "Yes, we do. We have known him even before his cousin married my nephew."

He groaned silently at Lady Astor's revelation that they were distantly related, even as Cintia brightened.

"Oh, *família*. Welcome to Port Selva. You must be my family's guests for dinner. I can only imagine the food you have had to endure on that boat." She scrunched her nose before turning around to where her man held their horses and motioned to him, no doubt to make the arrangements.

As he imagined what the rest of the day would be like, he wished himself and Marianna back aboard the *SeaSprite*, even though he'd barely been off the ship for half the hour.

Lady Astor saved him. "That is very kind of you, *senhora*, but we wouldn't wish to impose on you and your husband. We are, in fact, excited to see your town."

Cintia laughed. "Husband? Oh, no, I am far too young to settle on a husband. I live with my father, the *capitão do porto*, and my *avó*."

Lady Astor looked blankly at the woman, who didn't pay any attention.

He answered her unspoken question. "Both married and unwed ladies are called Senhora here. Senhora Rocha said she lives with her father, who's the captain of the port, and her grandmother."

Once again, Cintia took his free hand. "And she would so enjoy seeing you again." She pouted, looking up at him from under her lashes.

"And we would enjoy meeting her." Lady Astor stepped closer to Cintia. "Perhaps she could join us for dinner at the inn here. I know the captain plans to and it would be lovely to have your grandmother. In fact, we were just headed to the port captain's office right now to invite your father."

Cintia squeezed his hand, obviously not happy with the idea at all. And if it had been anyone but Lady Astor, he would say that they were oblivious to his awkward position, but Lady Astor was astute, if nothing else.

Cintia laughed as she waved her hand about. "*Minha querida avó* does not venture from our home. She cannot walk very well."

"Nor can she hear, if I remember correctly," he added. The last he'd been in Port Selva, the older woman had been deaf to her granddaughter's cries of ecstasy in the very next room.

"You remember too well, Theo. Perhaps you remember much of your visit here?" She licked her lips, as if remembering herself.

The blatant invitation in her eyes had his stomach tensing. Elsbeth had yet to say a word, though her tight grip on his arm told him she had many thoughts. "It has been a very long time and much has happened since my marriage and Marianna." He disengaged his hand from Cintia's to shift Marianna to his other arm.

She immediately backed away. "Do you not wish to give your daughter to your servant?"

He swallowed a growl. He'd like nothing more than to give his former lover the cut direct, but with her father's power over the port, it would not be helpful for their voyage. "I *like* to hold Marianna." His tone revealed too much of his anger if Cintia's narrowing eyes were any indication. He forced it to be lighter. "Perhaps you would walk with us to see your father?"

She glanced toward the office before looking at him. Clearly, she wasn't very amenable to that idea. "*Não*, I have not simply come to see our new arrivals. I also must see if the new hat I ordered has arrived." She waved them toward the office. "You go and reacquaint yourself with my *pai*. I will join you again in a bit."

Last he knew Cintia's father had no idea his unmarried daughter enjoyed many a liaison with a passing aristocrat. Had the man finally discovered her true nature yet or did he remain woefully ignorant? "We will look forward to your company later, then."

"Yes, of course." She turned on her heel and clapped, her man scurrying to do her bidding.

Finally, he turned to Elsbeth, but before he could say anything, she slipped her hand from his arm and strode toward the port office.

His heart sank.

Lady Astor shook her head. "Just when I had such hopes for your character." Then she followed her daughter.

Would he ever be able to leave his past behind? He'd found a new purpose in life with his daughter and he wished to be a reliable and loving parent, but if his past kept reappearing, how could he leave it behind? Then again, Elsbeth was his past too.

He spoke to Marianna. "What am I to do, *carina*?"

"You rid of her."

At Consuela's answer, he turned toward her, having forgotten she was there. "I would very much like to, but she is the daughter of the port master, and the captain needs assistance from the man."

Consuela pointed to the office. "Then go. I care for Marianna. You care for trouble."

Though her English wasn't that good, her thought process was. "You're right. But if you see Cintia coming back, I want Marianna."

The woman gave him a sly smile. "You hide behind daughter." She spat on the ground. "*Puta* not like babies."

Consuela was very observant. Though it was hard to admit it, she was right. Not only about Cintia's doubtful character, but also his defense against her. If having Marianna was the only way to keep Cintia at bay, then he would hide behind his daughter's skirts, or rather, napkins. "Yes, I do." He handed Marianna to Consuela then headed for the office.

"Señor Mabry."

He halted and turned. "*Sí*, Consuela?"

"You good man."

He let out a heavy sigh. "I'm trying." Shaking his head, he continued on his way.

CHAPTER FOURTEEN

"**I**'M NOT GOING." Elsbeth strode past her mother at the bow of the ship, too angry to stand still. All of her hurt and fury had not dissipated at all since the evening before when the "lady" Cintia had not only accompanied Teddy into dinner, where she sat next to him, but she also kept her hand on him the entire meal. To make things worse, she'd managed to get him outside alone.

Now that she understood passion, she knew exactly what they had done out there in the moonlight. And now she was expected to venture out in a coach to some secluded spot in the jungle with him? She turned and strode back. "He can take Senhora Rocha."

Her mother, who leaned her back against the railing, shook her head. "Elsbeth, you cannot tell me you are upset with that woman. She's obviously not a lady, and if I'm correct, I don't think Lord Mabry is interested in her—not that it matters to us."

"Please, Mother. I know you watch people. They have obviously been lovers. For all we know, they still are. For all we know, he may have left the ship in the middle of the night last night to see her." Though she'd been awake as her mother slipped out, she didn't leave her cabin all night. Even when she heard Teddy pull out a chair in the dining area, she'd stayed in her bed. When he tapped lightly on her door, she'd ignored it.

She never heard him go back into his cabin, but then again, she hadn't heard her mother return, either. She had fallen asleep.

It was one thing to know that he would one day marry someone else, but she expected it to be a woman of quality. Then she wouldn't have to suffer watching whispers and touches and whatever else Cintia had done beneath the table. But why would he care what she thought? It wasn't as if he were still in love with her. She wouldn't be surprised if he still harbored resentment toward her for turning down his proposal.

"So you will forgo seeing a cave with strata clearly visible because Lord Mabry is going and the *senhora* is not?"

She halted. "Perhaps we can go without him?"

"Elsbeth, you are far too much a lady to make an excuse now. I don't understand why you are so upset. We both know that Lord Mabry spent most of his time on the Continent in self-indulgent activities. Why are you bothered one of those activities has reappeared?"

Because I love him. She swallowed the words as she faced her mother. "I'm angry *for* him. He seemed to have changed and now it looks as if he's fallen into old habits. He has a daughter now. His behavior should be more circumspect."

Her mother chuckled. "I hardly think his activities on this ship will make any impression on his daughter. Not to mention there are many fathers in the *ton* who are hardly monogamous and their daughters do well. Meanwhile, you could be giving up the chance to see this unique site."

Something in her mother's arguments caught her attention. "You sound as if *you* are actually looking forward to seeing this cave."

"I am, though perhaps more the lagoon that is said to be next to it. The ship is still being repaired. It's a beautiful day. And from what the captain says, even those of us not interested in the geological wonders of Earth will find the area quite pretty."

Of course. How could she have forgotten that the captain was coming with them? Her mother had mentioned it when they broke their fast. Would they all stay behind if she refused to go? Or would her mother go, anyway? Surely, she would stay on board with her as chaperone since Teddy would stay. Then again, he was their guide, and she couldn't see him refusing to show the captain where the cave was. Which begged the question—how *did* the captain know how beautiful the cave was?

"Is this not the perfect morning for an adventure, ladies?" The captain strode toward them. "Are you ready for our expedition?"

Her mother looked to her and raised her brows. "Are we ready?"

It seemed there was no help for it, but she must go. Fine, she'd simply avoid talking to Teddy. She wanted him to feel her disapproval. Smiling at the captain, she gave a short nod. "Most assuredly. I'm quite tantalized by all the talk about this cave. Have you been there before, Captain?"

The man shook his head. "No, but I have heard about it for years. I'm pleased to have an excuse to visit it." He held his arm out. "Shall we?"

Her mother took the captain's arm. "We shall." The laugh that followed sounded almost girlish.

Following the pair, she looked about the deck, expecting Teddy to suddenly appear, but he wasn't in sight. Had he decided to spend the day with Cintia? At the thought, her belly tightened, as if a handful of granite rocks tumbled about inside. How could she want Teddy to come with them but also not want him to? She didn't like this feeling at all.

As they descended the gangway, she looked down the wharf, but didn't see him. It wasn't until they had walked onto the road that she spotted him. Relief, followed by irritation, shot through her. Teddy wore a dark, brocade tailcoat, a white cravat, tan pantaloons that showed off the muscles in his thighs, and black boots. He looked far too handsome for a simple outing into the interior.

"My ladies, I hope you don't mind riding. I'm afraid a coach will not be able to navigate the terrain." He smiled at them as he gestured to the four horses behind him, two with sidesaddles.

Her mother reached him first. "I would love to ride. I haven't ridden since last winter. Our forays into Hyde Park have all been in the phaeton." Her mother walked toward her mount with the captain.

"And what about you?" Teddy studied her as if trying to judge her mood.

"I would prefer riding over being cooped up in a coach." Now she wouldn't have to speak to him. She moved to her horse, too late realizing that she would need his assistance in mounting.

She turned to find him directly behind her.

"Allow me." He cupped his hands for her to step into.

Seeing no help for it, she took hold of the saddle and stepped into his hands. He lifted her into position as if she weighed little and held the horse as she arranged the purple skirts of her dress. She had no riding habit on board, so it took a bit longer to get comfortable in her day dress.

"You are looking quite beautiful today, Elsbeth."

She wanted to ask if she was more or less beautiful than Cintia but bit her tongue. Instead, she gave a short nod, not trusting herself to remain civil.

When he didn't move to his horse, she finally looked at him. "Are you walking?"

As if he realized they all waited upon him, Teddy turned on his heel and quickly mounted.

He led them down the road, her mother and the captain behind them. Once beyond the settled area, Teddy addressed her. "When we arrive at the path, we will need to ride single file."

"Is the way treacherous?" She imagined riding along a cliff with the dirt beneath her mount slipping away.

"No, not at all. It's simply that the path isn't used for anything but access to the cave, so it's not wide."

That made sense, since he'd described it as a shallow jungle cave, but for no reason, she found herself angry that she was just now learning of this. What was wrong with her? "Then you will have to lead."

He gave her a questioning look. "I had planned to."

Silently kicking herself for being inane, she clenched her jaw. It would be best if she kept silent. They traveled higher on the road before veering off onto a smaller one. Here, there were occasional residences of local people, much like cottages at home, only whitewashed and instead of thatched, the roofs were terracotta.

Teddy then led them off the road onto a narrow path. It was narrow because of the dense foliage, and she had to duck under a low branch of a tree at least three times.

At one point, Teddy jumped down from his horse and moved a large branch that had fallen over the path, proving how rare it was for people to search out the cave.

When the path widened substantially, he turned his horse around to address them all. "I've been told that if we follow this path past the entrance, there's the Blue Grotto, named such for its blue water and the way the sun reflects the color against the walls where the water trickles in. It's also supposed to have some unusual birds, though to be honest, I'm not sure I could pronounce their names."

Her mother moved her horse forward. "Now that is something I'm quite interested in."

She groaned silently. She had no doubt her mother would wish to see the birds, as she had been helping Georgina with her studies in ornithology.

"This way." Teddy directed his mount farther along the path.

Though the way had widened and could easily fit two abreast, she continued to hang back, earning her an odd look from her mother.

There was no opening in the foliage to suggest a cave entrance, but suddenly, it was there, in a large, dark rock rising high above them. She couldn't resist and rode forward, even passing Teddy. Since he had told her not to expect anything of significant interest, her expectations were quite low. However, as the large, arched opening came into view, she could see the cave was lit inside, which meant it must have an opening to the sky.

She slowed her horse. "It has an oculus!" She smiled, thrilled to have seen a sight she'd only read about.

Teddy rode up beside her. "Is that important?"

"Yes." Then, remembering she was unhappy with him, she frowned. "I need to investigate."

"Wait, let me help you down." He jumped from his horse and was by her side before she could argue.

With no alternative, she allowed him to help her dismount. His hands around her waist and the scent of him as she placed her hands on his shoulders reminded her of the night he'd shown her passion. Had that only been two days ago?

He let go of her as soon as her feet hit the ground, and she quickly turned toward the cave. Picking up her skirts, she walked briskly across the soft ground, her excitement too much to contain. As she drew closer, the rings of different rock strata became clearer. They started at the base and rose all the way to the giant hole at the top, large enough that the ship could fit into. The sun was almost directly overhead, highlighting the different-colored rock in the walls. She stopped beneath the opening archway, reviewing the inside with a practiced eye for width, depth, and height. "This is beautiful."

Teddy's chuckle behind her startled her.

"I believe you are the only woman in the *ton* who would say so."

He was most likely correct, but she saw no reason to confirm his opinion. "It's a geologist's dream." Picking up her skirts again, she strode forward until she reached the wall directly opposite her. Touching the lines, she wished she'd thought to bring her sample containers. She still had a few empty ones left.

"It looks like there's another alcove over here."

At Teddy's observation, she turned toward his voice. He was about fifty feet away, which was where she preferred him at the moment. "There are probably others. Caves are created in many ways. I'd have to study this one further to truly understand it."

She looked up. Had the hole at the top once been small, but water had enlarged it over time? If so, what could have been the source and why had it changed direction? Or had the ceiling simply weakened and caved in? Not seeing anything higher through the opening, she would guess the latter.

"So this is the Caverna de Pedras Perdidas." At her mother's voice, she turned, having almost forgotten her mother was with them. "It really is quite light and high. Much better than the Dragon Caves."

She pointed to the opening. "That's due to the oculus. My guess is that years ago, there was a cave-in and then the rain simply weathered the sides of the opening to the smooth surface we see now."

The captain stepped into the shade of the cave. "That cave-in must have been very long ago. Those edges appear almost polished."

She didn't think it was quite that smooth, having seen what water could do, but she wasn't going to gainsay the captain. Instead, she turned back to the wall and tried to chip out a piece of it with her fingers, but it was far too solid.

"Would this help?"

She spun at Teddy's voice. The moss-covered ground really did not readily convey the sound of footsteps. He held out a small penknife.

Not wanting his help, but too eager to take some rock back with her, she nodded and accepted it. Working carefully, she happily chipped away at five different strata that she could reach.

"I have pockets, if you'd like me to carry those."

Again, he was being helpful, but instead of being happy about it, it made her rocky stomach churn more. Turning once more to face him, she discovered her mother and the captain exiting the cave.

Her mother pointed down the path. "We're going to explore the lagoon while you collect your samples." The captain helped her mother mount, and they were soon out of sight.

That gave her the privacy she needed. She turned on Teddy. "Why are you being so helpful?"

He raised his right eyebrow. "Why would I not be?"

Curling her fingers around the rocks she'd collected, she set that hand on her hip. "Because you'd rather be dancing attendance upon Cintia than here in a cave with me." She couldn't bring herself to say *Senhora Rocha*. The woman was hardly a lady.

"Is that why you're angry with me? Because of last night?" Teddy held his hands out to the side. "Surely, you noticed I did not encourage her."

"I saw no such discouragement. She never stopped touching you, and I'm fairly certain I know what you did outside after dinner. After all, the moon was out, and she must have looked so much prettier in that light."

He shook his head. "I could do nothing overt while at the table. Her father is the port master. He can make things very difficult for Captain Gentry, but I promise you that we did nothing outside except talk."

"Truly?" She let her doubt fill her tone. "About what?"

"We spoke about mutual acquaintances."

She rolled her eyes. "You expect me to believe that a woman like that"—she pointed back toward town—"who has obviously felt much passion with many men, simply discussed mutual acquaintances? Teddy, you have a daughter now. How could you be with a woman like that?"

His brows lowered. "What do you mean *be* with a woman like that?"

She crossed her arms over her chest. "You know exactly what I mean. Did you sneak off the ship in the middle of the night? It seems much is done under the cover of darkness aboard a ship."

His eyes widened. "You think I went to her bed?"

The rocks in her belly turned into one solid boulder at his statement. "Of course. Why wouldn't you? You have before." She lifted her chin, more positive than ever that he'd done exactly as she suspected.

"So because over a year ago, I enjoyed Cintia's body, that must mean I can't resist her the moment I see her?" His voice had risen in volume.

Was that how it worked? Was that why even now she wanted nothing more than to touch him and wipe away any touches of his lover? She forced herself to shrug. "How would I know? I'm far less experienced than you. I can only make an educated guess."

His lip curled up. "Is that how little faith you have in me, how little you think of me?"

His tone and look changed him from the young man she'd always known to the formidable man he'd become.

She threw her free hand up. "I don't know what to think. One moment you're showing me what passion is, and the next you're outside in the dark with your lover."

"*Former* lover." He growled out the words.

Despite his emphasis on the first word, her heart hurt, her stomach ached, and her mind wanted to rail at him. She was confused on every level. "Don't you want to be with her now? It's a chance you didn't expect." She gritted her teeth to keep herself from asking if that wasn't what he wanted. What *did* he want? She had no idea why she kept attacking him when all she wanted to do was run away and cry.

"No."

"I don't understand. She's obviously willing." She waved him off. "I'm sure I can ride back with my mother. You can leave if you wish." Tears stung the back of her eyes, but she couldn't seem to stop.

He ran his hand through his hair before scowling, obviously losing patience with her. "I can't."

"Truly, Teddy. You have two legs with which to walk. I see no known impediment to your departure."

"Damn your cattiness. I can't go because I still love *you!*" His head jerked back, as if surprised he said such a thing.

He loved her? After she'd rejected him? If he felt that way, why hadn't he told her? She very much doubted it. The Teddy she knew would have told her repeatedly, unable to keep it to himself. "Truly, Teddy? If you love me as you say, then I guess we should just marry. It may be the only way to keep you from falling back into your depraved life. After all, you have Marianna to think of now."

He took a step closer. "Are you saying you would marry me?" His voice had lowered and softened, but his face revealed nothing.

Her skin pricked with a new sensation that had nothing to do with anger or jealousy. She met his silvery gaze. "Yes, I would."

"Then, Lady Elsbeth Rawley of Astor, will you do me the honor of becoming my wife and the mother to Marianna?"

Studying his face, she couldn't read anything in his expression. This was her chance to have what she'd started dreaming of the moment she discovered he'd boarded the *SeaSprite*. She took a deep breath and let go of the last of her doubt and anger. Finally, she gave him a single truncated nod. "I will."

She barely saw the flash of his smile before he pulled her against him to capture her lips with his own. Her passion rose swiftly. She wrapped her arms around his neck, tangling her tongue with his as joy burst upon her. He loved her and wanted her. She would be his *wife*! Her whole body lit with happiness, and she couldn't seem to get close enough.

His lips left hers to travel down her neck. "Ells, I want you now. Let me show you what I feel."

His words made her shudder with anticipation before she was suddenly lifted into his arms.

She should be worried about propriety, about them being in a cave, but she didn't care. She wanted him even more than she had the night he'd taught her about passion. She wanted to feel him like he felt her. She wanted to feel his body against hers. She wanted to be his.

As he turned to duck into the small alcove, she glanced toward the cave opening, wondering if anyone would come upon them and not caring. But then she was set on her feet in the hidden space, still lit by the hole above, and she couldn't wait. Her fingers found the buttons of his tailcoat and slipped them open, even as his hands on her back untied her dress.

When her neckline fell, she anxiously shrugged it from her shoulders, not realizing he'd untied her shift as well. She sucked in her breath as the material caught on her stays, keeping her covered.

Teddy lifted her chin. "I want to love you *now*. Do you know what that means?"

His words sent a thrill from her bared shoulders to her toes. She sensed more than knew what he wished to do, and it had her passion rising. "Yes. Please." Her words came out on a breath.

His nostrils flared before he lowered his head, and his lips sealed her fate.

CHAPTER FIFTEEN

Y ES, HE WAS being selfish, but he couldn't hold back from making Elsbeth his. He didn't know why she'd said *yes*, and he didn't care. He needed her like he needed to go home. It was instinct. A desperate need tinged his happiness. She'd always had his heart, even when he didn't understand why. But he did now, and she would be his. He couldn't lose her again.

Breaking the kiss, he ran his hands down her bare arms to the gloves she wore and discovered she still held her blasted rocks. Carefully, he took them from her and dropped them in his coat pocket before removing her gloves and kissing each palm.

"Oh, that's nice." She practically purred the words as she lifted her arms to rest on his shoulders when he was done.

At her response, he thought of all the other ways he could show her passion, but not now. They had little time. He should wait, take her in her cabin at the least, but he could no more wait than stop the tides from rising.

Running his hands over her smooth collarbone, he reached her stays and reverently cupped each breast from inside and drew it out. Using his thumbs to brush the taut peaks, he marveled at how she responded to him. So intent was he on her beautiful breasts that when her hand touched his bare chest, he jerked.

She pulled her hand back. "I thought you liked that."

He smiled sheepishly. "I do. I was simply so focused on how

you feel to me, I was surprised by your touch. Please." He shrugged his shirt down further and brought both her hands to his chest.

She was not shy about her feeling him. She explored his shoulders, his chest, and particularly his nipples. As she leaned forward and laved them with her tongue, his groin sac tightened. How he wanted her to do so much more.

She licked lower, distracting him as her fingers tugged at the buttons on his pantaloons. He caught her hands before he slipped out. "I know you're anxious, but I want you to know what it feels like to reach ecstasy."

She gave him a saucy smile. "You already showed me that."

Shaking his head, he backed her up to where a small outcropping was at the perfect height. "That was one way, but there's an even better way. A way to reach it together."

Her eyes lit with curiosity. "Show me."

A fissure of need spiked up his back, causing his growing erection to harden more. "Hop up."

She looked behind her then back at him with a grin before lifting herself onto the small, flat space. He had never thought of a cave as a good place to enjoy a woman, but he could see the advantages now.

Kneeling at her feet, he ran his hands up her legs, pushing her purple skirts higher, wanting her to remember his touch and how much pleasure it had given her the other night.

She held her skirts at her waist, giving him the freedom to do as he wished. As much as he wanted to taste her, that would have to wait. Gently, he coaxed her legs apart. Grateful for the light shining from above, he viewed the full beauty of Elsbeth.

It was far different being able to see her pink folds as he explored her with his fingers, feeling her readiness. Glancing up, he found her head back, her eyes closed, and her breasts beckoning him. Unable to resist, he took one in his mouth and sucked on it, even as his finger discovered her already-moist opening.

Moving his head to her other breast to nip lightly, he moved his finger to the place at the top of her folds where he knew she enjoyed his touch and circled it.

Small gasps issued from her. He wanted her on the edge, needing him as he needed her. Taking her nipple between his teeth, he rolled it. Her breathing grew short and fast, so he added pressure between her legs, listening to her every breath, feeling her every movement.

Her hips bucked up, and he lightened his touch. At her moan, his hardness became painful.

"Teddy, I need it."

He rose. "You need the ecstasy I promised."

Her eyes opened and she gazed at him with passion-filled eyes. "I need *you*."

Those words almost broke his control. Carefully, he positioned himself against her wet opening, wanting her to enjoy their first coupling. He continued his ministrations to her pleasure point, while he lowered his head to kiss her.

She wrapped her arms and legs around him, making it difficult to move slowly.

He filled her mouth with his tongue and pulled back, just as he would with his body. But he kept his hips still until her moans increased and she lifted her pelvis toward him. Just as she reached her pinnacle, he slid in.

The tightness of her sheath almost undid him, but he kept his wits enough to recognize her gasp. Immediately, he felt her tighten around him, her hips pressing against him as if she couldn't be close enough. Her fingers on his biceps dug in deep as her head fell back and she released a small scream.

He captured her mouth with his own before bringing his hips back.

Her legs tightened around him, not wanting him to go, and so he acquiesced. But he was soon moving out again, his own instincts impossible to resist. Elsbeth's moans of pleasure filled his head as he continued his journey toward fulfillment. He sensed her growing excitement when she moaned into his mouth, her hands holding his head as she sucked upon his tongue.

It was that last action that sent him careening into bliss, filling her with his ecstasy even as she tightened around him and arched against him, ripping her mouth away as they spun into joyous oblivion together.

Their fast, hard breaths seem to echo in the small alcove like the billowing sails of the ship, alerting him to the feel of her breasts against his skin and the warmth of her pleasure still surrounding him. He was loath to move.

"Teddy?" Her breathless question forced him to lift his head.

"Yes?" He brushed the loose strands of golden hair away from her face.

"You're correct." Her lips curved into a satisfied smile. "That *was* better ecstasy."

He chuckled softly, his heart filling with a joyful contentment the like of which he'd never known. "Ells, I love you." He lowered his lips to seal his words with a kiss, not wanting a reply, happy she would be his wife, and certain she could grow to love him in return.

The sound of a horse neighing reminded him of where they were and he lifted his head. "I know it's too soon, but we must make haste. That could be your mother."

Her brow furrowed. "I suppose we must dress, for appearances' sake." She gave a heavy sigh that he felt before her lips quirked upward again.

He stifled a full-out laugh and took the opportunity to pull out.

"Oh." Her eyes widened and she pouted.

That she was clearly not happy they were apart spoke to his male ego. "I promise next time, we will savor the moment longer." He wiggled his brows. "And find our bliss multiple times...in multiple ways." Buttoning himself in, he made sure his shirt was tight, listening for footsteps.

Her blue eyes lit with curiosity, as he'd hoped. "There are many ways?"

"Yes." He grasped her about her waist. "Now come down from there so I can tie you back up."

She held his forearms, and he lifted her down.

Still, she stumbled when he let go.

He caught her. "Did you twist your ankle?"

"No, but my knees feel weak."

Again, his ego rose to the fore. "That's because you enjoyed yourself. Now turn and hold on to the ledge."

She did as he instructed, and he had her clothes back in order, but as she faced him, the wrinkles in her skirt and her messed hair were a testament to what they had done.

He pointed to her dress. "I'm not sure how we can hide that."

At the sound of footsteps, they both froze.

"Elsbeth, are you still in here?"

Her eyes widened, then her normal confidence reappeared as she put her finger to her lips. Reaching into his tailcoat pocket, she retrieved the rocks, put them in his bare hand, and motioned for him to leave the alcove.

He understood and quickly exited.

Lady Astor was just inside the cave. "Lord Mabry, is my daughter still in here? We heard a cry and weren't sure if it were she or a bird."

He moved forward, his hand outstretched. "It must have been a bird." Though he knew that was not the case. "It wasn't Lady Elsbeth. She was busy chipping away."

Lady Astor rolled her eyes. "Still? That girl." She brushed by him, and he followed.

As Lady Astor entered the alcove, he could see Elsbeth on her hands and knees, using his penknife on the ground.

"Elsbeth, didn't you hear me call you?"

He grinned at the exaggerated surprise on Elsbeth's face. "Oh, Mother. You're back? I just need a little longer."

Lady Astor set both hands upon her hips. "You have spent far too long as it is. Now please rise. Your dress is probably ruined."

As Elsbeth rose, she looked at her dress, which now had dirt smudges as well as wrinkles. "I apologize. I did not expect this cave to be so exciting. I suppose this gown will need to be discarded." She grinned and held out her hand, which had three rocks, all different colors. "But look what I was able to gather."

Her mother threw her hands up and spun around, almost bumping into him. "Come at once."

Elsbeth gave him a sly smile before gathering her gloves and returning his pocketknife. "No harm done."

As she followed her mother out of the cave, a niggling doubt wormed its way into his brain. While he appreciated her cleverness in hiding what they had done, it also seemed *too* clever. Shrugging off the odd thought, he followed her to the opening, where the captain and Lady Astor waited.

"Did you find the cave more interesting than you expected?"

At the captain's question, Elsbeth's smile was wide. "Indeed, I did. I must thank Lord Mabry for finding it for me. I do so enjoy caves."

Teddy barely stifled a groan.

The captain studied her. "I fear I have been out of society for too long. I have never met a young miss so interested in caves."

Lady Astor touched the captain's arm. "My Elsbeth is not typical. I have encouraged her pursuit of knowledge in the same subjects I have found of interest."

"You study caves?" The captain's brows rose.

Lady Astor laughed, again touching the man's arm. "Hardly. Elsbeth has gone beyond what I could teach her and found her own interests. Caves and rocks happen to be two of those."

"It's geology, Mother."

"Yes, I know. Now, are you done with the cave, and can we return to the ship?"

Elsbeth looked at him before answering. "I would like to see this blue grotto. Perhaps I can guess at why it is blue."

Based on the twinkle in her eyes, he could see she truly was quite interested in exploring the feature. "I would be happy to take you if Lady Astor deems it worthy of your time."

The older woman looked pointedly at him. "It *is* worth her time. But I shall ride down with her, as I don't wish her to impose upon you any longer."

His stomach tensed. Had Lady Astor suspected what he and Elsbeth had truly done in the cave? He did not want Elsbeth's reputation damaged before they wed, even if he was the one who had compromised her. "Of course. As you wish."

Elsbeth was clearly not happy with the arrangement. Had she been interested only as a chance for more intimate activities? What if her acceptance of his proposal was purely because of the passion he'd shown her? Part of him balked at that idea, but his saner self told him she wasn't the kind of woman who responded to any man. She had to have feelings for him. It was just that passion was new to her, much like a cave in which she'd never before set foot was new to her, and she was excited about its newness.

But he wanted her to *always* be excited by him.

As soon as the two ladies were out of hearing, Captain Gentry turned to him. "You love her."

Surprised, he turned startled eyes to the captain. For a moment he thought to deny it, but if the man had guessed, then no doubt his feelings for Elsbeth were obvious. That may have even been why Lady Astor had determined she should take Elsbeth to the grotto instead of himself.

Tired of hiding what he felt, he answered truthfully. "Yes. I've loved her for years. It's only now that I believe she may return the feeling. I'm going to ask her mother for her hand."

The captain pondered that before speaking. "I'm not sure her mother is ready to let her go."

His heart skipped a beat at the prospect of coming so close to having Elsbeth for his wife, only to be denied by her mother. "She is of age. I'm sure Lady Astor would prefer Lady Elsbeth not become a spinster."

The captain's hesitation in replying made him wonder exactly what was motivating Lady Astor.

Finally, the captain spoke again. "I encourage you to speak to Lady Astor. She is a reasonable woman and if Lady Elsbeth also cares for you, I'm sure she will listen."

It was more what the captain didn't say that told him he'd have an argument on his hands. If logic didn't persuade the woman, he would use pathos, though he was quite sure Lady Astor would recognize his strategy at once. Still, he appreciated the information from the captain. As Elsbeth had said, forewarned was forearmed. "Thank you. I appreciate your counsel."

"And I appreciate your willingness to help during the storm. Wiley told me what happened. It appears you also saved one of my crew. If I can be of assistance to you, I hope you will not hesitate to request it."

He wasn't sure if the captain meant with Lady Astor or not, but either way, he appreciated the offer. "I'm grateful for your skill in getting us through that storm. If you can deliver all of us safely back to England, I'll be content."

The captain stroked his beard. "I have confidence in my ability to deliver everyone safely back to England. The question I have is will that be enough for you?"

He understood what the man meant. His need to have Elsbeth as his wife had only grown with her acceptance and her willingness to be compromised. If he encountered resistance, he would do what was necessary to overcome it...no matter what that meant.

CHAPTER SIXTEEN

THREE NIGHTS LATER, he sat in the dining area after leaving Elsbeth satisfied and asleep, resisting the call of his own bed as the ship rocked rhythmically over the waves. He crossed his ankle over his knee and leaned back, his view that of the entire dining area, or as much as the hanging lantern illuminated. He wasn't sure if the captain had warned Lady Astor of his interest or if the woman had sensed a change in his and Elsbeth's relationship, but the older woman had avoided being alone with him. Even when he'd asked specifically for time to discuss an important matter with her, Lady Astor had declined, claiming a headache.

Did the lady still have doubts as to his character as a gentleman or had his obvious past with Senhora Cintia make him now unacceptable? Even at the thought of his former lover, he grinned. The last day in port she had tried once again to interest him. Unfortunately for her, he had Marianna while Consuela was in a shop buying additional material for his daughter's napkins.

Cintia's interest in touching him was forestalled by his daughter's presence. However, it was when he asked her to hold Marianna so he could enter the store to gather up the packages that she had gone into a tirade. She claimed he only wanted a woman for making babies and doing, as she put it, unthinkable things, which he interpreted as changing baby napkins.

He wasn't sure if his days on the Continent was what made Elsbeth's mother hesitate or if it was something else. His past was an important part of him because it made him into the man he was. But it was the *past* and he had no interest in returning to it. If Lady Astor needed that reassurance, he'd be happy to make it. However, he was done waiting.

Elsbeth had also noticed her mother's avoidance. Her suggestion was for them both to talk to her mother together. He had promised to consider it, but he no longer had any patience left. It was as if Lady Astor hoped to avoid having to crush Elsbeth's dreams until they were safely back on land. He had no doubt that the lady planned to enlist the duke's support in her refusal of his request, but he would not allow that. Elsbeth was his. More importantly, Elsbeth wanted to be his wife, and he wouldn't let anyone stand in the way of that, not even her own mother.

The sound of quiet footfalls approaching the door that separated the passage to the captain's cabin and the dining area had him tensing. As the door at the other end of the rectangle table opened, Lady Astor in her dressing gown slipped out and silently closed it behind her. Turning, she started for her cabin. She was just a few feet away from her door when she noticed him and halted abruptly.

Her eyes rounded as her cheeks flushed.

He held his hand out toward the chair on his right. "Please, join me. I highly doubt anyone else will be up and about for a few hours yet, except perhaps the captain."

Her mouth opened as her cheeks brightened, but she closed her jaw quickly and pulled out the chair he had indicated. "Were you waiting for me, or is this just a happy happenstance?" The sarcasm in her tone could hardly be missed.

"I've been waiting for you to return to your cabin after spending time with the captain." As much as he wanted to be blunt about what she was about, he controlled his irritation with her enough to be civil.

"This is hardly the time for a conversation." She lifted her chin, much like the duke and Elsbeth did when they expected to be in control.

But she wasn't in control. She had made a misstep by trying to avoid him. Perhaps if they had spoken under normal circumstances, she might have held some minor power, but her strategy had left her vulnerable, and she was quite aware of it, as was he.

"Actually, this is the perfect time and place for the conversation I have in mind, and it won't take long. I simply wished to inform you that Elsbeth has agreed to be my wife. I will, of course, be happy to sign a settlement agreement once we arrive in London, but I thought you should know that I will request a special license as soon as we land so that we may be married posthaste. So whatever negotiations you or your nephew, the duke, wish to engage in, will need to be accomplished quickly."

Despite her state of undress, she straightened her shoulders, her blue eyes keenly judging him. "It is normal for the suitor to *request* permission to marry."

He acknowledged her strength of character to be able to send a warning shot across his bow as if she could head him off course, even with her hair hanging down her back and her skin, no doubt, still flushed from the captain's touch. But he would not be thwarted. "I do not make a *normal* claim upon Elsbeth. We have known each other in the past and in the present. We complement each other well, and it is both our wishes. In our minds, we are already married. We simply await the legal proceeding before making our union public."

Lady Astor's intake of breath told him she understood that he and her daughter had already consummated their promise to each other.

Now that she understood, and before she could throw any impediment before them, he needed to be sure she supported them. "Of course, I would expect that my future mother-in-law would be very circumspect in her public behavior so as not to tarnish my bride. I will, after all, be inheriting the titles of earl and marquess in the future and want to be sure that both Elsbeth and

Marianna are looked upon in favorable light."

The lady's color rose again, but her gaze narrowed, a reminder that her daughter was of equal fortitude. "I can assure you that your *own* behavior is far more likely to reflect upon her than mine would."

He raised his right brow. "Then it appears we have come to an understanding."

She gave him a stiff, shortened nod. "It appears we have."

Pleased that his strategy had worked as he'd wished, he relaxed. "I am pleased that Marianna will have such an intelligent and strong grandmother in her life."

For the first time since she'd entered the room, her shoulders relaxed, and a smile tugged at the corners of her mouth. "*That little girl* will be a welcome member of our family."

That she made a point that *he* wasn't so welcome did not bother him in the least. "I can ask for no more than that." He rose and held out his hand. "Now might I suggest that we both retire for what is left of the night? If you wish, you may announce our betrothal in the morning."

She stiffened once again but took his hand and rose. "Am I to assume if I don't make such an announcement that come afternoon, you will do the honors?"

He grinned. "My lady, you are most astute."

"Hmph. I expected no less." Giving an exaggerated sigh, she allowed him to walk her to her door.

Once Lady Astor slipped into her cabin, he leaned against the wall, his relief almost taking all his strength. Yet as the reality of his forthcoming marriage took hold, he pushed away from it, suddenly filled with excitement. What he wanted to do was climb to the top of the crow's nest and shout his news to the world.

He shook his head, even as he grinned and headed for his cabin. Elsbeth would soon be his wife and the mother of his daughter, the woman he loved and the child he loved under his roof. Just a few more days at the most to arrive in England and a few days for the license, and he would achieve his greatest dream.

He could ask for no more.

London, Craymore Hall
First of June

TEDDY BOUNDED UP the steps to Craymore Hall, his daughter in his arms giggling at the motion. At the top, he looked back to find Consuela peering out the coach door. She waved him on, not in the least interested in meeting his family all at once. Though to be fair, he had no idea how many would be inside.

The door opening had him turning to find the butler, Channing, who stared at Marianna, his mouth open. As if recalling his duties, he smiled. "Lord Mabry. Welcome home. I don't believe Lady Wakefield is expecting you."

He strode into the entryway, shifting Marianna to the other side. "She is receiving visitors, though, is she not? It *is* calling hours."

"Yes, of course, my lord." Though the man tried to hide his curiosity, his gaze kept flitting to Marianna.

"And does she have others in attendance?" He'd love nothing better than for word to get about Town that he had arrived home with a daughter.

"She does. But Lady—"

That was all he needed to hear. Protocol regarding children, be damned. "I'll show myself in." Waving off the butler, he strode forward and opened one door to the parlor.

Inside was his aunt, the Marchioness of Wakefield, looking as youthful as she ever did. Her chestnut hair showed no more white than it had when he'd left and her blue eyes burned with curiosity. Across from her was her dear friend, Countess Dulac, whom he'd been known to praise unmercifully in the past and who looked to have aged quite a bit more. Her hair had thinned considerably and her forehead wrinkles were much deeper, most likely from frowning in judgment of others.

But the woman he was beholden to sat next to his aunt, his closest cousin, Her Grace Joanna Mabry, now Joanna Huntington, the Duchess of Northwick, as she'd married Elsbeth's cousin James and opened the school for Curious Ladies. His cousin looked as robust as she always had, her black hair up with the single curl left to fend for itself and her hazel eyes almost green with her happiness at seeing him.

His heart pounded with excitement, but he curtailed it, something he wouldn't have done last time he'd been in the ladies' presence. Behaving as a lord should, he addressed them each by status. "Your Grace, Lady Wakefield, Lady Dulac, it is such a pleasure to be in your presence once again."

"Teddy!" Joanna sprang up from the settee and ran to him, but before she could hug him, she halted, still grinning. "And who is it you have here in your arms? You must know she is a little too young for my school."

He couldn't stop grinning. "This is my daughter, Lady Marianna Mabry." He made sure he spoke loud enough for even Lady Dulac to hear. "Unfortunately, my Spanish wife has passed and so it is just the two of us."

"Daughter? Wife? Oh, Teddy, you must tell us everything." Then, as if almost two years hadn't passed, she enveloped him and his daughter in a warm hug. When she pulled back, her eyes glistened and she sniffed.

"Joanna, do not take all of my nephew's attention. Come here at once, young man."

At her mother's command, Joanna stepped aside, and he strode forward.

He gave his aunt a kiss on the cheek, truly pleased to be in her home once again. She had become his mother after his own had passed, welcoming him into her family, giving him sound counsel, and comforting him when he was too embarrassed to show his upset to his cousins.

"Sit." Lady Wakefield gestured to the settee.

He waited for Joanna to take her seat before he lowered himself next to her, within arm's length of his aunt. "It is a warm welcome I have come home to." After adjusting Marianna so she sat on his lap where she could see everyone, he continued. "I was not sure after the way I left."

Lady Wakefield waved off his comment. "You are a Mabry, Teddy. You are always welcome. And so is this little one." His aunt reached out her hand to touch his daughter, but Marianna grabbed on to her finger.

"Oh, what a strong grip she has." His aunt smiled warmly, and her gaze softened. "It has been too long since this house has seen a little one such as this. How old is she?"

"She will be five months in a fortnight, when I marry for a second time."

"Marry?" Lady Dulac's voice, still as strong as ever, filled the room. "But you have just arrived, have you not? Surely, you do not know who is available."

"Wait." Joanna touched his shoulder. "Let us hear the story from the beginning. No jumping about and you must give us every detail."

He laughed and Marianna giggled at the sound. A new feeling began to grow inside, but he wasn't quite sure what it was. Contentment? Perhaps. Or maybe something more. Could it be peace?

"If we are to hear every detail, we need more tea." His aunt looked to Joanna. "Do have Channing fetch us a new service."

Joanna rose, pushing down on his shoulder to keep him from rising as well. "You stay there. Marianna need not learn to be a gentleman. I'll have Channing send for Amelia and Mariel as well."

Marianna let go of his aunt's finger and leaned over to the side to grasp at his tailcoat.

The marchioness sat back and addressed Joanna. "When you send the messages to your sisters, tell them we are not waiting for them to hear all about Teddy's adventures."

Joanna winked, reminding him of his betrothed. Elsbeth and her mother had headed for Haven House while he came to Craymore Hall, and they were no doubt telling James about their adventure even as he sat here telling his family.

"Mother, I will simply instruct them they need to arrive post-haste."

As Joanna slipped out the door, his aunt leaned in. "You know she will make it sound like someone is dying."

He laughed again. "Should we send our own message, then?"

"No. They'll forgive her. They always do."

That was true. He hadn't truly realized how fortunate he was to have been welcomed into his cousins' family, to have what felt like four sisters, not cousins. That realization had occurred before Marianna had been born after hearing of what might befall his daughter if he didn't marry Francesca. Even if half of what she and Señora Bello had told him was fabricated, it didn't matter. He never wanted Marianna to feel alone. Hopefully, she'd even have a sister or brother someday.

As Joanna strode back in, he began his tale, telling them everything he wished to tell, generalizing his past escapades, and focusing on Francesca, Marianna, the dragon teeth, and the travels home, including the storm. But not once did he mention Elsbeth.

"Teddy, I'm very proud of you." His aunt patted his arm. "Not only are you a caring father, but a hero as well. It appears your decision to travel abroad was for the best."

"Humph." Lady Dulac scowled. "But whom are you to marry?"

He turned to Joanna. "Have you not deduced who it could be?"

"Me?" She widened her eyes in surprise as she put down her tea cup. "Why me?"

He smirked. "Surely, you know something of dragon teeth."

"Dragon teeth. Do you mean in a fable book?"

Shaking his head, he raised his brows, looking at Lady Dulac and his aunt before returning to Joanna. "Do you know anyone else who is interested in dragons?"

Joanna's brow furrowed. "A woman who is interested in dragons. They are nothing more than mythical creatures who breathe fire, live in caves, and—"

As her lips turned up into a smile, tears glistened in her eyes and she clasped his arm. "Oh, Teddy, I'm so happy for you." She leaned in and gave him a kiss on the cheek.

"Well, who is it?" Lady Dulac's question rebounded off the walls of the room. "I'm not leaving until I have a name."

His aunt reached over and grasped her friend's hand. "I'm sure Joanna will tell us. Only she is clever enough to solve the riddle."

His cousin beamed. "I'm happy to announce that our very own Theodore Bartholomew Augustus Mabry is marrying the woman he's loved for years, Lady Elsbeth Rawley, my husband's cousin."

Lady Dulac's hand flew to her chest. "Lady Elsbeth? She's in your school, is she not?"

"Indeed, she is." Joanna patted the woman's arm. "She is an excellent student, but obviously, she has found dear Teddy to be of far more interest."

He sincerely hoped so, but he didn't discount the number of times Elsbeth had talked about missing the school and her classmates while on their voyage. She considered them sisters, much like he considered his cousins sisters. Though he'd missed his family while abroad, he knew he'd be coming home eventually. Elsbeth would be in the same country and in London for the season and so would have access to her friends then.

"What made her change her mind?" His aunt studied him. "Was it Marianna or your actions on board the ship?"

He shrugged. "I'm not sure I know. I'd like to think it is the man I have become despite my poor start."

"I agree." Joanna, as usual, took his side. "Elsbeth did care for you, so I'm sure when you lost your dramatic ways and self-indulging tendencies, she couldn't quite resist falling in love with you."

He was about to argue the point about his tendencies, but the door to the parlor opened and his cousin Amelia swept in with her husband Andrew Caulder, Earl of Sommerset. "Who's dying?"

He exchanged a look with his aunt and rose. Marianna, having fallen asleep during his tale, was now awake and fidgeting. He moved her to his shoulder to greet his cousin, who wore a pretty spring green gown that made her blonde hair appear brighter. "You look lovely, Amelia."

"Teddy! You're home." She gave Joanna a scowl, her small nose wrinkling before turning back to him. "I trust your travels were beneficial. And who is this beautiful child?"

That his cousin, the artist, thought Marianna beautiful had him smiling proudly. But he knew it was time for her to eat. "I'm afraid I must allow my cousin to tell my story, as I need to find Lady Marianna's wet nurse posthaste."

Even as Teddy said the words, Marianna started to cry. Quickly, he strode out of the parlor to give Channing directions to fetch Consuela and bring her to the upstairs sitting room. A place he'd played as a young child.

Once there, he tried to entertain his daughter until Consuela arrived, but there was no distracting her.

"It is past time." The woman strode in and held out her hands for Marianna. "You wait too long."

He felt his cheeks heat. Joanna stated he was no longer selfish, but he had not thought of Marianna's comfort until she'd become uncomfortable. "I will try better next time."

Consuela took Marianna and crooned to her. "You learn."

Yes, he would, as he had been for years.

She sat in an armchair and gave him a stern look. "Go to your *familia*."

Yes, he would go to his family. "*Gracias.*" As he walked out of the room, he heard Consuela grumble something about strange

Englishmen.

Despite his misstep with his daughter and Consuela's scolding look, he knew at once that what he was feeling was truly peace. He'd found the path he was meant to travel in life, and despite the rocky road and detours, he couldn't be more sure that all would be well.

Descending the stairs, he walked back into the parlor to discover Lady Dulac had left, most likely to spread the news, and his oldest cousin and last living cousin, Mariel, or rather, Lady Blackmore, had arrived with her husband, Marcus Stratton, the Viscount of Blackmore. Upon his entrance, Mariel stood, the skirts of her pale blue day dress not revealing her status as an expectant mother yet.

Her green eyes held warmth and happiness as she met him halfway across the room and cupped his head in her hands. "I'm so happy for you, Teddy. You have found forever love."

Mariel, as the champion of love in their family, had always kindly lectured him on its importance, so he was not surprised by her greeting. "I appreciate your felicitations. I am to understand that you are also to have a new person to love."

His cousin removed her hands and blushed. "Yes. Marcus and I are expecting a child in February."

"Then my daughter will have a cousin with whom to steal pies and slide down banisters."

Mariel's eyes widened before her hands found her hips. "You have a child? But you aren't married yet."

Amelia's husband, Andrew, who she fondly called her golden Adonis, came to his rescue. "Marianna is from a previous marriage. Your cousin Teddy, Lady Blackmore, is a widower."

Immediately, Mariel dropped her hands and gazed at him with compassion. "Oh, Teddy. I'm so very saddened to hear such news." She took his hand and walked him to the settee where Joanna was seated. "You must tell us everything."

A bit uncomfortable with Mariel's compassion over Francesca's passing, he looked to Joanna for help.

She knew exactly what he needed and proceeded to explain.

He wished he could have loved Francesca as she deserved. She'd been a beautiful and caring young woman. Though not a virgin, she'd not been as promiscuous as Cintia. What he remembered most about her was her laughter, which was vibrant and uninhibited. That and her smile had captured his attention. Though she'd enjoyed his company, it was her concern for their baby that brought them together again. Now, he would honor her by loving their daughter and giving her a life Francesca never had. He was glad he could give Francesca peace in the end that Marianna would be well cared for. Perhaps he could do more by creating something in her honor. He would need to discuss the idea with Elsbeth...after they married. He wouldn't feel completely confident that she was truly his until they'd said their vows and signed the register.

As the conversation went on around him about him, his thoughts continued to drift to Elsbeth. He wished she were with him, but understood she had her own family, which would soon be even more connected to his. Turning to Joanna, he kept his voice low. "Would you and James be willing to sign as witnesses at the wedding?"

She turned her head to meet his gaze. "We would not only love to, but we'd insist upon it." Her chuckle brought the attention of the room back to them.

"Nephew, what trouble are you concocting with Joanna now?" His aunt tried to look stern, but her blue gaze filled with laughter.

"Nothing more than discussing the wedding, which I expect you all to attend."

All at once, questions abounded about place, time, and where the wedding breakfast would be held. He laughed freely, enjoying the excitement on his behalf. Soon Elsbeth would be a part of all of it.

"Teddy, we must schedule a week for me to paint your portrait after the wedding. I do hope it will simply be you, Lady

Elsbeth, and Lady Marianna." Amelia gave Mariel a sly smile.

Not sure what that was about, he simply nodded. "I will leave that to my wife." He couldn't help grinning at the phrase. "I am honored that you would take the time to do so."

Amelia waved him off. "As long as you promise not to include an exotic animal or a boulder, I will be pleased to capture you all as you begin your lives together."

The mention of a boulder gave him an idea. "I promise no exotic animals or boulders, but there may just be a dragon tooth in it."

As Amelia's eyes rounded, Joanna chuckled, but he refused all entreaties to explain. This would be a surprise for his wife, and the only way to keep it that way was to not tell his family. He grinned as they continued to chatter on. Soon he would have a second family. One that he would be responsible for and rather than be intimidated by the prospect, he embraced it wholeheartedly. Now if he could just make it through the next fortnight without having Elsbeth in his arms.

CHAPTER SEVENTEEN

Elsbeth couldn't stop smiling as she and Dory walked arm and arm to the retiring room for ladies. She didn't remember much about the wedding except for signing the registry, but she did remember all the warm hugs from the Mabrys. They genuinely seemed excited that she was part of their family. So much so that she had started crying with joy. It had always been just her cousin James, her, and her mother, and now she had a large and growing extended family.

"Must I call you 'Lady Mabry' now? It just doesn't sound right to me. You will always be Elsbeth in my mind."

She patted Dory's arm, so thankful that she'd been able to attend the wedding despite how little time there'd been to let others know. "I'm still Elsbeth. No need to change that."

"Oh, I'm so relieved. Just because Shakespeare thinks a name is of no consequence, I am convinced it is of the utmost importance in friendships and reputations. Did you know that Miss Foster was given the cut direct at the theatre while you were abroad? There was quite a lot of chatter about it. It was at the play *Troilus and Cressida*. I find that play rather dull. It is far too simple. I much prefer more complex plots. Not that it isn't complex as it is, but the theme really is far too easy to understand."

She hadn't realized how much she'd missed Dory's penchant

of jumping from topic to topic. "Here we are." She opened the door, and they stepped in. "Is there any news on the rest of our classmates? I feel as if I've been gone a year instead of just five weeks."

Dory heaved a sigh as she moved behind a screen. "There's not much to tell. It has not been nearly as exciting as your adventures. We did get Sophie to attend one ball, but she didn't dance. Eleanor broke a bust in the Burham's library and spilled the punch bowl at the Worthington sisters' recital. Lissette is quite nice and told us a little of her life in France, but she's more interested in learning about us. She's always watching others. At first, I found it rather unsettling, but now it's rather flattering. She says she wants to learn all there is to being a lady in England, even from me."

Elsbeth stood before the full-length mirror admiring her bright-pink wedding dress. The very day they'd landed in London, her mother had sent for a seamstress to create it. She hadn't expected her mother to be so supportive of her marrying Teddy, but she'd even argued against James, who had been quite taken aback by the idea. Unfortunately, James thought Teddy was still the same man he'd been before he left for the Continent, but her cousin would come around eventually, especially since Joanna was so happy about it.

Dory came up behind her. "You look so beautiful. Of course, you always do, but today, there is something different about you. You seem to glow from the inside. Is that happiness?"

She nodded, reaching back to take her friend's hand. "It is. I'm so excited to be a wife and mother."

"Lord Mabry seems much changed from last he was in London. I'm glad he is acceptable to you now. Did you mention your aversion to being with child?"

"I did." She turned away from her reflection. "But it wasn't in the context of being his wife. I'm not sure he even remembers the conversation, which means I must broach it again."

Dory winked and a sly smile filled her face. "You best do so soon since tonight is your wedding night." Dory squeezed her hand and lowered her voice. "You must tell me everything."

She could feel her cheeks heat at the idea of telling such intimate details.

Dory gasped. "By Jove, you've already consummated!"

"Shh." She clapped her hand over Dory's mouth and listened intently for any footfalls in the corridor. Hearing no movement, she released her friend.

Dory's eyes were wide with astonishment before they narrowed. "You, my lady, must explain."

Unable to deny it, she followed as Dory pulled her by the hand to a settee set against one wall of the room. Her friend sat, pulling her down beside her.

"Tell me. No, wait. First, did you like it? No, I mean, did it feel awful?" She waved her hand. "I mean, does he really put... Is it like what we read? Did you see him? Were you—"

"Dory, if you wish to know, you'll have to stop talking. Remember, we discussed this before. You can't have a conversation if you don't listen."

Dory butted her shoulder against hers. "I know, but this is different. I need to know. All of us do. Well, maybe I don't if I become a spinster, which will no doubt happen if I can't keep quiet. Mother has already said if that comes to pass that she will send me to our estate in the country to live out my days. I know she thinks that would be a terrible threat, since it would be to her, but I rather like the idea. As you know, I could carry on a conversation with a rosebud. I really don't need anyone to pay attention to me, except, I do admit that Lissette's admiration and ability to understand me has been rather surprising and quite welcome."

Though she didn't actually wish to explain herself, she couldn't let her friend forget their topic since she needed to extract a promise of silence. "Dory."

"Yes?"

"I need you to promise me that you won't tell anyone. Teddy

is going to inherit two titles and I do not want people to think ill of me. It could reflect badly on him and Marianna."

"Marianna? Oh, yes, your new daughter. Your secret is safe with me." Dory paused, an unusual occurrence.

She waited, her instinct telling her that there was something important coming.

"Can you tell me what you thought about consummation?" The uncertainty in Dory's voice made it clear the subject had weighed on her mind. That wasn't surprising, considering Countess Preston's whispered reputation.

"I do not know how it is for every woman, but for me with Teddy, it was wonderful, glorious, and very satisfying. In fact, I cannot wait to be alone with him again."

Dory studied her as if judging if she spoke true. That in and of itself was telling because Dory took most of what everyone said as truthful. For her to doubt proved how important it was. Finally, she nodded. "Then I will wait for the details until another time. Thank you for being honest with me."

She gave Dory a hug. "I always will be." Though there were some things that would remain just between her and Teddy.

Dory hugged her back then rose. Striding to the mirror, she began tucking in the loose, mahogany strands about her face. "I know this is supposed to make me appear soft and comely, but it seems messy to me."

Unsurprised by Dory's change of focus, she rose to give her opinion. "I believe you look quite pretty either way. That maroon dress makes your hair fairly shine. Is there someone in particular you wish to impress?"

Dory stilled. "At your wedding breakfast? Of course not. But Mother says I must always be ready."

She barely kept from rolling her eyes. Dory's mother, Lady Preston, was always far too ready to attract male attention. Unfortunately, unlike her own mother, Lady Preston was married.

Satisfied with her neat look, Dory turned toward her and

hooked her arm in hers. "Are we ready to return?"

She smiled. "Yes."

As they headed back down the grand staircase of Craymore Hall, Teddy's uncle's London home, she marveled once again that she was part of the Mabry family. Though Teddy's father had come to the wedding and been quite polite and welcoming, he'd headed home to his country estate directly afterward. He was nothing at all like Teddy, which made her assume her husband had developed many of his characteristics from his mother. Or perhaps from his female cousins, whom he spent most of his time with in his growing years.

As if Teddy's oldest cousin had read her thoughts, Lady Blackmore approached the stairs and looked up at them, the skirt of her pale-green dress in one hand. "Ah, there you are. Teddy was just asking where you had gone off to." The woman smiled kindly. "He obviously doesn't understand the details of married life yet, but I have faith you will teach him."

She drew closer. "I can only try. From what the duchess has said, teaching a husband anything is a lesson in patience. However, I do believe that Lady Marianna has already taught him much."

Lady Blackmore's face softened, and her hand found her belly. "Yes, a child can work miracles."

She wanted to ask the viscountess if she wasn't afraid to deliver but held her tongue. Now was not an appropriate time. She could always seek counsel from Teddy's cousins in a more private setting.

As they reached the entry way, Lady Blackmore laid a hand on Dory's arm. "Lady Dorothea, I greatly appreciate you being such a friend to Lissette. The transition to England has been difficult for her."

Dory's eyes widened in surprise before she beamed. "It is truly a pleasure, Lady Blackmore. Lizzy is anxious to learn. I'm pleased to assist her in any way I can. Of course, I'm not the most knowledgeable"—Elsbeth squeezed her friend's arm, knowing all too well where the conversation would lead if she left Dory to her own inclinations—"but what I do not know, we learn together."

Lady Blackmore smiled kindly. "We are very grateful. Now, you two best get back to the parlor or I fear a groom's patience will be sorely taxed."

She grinned, too happy to do otherwise. That Teddy was anxious to have her back in sight after so little time apart just proved how much he loved her. She remained amazed that he always loved her, when she thought he would hate her for having rejected his first proposal.

As they entered the parlor, Teddy immediately came to her from across the room. He looked resplendent in the deep-blue brocade tailcoat, matching waistcoat, solid-blue breeches, and white shirt with cravat. "I was about to search the house for you." Though his voice was stern, there was a twinkle in his eyes.

"We were not gone so long." She smiled up at him before lowering her voice. "But I did miss you." She tried to keep her lips from quirking up, but from his chuckle, she'd failed.

"I do believe you simply enjoy Lady Dorothea's company far more than mine."

Dory pulled her arm out and grasped Elsbeth's hand, holding it up as if Teddy needed spectacles to see. "This, Lord Mabry, says otherwise. Wherever did you get such pretty gems? I don't think I've seen these before. Have I, Elsbeth?"

Dory released her hand, and she held it in her other to better admire the wedding ring Teddy had slipped on her finger. She'd expected a piece of ancestral jewelry, but instead, he'd taken one of the dragon teeth and had a ring made with the stone split in three, each piece a slightly different size. "No, Dory. I have never owned this stone before. It's yellow calcite, not something easily obtainable here. There are three different sizes of the stone, one each for myself, Lord Mabry, and Lady Marianna." She looked at Teddy, still touched by his explanation of the three stones.

"Oh." Dory clasped her hands and brought them to her chest.

"That is truly the most beautiful thing. I must tell Lissette."

As her friend scurried off to share her knowledge with her new classmate, she felt a tug at her heart.

"What is it, Lady Mabry?"

Teddy's softly spoken question had her turning toward him, amazed at how easily he understood her. "I was just thinking that Dory now has a new friend, which is wonderful, especially because I will no longer be attending the school."

He studied her, clearly aware there was more. "But…"

She gave him a crooked smile. "But I will miss her and the others. We all have a thirst for knowledge in common, but more than that, we feel a bond because we are considered different because of that very interest. It's hard to explain."

He tucked her hand into the crook of his arm. "I understand. It is much like the bond I have with my three cousins. Mariel, Joanna, and Amelia welcomed me as a brother and despite being a different sex, seemed to understand me far better than my father. Belinda, my other cousin, was the sweetest, and always found a way to explain how I was a good boy, though I was always in trouble. I know what it's like to miss someone so comforting." He paused, obviously mulling something over. Finally, he spoke again. "If you like, you could invite your classmates to tea in a couple days' time, if you think you can be settled into our townhouse in Mayfair that quickly."

"Oh, Teddy. I would very much enjoy that. Are you sure? We have so many calls to make, and I'm sure we'll need to make many changes to your house to accommodate myself and Marianna."

His right eyebrow rose. "I will have you know that in the two weeks it has taken to agree on the marriage settlement—which, by the way, was quite enjoyable, as my cousin Joanna negotiated with your cousin—I have enlisted the aid of Mariel in making immediate changes. I'm sure you will want more, but with the season almost over, I wanted you to be able to enjoy what is left of it as my wife in all that status entails."

The sting of tears started in the back of her eyes. "Your thoughtfulness is beyond compare. I keep uncovering more about you."

He cupped her cheek. "I hope you are happy with what you find."

Thinking about exactly what she did find upon divesting him of his clothes a full fortnight ago on the ship, she couldn't help a sly grin. "I do think I need to study you further."

His jaw tensed and his Adam's apple bobbed, both signs she had learned meant he was thinking of taking her to bed again, which was exactly what she wished for. "I believe you also require further study."

"Who's studying what?" Lady Sommerset, Teddy's youngest cousin, interrupted them, her husband joining her. "This is a day of celebration, not studying. I never did understand Joanna's penchant for all that studying, but it appears she's found plenty of students to join her in that endeavor. Still, today is your wedding day and I have a gift for you."

Since the countess was not much older than herself and held nothing in her hand, she had to guess that it was advice. She'd never received so much advice in a single day as she had since they left the church. "That is very kind of you."

Lady Sommerset's violet eyes sparkled with mischief. "This is a very unique gift, so if it is not what you care for, I'm sure we can find something else."

Her husband, the earl, who was quite handsome in a blond, Greek-god fashion, shook his head. "Do not tease, Amelia. Out with it before this young lady dies of curiosity."

Lady Sommerset laughed and gave Teddy a knowing look. "My cousin already knows. I would like to paint your portrait. That is you, Teddy, and little Marianna."

She'd forgotten that the countess was becoming known for her paintings. "My lady, that would truly be an honor."

"I predict it will be magnificent." Lord Harewood's sudden interjection had her and Teddy turning.

The lord was a very close friend of the earl, and an earl him-self. However, in temperament, the two were as different as the way they dressed. Whereas Lord Sommerset usually wore browns and tans, and smiled often, Lord Harewood was forever in black and never smiled. She and the curious ladies rarely interacted with him as his somber demeaner and cynical wit were not to their liking. As it happened, he'd grown up as a neighbor to the Mabry ladies and so was also a friend of Lady Sommerset.

Lady Sommerset held her hand out, palm up. "And so it shall be since Lord Harewood has said so. His predictions are never wrong."

The man shrugged. "I simply state the obvious."

Lord Sommerset frowned. "Please do not add that to the book at Whites."

Teddy leaned in and whispered. "Harewood is almost never wrong in his predictions."

She studied the man further. Could he predict if a woman would live through the bearing of her child?

"Lady Mabry and I will be as still as possible, but I'm afraid I cannot guarantee my daughter's behavior."

The countess waved her hand, as if dismissing the issue of his daughter's active nature as of little consequence. "If I can paint Mariel and Marcus with three horses, I can certainly paint your daughter." The woman's face changed from slightly arrogant to caring in an instant. "I'm very proud of you, Teddy. Not only have you changed for the better, but you bring both this lovely woman and a child to our family." Lady Sommerset stepped forward and pulled Teddy's head down so she could kiss his cheek. "I will be prepared to paint future portraits as you add additional children to your family."

Though the lady whispered the words, Elsbeth felt her cheeks heat even as her stomach hardened at the thought of bearing a child. She must talk to Teddy very soon.

"Thank you, cousin. What about the setting?" Teddy smirked. "Would you mind terribly painting in a cave?"

Lady Sommerset's eyes rounded. "Very well. We can find a pleasant outdoor location, preferably with rocks."

Teddy laughed.

She squeezed her husband's arm then addressed Lord and Lady Sommerset and Lord Harewood. "I do know quite a few areas in England where one can find the most wonderful rocks."

Though Lady Sommerset had a secret smile and Lord Sommerset nodded, Lord Harewood frowned. "Rocks? Why would you want to be painted next to rocks?"

"My lord," Teddy looked at her with pride before returning his gaze to the earl, "you are probably unaware, but my wife studies geology."

For the first time since he'd joined them, Lord Harewood actually appeared interested. "Then may I ask, is that why the unusual stones in the wedding ring?"

Surprised the man had noticed, she smiled. "Indeed." She looked up at Teddy then back to Lord Harewood. "These, in Mallorca, are known as dragon teeth. The more common name is yellow calcite. They were the reason we became reacquainted."

"Or rather, my need for a wet nurse and her superstition regarding them," Teddy added. "And speaking of superstition, I do believe another one found in Spain is that if newly married couples stay too long with their guests, they will have difficulty producing heirs, so I believe we should be leaving."

She hadn't heard anything like that but kept her own counsel as they said their goodbyes to Teddy's family. When she reached her mother, she found the woman with tears in her eyes.

"Mother, what is wrong?"

"I feel as if I'm losing you. It has been you and me for so many years."

"And James."

Her mother nodded as she dabbed at her tears. "Yes, that is true, but now you are both married and will forget about me."

This was not like her mother at all. "How can you say that? You are a teacher at James and Joanna's school. They can't forget about you."

"I suppose." Her mother's gaze moved to Teddy and became quite stern. "I expect you to treat my daughter with the utmost care."

His arm slipped around her waist, and he pulled her against his side. "Of that, Lady Astor, you need not worry."

CHAPTER EIGHTEEN

After further well wishes, she and Teddy were finally in their coach and on their way to her new home.

Sitting next to her new husband, she cocked her head at him. "Teddy, I'm curious. In Mallorca, I didn't hear that leaving a wedding breakfast early would ensure heirs. Did you learn that while living there?"

He grinned as he shook his head. "I made it up."

"What?"

"I know my family, and they were settling in for a day of visiting. I don't want to share you with anyone else right now. I just want to bring you home so I can show you how much I love you. It has been too long."

An excited shiver ran along her arms. "I would like that."

He leaned in for a kiss, but she placed her hands on his chest, and he halted. Raising his right brow, his gaze took on a devilish gleam. "We don't have to wait to arrive. We can start now."

His words had her mind buzzing, but she brought her thoughts back to her main concern. "I need to ask something first." Now that she was about to make her request, she felt silly, but she couldn't shake her fear.

He sat back, but continued to hold her hand as he studied her. "Ask and I will answer. I can tell it is something that weighs upon you."

"Do you remember that I've read a lot about childbearing, which has made me nervous?"

"Of course. You told me while aboard the *SeaSprite*. What of it?"

This was harder than she expected. She yearned to give him what he desired, what he needed, an heir. But her fear kept her from fulfilling that. "Would it be acceptable if we didn't have a child immediately?" She wanted to ask to wait for years but refused to let her fear rule her life.

"It is not an exact science, but if you like, we can attempt to avoid it for a while." He frowned. "You do still want to enjoy passion, though, correct?"

The relief she felt was almost overwhelming. "Oh, yes. Please."

His shoulders relaxed at her answer, and he squeezed her hand. "Good. It'll be a bit different than what we've been doing. You may even have already conceived."

She had not, as she'd learned the previous week, and her face flushed as she shook her head. "No, I have not." She couldn't even look at him. Discussing such an intimate subject with Teddy felt intrusive. Was this how all wives felt?

He looked blankly at her before understanding dawned. Then a wide grin lit his face. "All the better for our first week of married life."

As he wiggled his brows, she laughed. "I never realized you had such singular focus on—oh." His hand on her bare thigh beneath her dress both startled her and sent anticipation to her core. Her breath seemed to become stuck in her chest.

"If we're not to procreate, then I can take time showing you all the ways we can enjoy each other. We can discover your favorites together."

His words sent a thrill racing through her. She opened her mouth to answer, but his fingers moved to the space between her thighs. Unable to speak, she stilled, afraid he might withdraw.

His gray gaze turned silvery as it intensified. "Kiss me, Ells."

His words sounded as if he were a dying man, and she couldn't deny him. Grasping his neck with her hand, she pulled him toward her and kissed him. She didn't hesitate to open her mouth and invite him in.

His body tensed, her only warning before his fingers found her folds and the tiny spot above them that had her muscles weakening. As he continued to play with her, his tongue tangled with hers until his finger moved lower and slipped inside her.

Her body lit with need, unaware of how much she had missed his touch in the last fortnight. It was as if she were kindling, and he'd just lit a match. Anxiously, she deepened the kiss, diving into his mouth, showing him how much she wanted him.

As his fingers thrust inside her, he groaned, pulling her closer, as if he'd never be satisfied.

Excitement filled her even as her clothes began to feel rough and heavy.

The coach lurched to a stop and Teddy pulled back, his lips leaving her even as his finger slipped away.

She blinked, trying to remember where they were. The rocking of the coach had felt so much like the *SeaSprite*.

"We're home." He gave her a soft smile. "I hope you will be pleased."

Pleased? With the house? "I'll be pleased when I can take off these clothes and feel your naked body against me." Though she'd said the words in a pique, the flaring of his nostrils in reaction had her feeling something else entirely. It almost felt as if she were powerful. It was definitely something she needed to explore further.

The coach door opened and Teddy moved to exit. Once he helped her down, they ascended the four steps to his townhome.

Pushing aside the feelings he'd evoked inside her, she made herself focus on her new home. This was important to Teddy and to her. She was now mistress of her own home and she pulled upon the training her mother had instilled over the years.

As they entered, she took in the stairs that rose to the next level and the staff lined up before them. These were *her* staff. This was now *her* home. Wishing to make the appropriate impression, she graciously spoke to each person down to the final maid. Thanking them all for welcoming her, she looked to Teddy to dismiss them.

Once they left, he began by giving her a tour of the rooms on the main floor which included a parlor, dining room, and study. Lady Blackmore had helped him, but she could see his direction in everything. The pale-blue parlor had been transformed with purple drapes and various shades of that color in pillows, throws, and vases. The dining room was a pretty golden shade, and the study contained a walnut desk and blue chairs and curtains.

They ascended the stairs together, and he led her past one door, which she assumed was his bedroom, to the second door.

"I wanted you to feel at home, so I asked your mother for advice."

"My mother?" Her surprise came from the odd tension she'd felt between Teddy and her mother since giving her blessing on their marriage.

"Yes. Though she's not completely happy you agreed to be my wife, I wish her to feel free to visit you whenever she'd like, so I thought asking her advice on your bedroom would help her feel welcome here."

Her heart skipped a beat at his thoughtfulness. She had also sensed that her mother wasn't happy she'd decided on Teddy, but that he knew this and tried to mitigate the tension had her loving him even more. "You are truly a remarkable man."

He gave her a humble smile. "I am a man with many faults who has learned from many mistakes. And I must warn you that I will continue to make mistakes until my hair matches my eyes, but I promise I will always try to make you happy."

Her eyes filled with tears, and she brushed them away. "I promise to try to make you happy as well."

He pulled her into his arms. "You already have." He brushed

her lips with a sweet kiss. "Now, shall we?" He let her go and opened his arm toward the door.

She sniffed then nodded and turned the knob. As the door opened, a room filled with bright and pale pinks was revealed. She brought both hands to her chest. "Oh, Teddy. It's beautiful."

She took two steps inside studying the room, amazed at the design and how well it blended together. The pale-pink dressing table had a chair with a bright-pink cushion. The walnut bed had pale pink curtains but a bright pink quilt. It made her feel as if she were truly home. Sniffing back more tears, she noticed the door that must connect to Teddy's room. She sincerely hoped they would use it often.

But someone was missing. "And Marianna? Where is she?"

His gaze shifted from proud to loving in an instant. "She is upstairs in the nursery, where Consuela is tending to her."

Though she already knew Consuela and Marianna, she didn't know the protocol for the new wife of a viscount. "Should I then go there and....?"

Teddy took her hand and pulled her to him. "Not yet. I'm feeling selfish and want you all to myself first."

She looped her hands around his neck and looked into his eyes. Perhaps now was an appropriate time to experiment with that feeling of power. "I want you too, but I much prefer you without clothes."

Immediately, his soft-gray gaze turned sharper. "I prefer you naked as well."

A shiver of anticipation ran up her spine. "I may need help undressing, as my stays are tighter than usual, and my breasts are aching to be released."

His nostrils flared, causing heat to pool between her legs at her ability to elicit such a reaction with mere words.

"Lady Mabry, you know not what you do to me."

Actually, she was rather sure she did. Letting go of his neck with one hand, she moved it to the buttons on his breeches. "But I think I do."

His eyes widened before she found herself scooped up in his arms. She screeched, then laughed as he dropped her on her bed. Still grinning, she looked up into his determined face. "You do know my stays are in the back, don't you?"

The only warning she had was a low growl that had every nerve ending tingling before she found herself on her stomach.

"As I will show you, I know exactly what I'm doing."

Despite the fact that he straddled her legs over her skirts, excitement had her nipples reacting, truly wanting out of her stays.

Fortunately, Teddy spoke true. He knew exactly what he was about and within moments, her dress had loosened, and her stays were untied. Despite the fact she was on her stomach, his hands buried into the bright quilt and found her breasts, squeezing them before his fingers found her taut peaks.

Desire shot straight from her nipples to her core. Wriggling, she pulled her arms up to lean on her elbows and arched, giving him full access, which he took advantage of.

He teased her as his palms brushed across her nipples then took her entire breast in his hands before returning to her hard nubs to pinch them lightly, sending strong bolts of excitement to the juncture of her thighs. His mouth found the back of her neck and she wanted to melt.

When suddenly, he removed his hands, she opened her mouth to protest but snapped it shut as he grasped her hips and pulled her onto her knees. She started to sit back, thinking he wanted her in his lap, but he held her there.

"Lift your knee."

Curious, she did and felt her skirts pull out from beneath her and over her to bunch at her waist. When he tapped her other leg, she understood and lifted it. No sooner had he bunched her dress, baring her arse, then his hands clasped her behind.

"Beautiful." His voice sounded reverent.

It made her blush to be in such a position, her behind higher than her head, but her body only heated more with anticipation.

One hand stroked up to her waist and around her leg to search out the point at the apex of her folds that gave her so much pleasure. As his finger played with her, she dropped her head, noticing for the first time that he was still fully clothed, his boots a stark black on the pink quilt. Something about the contrast made her excitement spike.

As if he sensed it, his hand on her behind left and soon she felt the hardness of his erection at her entrance. She wanted nothing more than to rock back, but she kept still, breathless with the wonder of the feelings coursing through her in such an odd position.

His finger worked magic and soon all she knew was a heady need. That was when Teddy finally slid inside her to his hilt. The sparks he'd ignited inside her burst into flames, and she yelled as her body broke into millions of pieces like an exploding volcano. As the molten lava of her ecstasy flowed, she floated in the heat and pleasure of pure satisfaction.

As her body seemed to come back together, she continued to pant, unable to fully relax. It was then that she realized Teddy had yet to move, his hands now locked on her hips. The knowledge that he had yet to find his release had her tensing with excitement. There was more to come!

"Don't."

The single word from him made no sense. She looked over her shoulder. "Don't what?"

He didn't answer. Instead, he pulled back, causing tiny sparks to light all over her body. But when he thrust in again, he pulled her hips toward him as his pelvis hit hers.

She dropped her head as her sated body suddenly burst into flame once more. "Yesss." The hiss was torn from her, as if her body had taken over her mind.

It seemed to be all he needed. He quickly pulled back again and thrust forward, but this time, he didn't stop.

She caught his rhythm, anxious for the next explosion he set off with every thrust. As he rocked into her, she grasped the quilt in both hands, feeling her need building, driving closer to the pinnacle she knew was within reach.

As if he knew she was close, he bent over her and pushed her arms forward, his weight pinning her to the bed.

The buttons on his tailcoat pressed into her back, the fall of his breeches rubbed against her thighs, all adding to her pleasure. Despite her position, her hips still arched toward him, loving the feel of him thrusting into her, and of him holding her as they traveled toward their destination together.

And then his lips came down on her neck and he sucked. It sent her over the edge as she let him have all of her.

He thrust once more and then withdrew, muting her ecstasy. Turning her head to the side, she could see he knelt behind her as wet drops fell on the back of her thigh.

After a few moments, he left the bed, and she forced her still-heated body to roll onto her side. "Teddy?"

He stood there naked, hanging his shirt upon the back of a lovely armchair. "Yes? I'll help you with your dress."

Forcing herself to sit up, she dropped her legs over the side of the bed but didn't dare try standing.

He cupped her face and tilted her head to look at him. "What is it, Ells?"

Her cheeks heated, but she refused to be quiet due to embarrassment. "Why did you leave so suddenly?"

He brushed her cheek with his thumb. "So you wouldn't become pregnant. It is the only way to ensure that. That is what you want, correct?"

It was, but she didn't realize how it would feel. Maybe she needed to think upon it again. Finally, she answered. "Just for now."

"Just for now." He let go of her face and took her hands. "Come, let us get these clothes off."

Chapter Nineteen

TEDDY FOUND HIS wife in the nursery again with his daughter and Consuela. His heart swelled to see Elsbeth holding Marianna and telling her how the Earth was made of many different rocks. That Elsbeth was finally his and appeared happy was more than he had hoped for. Though he knew there was one thing missing for her. It had been a fortnight of wedded bliss, but he'd seen her happiness dim the closer the end of season came. It hadn't been hard to discern why when a date had been set for her to host her old classmates for tea. Ever since then, she'd been preparing for it, almost as excited for that as she was during their intimate time spent in bed.

Striding into the room, he stopped before his wife and daughter. "I hope you're planning her lessons for the next eighteen years until she can attend the Belinda School for Curious Ladies."

Elsbeth's eyes lit with excitement. "I would love to do so."

He bent to take his daughter and lifted her high in the air. "You are such a fortunate little girl to have such a smart mother."

"Señor Mabry, not so high. She spit up. She just eat."

At Consuela's command, he lowered Marianna. Not that he cared a whit if she spit up on him, but he didn't wish her stomach to be upset. Settling her in the crook of his arm, he rolled his eyes at Elsbeth.

She laughed. "I can't wait for Lady Blackmore to have her

child so they can play together. I wonder if the viscount and viscountess have chosen names yet."

He grimaced. "From what I was told, they have but won't tell anyone. They're making us all guess."

"Well, that could be quite fun." She cocked her head. "Where did the name 'Marianna' come from?"

"That was Francesca's doing. She said it was a combination of Maria and Anna, which were her mother's and *abuela*'s names."

Elsbeth's face softened. "What a fitting tribute. I don't know that I would want to name my daughter Louisa or Augusta, my mother's and grandmother's names. I'd prefer to do something a bit more fun, like the Blackmores."

He raised his right eyebrow. "Not quite as fun as your tea. I believe it is soon, is it not?"

She rose immediately. "Oh, my, yes." She leaned in and gave him a kiss before kissing Marianna. "I'm quite sure Dory will arrive early. I best warn the cook." Elsbeth strode out the door without a backward glance.

"She very excited."

He turned toward Consuela. "Yes, she is. These ladies are like sisters to her."

Consuela held her hands out for Marianna. "Then she will miss them when we go to country, *sí*?"

"Maybe." Ignoring Consuela's confused look, he handed over his child. "I'll be back after my errand to spend more time with my daughter."

"You spend more time than other papas."

He grinned before kissing Marianna on the cheek. "*Te amo, mi pequeña*." Pleased with his daughter's giggle, he turned and left the nursey, anxious to talk to Joanna about his new idea.

After gathering his gloves and hat, he entered his coach and sat back. His life had changed so much since he'd left London with a broken heart. Not only had he continued down a selfish path at first, but he'd taken a detour and learned from his mistakes, already thinking about his future before he received the letter from Francesca. He couldn't be happier to have his daughter and the woman he'd always loved to mend his broken heart.

Elsbeth had not said the words, but her gaze revealed how much she cared for him. She must love him. She wasn't the kind of woman to marry any man she didn't love. If she was, she would have married him the first time he asked for her hand. He grimaced as the coach pulled into the drive of Haven House, where Joanna and James resided.

It was only when his footman opened the door that he remembered Lady Astor also resided at Haven House. Part of him felt guilty that he'd put her in such an awkward position, but her own actions had forced him to it. Now, he needed to make peace with her, if she was open to it. If she resented him marrying Elsbeth and taking her away, there wasn't much he could do.

Running up the steps, the door opened, and he stepped inside.

"It is good to see you again, Lord Mabry." The duke's butler took his hat.

"Thank you, Harrison. Is the duchess at home?" It hadn't occurred to him that she might be about Town.

"Yes, my lord. Her Grace is in the library." The tall thin man held his hand out, intending to lead him there.

He grinned. "Of course, she is. No need to show me the way." Immediately, he headed for the double doors that opened into a scholar's dream, the two-story library of His Grace James Huntington, the Duke of Northwick. Giving a quick knock on the door, he waited.

Finally, it opened, and a maid scurried out. "Oh, pardon me, my lord. Her Grace is on the second level. She didn't hear you knock."

"Thank you." He stepped inside the room with so many books, there wasn't even room for a bust of Caesar and headed toward the stairs in the far corner. Taking them two at a time, he stopped to scan the balcony. "Joanna, are you up here?"

Footfalls sounded toward the front of the house, and he headed that way.

Joanna stepped out from an alcove, a book in her hand she'd no doubt been reading. "Teddy, how wonderful to see you. Is Elsbeth with you?"

He strode toward her shaking his head. "No, she's hosting her classmates for tea."

"Oh, I suppose that's fine. I'll see her tomorrow when they visit me here."

He stopped a foot away and gave her a kiss on the cheek. "Why do I have the feeling that you're happier that she's in the family than that I came back from the Continent?"

"Now, Teddy. You know that's not true." She took his arm in hers and guided him farther down the balcony. "I'm equally pleased with both events."

"As I suspected. I had hoped that I still held some special place in your heart, but I can see I have lost it." He sighed dramatically like he used to, unable to keep from teasing her.

They stopped at a settee in another alcove. She sat and pulled him down beside her. "Now stop expecting reassurance. You are not that man anymore. Did you come for my advice?"

He chuckled, not surprised she would think so, as she'd always been the one he came to first. "No, actually. I've come to make a request."

"You know if it's within my power, I will be happy to grant it. What is your request?"

"I would like to use the Dowager House at Silver Meadows for the winter if you haven't already let it out or used it for something else."

Joanna rose suddenly and faced him. "If this is for your mistress, I cannot condone it."

Startled, he stared at her blankly. "Mistress?" The thought was so absurd, he laughed, causing much consternation on his cousin's part.

"Why are you laughing? This is hardly humorous." She set

both hands on her hips.

He had no doubt that if she'd had a switch, she would have taken it to him despite the fact that he towered over her when standing. "But it is. You see, cousin, I wish to use the house so my wife can be closer to her former classmates and perhaps visit them on a regular basis. They're the first sisters she's had, and I think it would make the first year of our marriage more bearable for her."

Joanna's eyes misted. "Oh, Teddy. I misjudged you. Of course you want it for Elsbeth. I forgot how much you love her." Her brows lowered. "You do truly love her, correct?"

He gladly nodded. "With all my heart, body, and soul." He raised his hand as she opened her mouth to speak. "And yes, before you ask, I know her favorite book, that she's kind to all people, not just those of the peerage, and she loves my daughter very much. But I also recognize right now, Marianna and I are not enough. I think the transition from student to wife would be easier for her if she could easily visit her friends at your school."

Joanna sank down onto the settee next to him and took his hand. "I always knew you could one day be a thoughtful, intelligent, and protective husband. I had just despaired that it would take another score of years."

He gave her a lopsided grin. "Or two?"

"Or two." She squeezed his hand. "I would very much enjoy it if you were to take up residence at Silver Meadows. Not only would I be able to see you and Elsbeth, but I could get to know my baby cousin better and introduce her to reading. As I'm sure you're aware, rocks are fine, but books are better."

He shook his head and gave her a sad smile. "I'm afraid my days of agreeing with you are in the past. I fully support my wife on such weighty matters, so rocks will forever be far more valuable." He kept his face serious, though it had been a silly response.

She studied him a moment before giving him a nod. "I'm proud of you. You have surpassed my expectations, Teddy, and for that, I can only applaud you. We shall simply disagree on this subject from now until eternity."

Though they spoke of trivialities, the underlying meaning was clear. He had learned all he could from his older cousin, and it was time to take the lead in his own household. "Thank you." He let his smile grow. "If you ever have questions about raising a daughter, I will be pleased to give you guidance."

Her eyes rounded in surprise. "Now *that* is something I would have never predicted. That you, of all of us, would have the first child."

"If it makes you feel more satisfied, I would have never predicted you would have a successful school for ladies that taught the subjects of Oxford."

She smiled proudly before releasing his hand. "And we will adore having you and your family living at Silver Meadows."

Excited that he could give Elsbeth such good tidings, he rose. "Thank you. And please thank the duke as well."

"I will. Tell Elsbeth I look forward to her visit tomorrow."

Taking his leave, he ran down the stairs, leaving the library door open as he strode out and reached for the outside door, almost forgetting his hat. Luckily, Harrison thrust it toward him just in time, and he settled it on his head before jumping into his coach.

All the way home, he anticipated Elsbeth's reaction when he told her they would be living on the grounds of Silver Meadows over the winter. By the time the coach stopped at his townhome, his patience was at an end. Running up the steps, he opened the door before his butler could and headed for the parlor when voices inside had him stopping in his tracks.

He'd forgotten she had guests.

"Elsbeth, I am so grateful to you. Your sacrifice of marrying before the end of the season and so impressively has my mother convinced now that I should stay at school. I know you promised you would marry for our sakes, but I know how difficult it can be to capture a man's attention to the extent that they offer marriage."

His heartbeat slowed as cold doubt filled his chest.

"Eleanor, there is no need to be grateful. I—"

"Of course, we're grateful." That was Lady Dorothea's voice. "If you hadn't married Lord Mabry, we'd be spending the winter preparing for next season and our mothers forcing us into untenable situations in order to marry us off instead of enjoying our studies. Granted, you had it easier than expected since you had already had a proposal from Lord Mabry once before."

"Oh, dear." He didn't recognize the soft voice. "Your husband was someone you turned down before? Truly, tell me you are not too miserable."

Miserable? Sacrifice? His heart stumbled a beat as he stood frozen in place.

"Sophie, it is not so bad as that. You see, when I turned down Lord Mabry, he had become quite dramatic about his feelings for me and overly jealous of any men I spoke to. So when I met him again in Mallorca, I was quite pleased to see him as he is, a dear friend."

She'd married him because he was her friend?

"But the rumors." It was Lady Eleanor again. "We heard Her Grace talking, and it sounds like he'd become quite the cad on the Continent."

"Oh, no. Well, I mean, Teddy wasn't—*isn't* a cad. He…"

He found himself leaning forward. What was he? What did his wife think of him?

"The best way to describe Teddy is 'changed.' Yes, he enjoyed his adventures, but he also married."

More than one gasp could be heard.

"He left his wife for you?"

He couldn't let this go on. He took a step forward.

"No, no, Eleanor. His wife passed away and he now has the most charming daughter. I'm so in love with little Marianna."

And what about him?

"But what about Lord Mabry? You said he's changed. Does

that make him more palatable? Really, Elsbeth, you can tell us. We all understand a friendly marriage of convenience. You needed a husband and he needed a mother for his child so he could continue to enjoy his paramours." Lady Eleanor was quite insistent that he was a cad.

Anger began to cover the hurt. Would his wife defend him or not?

"No, it's not like that. Teddy is devoted to Marianna. I feel fortunate to be her mother."

"Elsbeth, did you tell him?" That was the soft-spoken Sophie.

"Tell him what?"

"That you married him to help us all stay at school?"

Elsbeth answered immediately. "No, I haven't."

"Will you?"

He held his breath. Maybe she hadn't thought to tell him?

There was a long pause before his wife, the woman he loved, answered.

"No."

He could forgive her for not loving him yet, but to hide the true reason for their marriage from him was too much. Unable to listen to any more, he turned on his heel and took the stairs two at a time as he made straight for the nursery. He strode through the open door and searched the room for Marianna.

She was napping.

Consuela set aside her mending and rose from her chair. She put her finger to her lips to indicate he be quiet.

He didn't want to be quiet. He wanted to yell as loud as he could as his chest squeezed with a pain far harsher than any he'd known before. He took a deep breath to find some kind of control, but the best he could do was lower his voice to an infuriated whisper. "Pack your clothes and Marianna's and meet me in my coach in ten minutes."

The woman's eyes rounded, and she opened her mouth but seemed to think better of it.

Lifting his daughter carefully, so as not to wake her, made his heart pound harder. He wanted to throw furniture, not be gentle, but Marianna's little body in his arms kept his fury at bay. Walking from the room, he strode down the stairs to the front door where he had his butler send for the coach again. Not wishing to hear any more from the parlor, he exited the house. The last sounds on the way out were the laughter of the ladies with his wife.

Within minutes, the coach arrived, and Consuela emerged from the house. Once they were settled in, they headed back to Haven House.

What a fool he'd been, thinking Elsbeth actually cared for him. Now it made sense that she had been the one to suggest marriage. She made a promise to get married by the end of the season. How convenient it was for her that he had stumbled upon her. Had she decided he would do for a husband that very afternoon? Was that the real reason she'd taken the dragon teeth, so he would be forced to follow her? Did she know there were no other ships headed for England? The questions whirled around in his head like the lashes of a whip, each one digging into his heart.

He'd only seen what he wanted to see, but now that her true motivation was revealed, everything came to light. Her interest in passion. Was that to have him compromise her? Had she hoped her mother would return in time to catch them, but he'd withdrawn? The slyness of her mind when she pretended to have been looking for rocks to hide her wrinkled dress? That would have been the perfect opportunity for her, but she had felt confident in him by then. After all, she'd said *yes* to his proposal. Even her nervousness about her mother accepting him. Obviously, she'd not told her mother that she'd made such a promise to her friends.

As the coach rumbled through London, his own self-loathing came to the fore. He'd been blind. Now all he wanted was to be as far from her as possible. He looked down at Marianna, sleeping peacefully, oblivious to his turmoil. His heart lurched. Elsbeth sounded as if she truly cared for his daughter, but how could he trust her when he'd thought she'd cared for him?

The coach came to a stop and he looked out the window to see the blurry front door of Haven House. Blinking rapidly, he squelched the pain in his chest and the loss of his dreams as the footman opened the door. Carefully, he descended and headed inside.

"Lord Mabry, you have returned."

He nodded to Harrison. "Yes. Please have someone fetch my cousin. I will wait in the parlor."

He watched Harrison move down the corridor before turning to enter the parlor.

"*Señor.*"

At Consuela's voice, he halted, having forgotten about her in his misery. "*¿Sí?*"

"Give me *pequeña.*"

He hesitated. He didn't want to. He needed her.

"*Señor*, you upset. Not good for *bebé*. Or you."

She was right. His daughter was innocent in the debacle he'd made in his marriage. Reluctantly, he handed her to Consuela. Straightening his shoulders, he addressed Harrison, who had reappeared. "Please find a quiet room for Miss Consuela Castilla and my daughter."

"Of course, my lord."

As Consuela and Harrison ascended the grand staircase, he walked into the parlor, silently wishing he'd suggested meeting Joanna in the library, where the duke kept his scotch. He didn't even know what he'd say to his cousin, but he couldn't go home. His heart hurt so much, he couldn't think. How could he have been so wrong?

"Teddy?" Joanna strode into the parlor, her brow furrowed with worry. "Harrison said you appeared upset and you brought Marianna. Did Elsbeth not like your idea?"

He snorted, unable to help it. He'd completely forgotten that he'd wanted to enhance Elsbeth's happiness by moving them to Silver Meadows. "I've been a fool."

"I believe you many things, but a fool is not one of them."

"Now, you're free to believe me a fool as well. I thought Elsbeth loved me. I just discovered I was wrong."

"Tell me." She sat on the straight back chair closest to him, her gaze steadfast as she gave her full attention.

He couldn't sit, but he couldn't move, either. He remained where he was, in the middle of the room, as if lost. He *was* lost. He didn't know what to do. "I arrived home to share my news with my wife, only to overhear her being thanked by her former classmates for making such a horrific sacrifice for them."

Joanna's brows furrowed. "What sacrifice could she have made?"

His hands curled into fists of their own accord. "Marrying me."

"Truly, Teddy? Why would—"

"She married me so her classmates could remain at your school. Apparently, their mothers weren't going to allow them to return if one of them didn't marry by the end of the season."

"No." Joanna rose. "I cannot believe that. I have heard no such threat."

He snickered, not at all surprised. "Of course you wouldn't. Those ladies enjoy your lessons so much, they would do anything to remain. Even you must know that."

His cousin shook her head, but she didn't look at him. "Even if that were the case and they didn't tell me, that doesn't mean Elsbeth married you simply for that. Elsbeth is a smart woman and wouldn't sacrifice her entire life's happiness for her classmates."

"Wouldn't she?" He ran his hand through his hair, not sure how to make Joanna see what he could see. "She just now confirmed that she would never tell me about this pact they had. Do not mistake intelligence for rebelliousness, Joanna. I believe she used that mind of hers to trap me well. Who better to marry than an old suitor whom she knew loved her?"

His cousin started to pace, as was her wont to do when thinking. "I cannot believe this of her. Elsbeth may be intelligent, but she also has a heart. She was devastated by how you took her rejection before you left and blamed herself for you leaving. She cared for you even back then, despite the fact that she declined your offer of marriage."

He slumped down into the armchair by the fireplace, Joanna's pacing making him dizzy. "There's a difference between caring and loving. She did what was right for her at the time, which was to turn me down. I wasn't good enough. But now, I fulfill her need for marriage."

Joanna stopped and studied him. "I was at your wedding. She appeared very happy."

"Yes, but about what? That she landed a husband in time?"

"No, she looked like a woman who'd just married the man she loved." Joanna stopped and crossed her arms as if to stand her ground on her observation.

Just as a spark of hope flared inside his chest, a chill washed over him. Though he'd told her he loved her multiple times, she'd never expressed her own feelings. He dropped his head in his hands. It hurt too much.

"Teddy." Joanna's hand on his shoulder did not entice him to look at her. "You should go home and talk to her."

"No." He didn't want to see her. He felt as if his chest had been cracked open and his heart bared for all to see. Somehow, he had to find the strength to exist, if only for Marianna. His throat closed on the anguish that wanted out.

Joanna's hand left him as she stepped back. "Now, I'd have expected that answer from the Teddy who left for the Continent, not from the one who returned with a daughter in his arms."

Her words lit a fuse that had been begging to flame to life and he jumped up. "They are the same person! One cannot be separated from the other. The pain is real." He slammed his hand against his chest. "Talking to the woman who caused it will only make it worse. Do you understand that?"

Joanna stepped back, her eyes wide. Finally, she nodded. "I

think I do. Please stay the night. I promise we won't bother you. I want you to be safe."

He held back a snicker. For all that she thought of him as the young and former Teddy, she feared him going to some pub and drinking himself into oblivion, as he'd done last time Elsbeth had rejected him. But she was wrong in her assumption. He had Marianna to think of now, and all his actions hinged on that. Nevertheless, there was nowhere else he'd prefer to go. And despite her strong opinions, Joanna was someone he would trust with his life. "I accept your invitation."

Her relief was obvious. "Let me tell Harrison."

As she hustled out the parlor door, he fell back into the chair. He had no choice but to live a life separate from his wife. Part of him ached for his ignorance. If he hadn't overheard, he could have lived his life in blissful oblivion.

But he had. And now a part of him had died.

CHAPTER TWENTY

T HE SILENCE LASTED far longer than was comfortable for Elsbeth before Eleanor cleared her throat. "That sounds appropriate, given the type of marriage you have entered into."

Not a little irritated by her classmate's insistence that Teddy was irredeemable, Elsbeth held up her hand. "It has nothing to do with my *type* of marriage. I don't plan to tell my husband because I don't want to hurt him or have him doubt my feelings." She turned toward Sophie. "No, I'm not miserable. In fact, I'm the opposite."

"Then you are actually happy?" Georgie put down her tea, brows raising high above her round eyes. "To be married to the man you rejected?"

Lissette, who had been quiet to this point, spoke. "Pardon me, but am I to understand that you promised to marry by the end of the season so that these ladies' mothers wouldn't pull them from the Belinda School for Curious Ladies?" Her shock was obvious, but the reason for it less so.

"That is correct. However, I did not make a sacrifice, Eleanor, nor was it hard, Dory. And yes, Georgie, I am happy to be married to the man I rejected. That's because he's become a courageous man with great integrity. The best way to describe the transformation is that he's gone from a spoiled young man to a responsible and caring individual. So to be quite honest with you all, I fell in love."

They stared at her in disbelief. Finally, Sophie spoke, her voice even softer than normal. "Truly? How do you know?"

She smiled, feeling far wiser than her friends in this subject matter. "I'm sure it's different for everyone, but for me, it was the moment I thought he'd be washed overboard."

A chorus of exclamations followed her statement. Having finally caught their undivided attention, she spent more than half the hour painting the scene in words, from the moment of Teddy's knock on her door to the moment she realized she loved him. She had their rapt attention for the entire story. When she finished, everyone except Lissette had a look of dreamy yearning in their eyes.

The dark-haired woman who appeared far older than her stated age of nineteen cocked her head. "Are you saying that we won't know if we are in love with a person until their life is threatened?"

"Oh, not at all. I simply wanted to explain how I came to my own understanding." She smiled encouragingly. "Hopefully, you'll know in a much less dramatic way. I think I was a bit of a nick-ninny to take so long to realize how I felt about him."

"How wonderful that you fell in love and we are able to return to school." Georgie grimaced, rearranging her skirts as she did so. "Yes, I just discovered my mother had the same reserva-tion about me returning. She only mentioned it when your marriage was announced in *The London Gazette*."

If she understood correctly, Joanna would have had no stu-dents if she hadn't stumbled upon Teddy. The thought of how the duchess would have felt, not to mention her friends, brought tears to her eyes.

"My grandmother has no such stipulations." Lissette shrugged. "I guess not having a mother gives me more freedom, though I'm not sure how this school will help me acquire a husband."

Dory reached over and squeezed Lissette's hand. "It's not that kind of school. It's a school that teaches you how to think. I believe learning how to observe and analyze will help us all find the right men for us, but that is not the purpose."

"I see."

From the way Lissette said the words, Elsbeth was quite sure she didn't, but the woman would soon learn how wonderful it was to follow her interests. With Dory to help her adjust, she'd be as excited about returning as the rest of them.

The thought that she, herself wouldn't be returning cooled her happiness a bit. It would be far too much to expect to have a loving man and go to school. She would simply need to adjust. Lifting her hand, she stared at the beautiful yellow stones in her wedding ring. Teddy and Marianna were her school now. She had so much to learn about being a loving wife and a mother that couldn't be read about in books. Though she was afraid of giving birth, she'd found herself longing to give Marianna a sister or brother. That made no sense, yet the urge had seemed to grow stronger over the last sennight.

Eleanor, who sat next to her, covered her hand. "What do you think so pensively about, Elsbeth?"

She was not surprised Eleanor noticed her change in mood. Her friend always seemed to sense such things. She pulled her hand out from Eleanor's and held it up for them all to see. "I was thinking about the superstition regarding the stones in my ring."

"The dragon teeth." Dory nodded knowingly. "You can make one wish upon them. Elsbeth, have you wished for anything yet?"

She hadn't given the myth much thought, but she knew Consuela firmly believed in the power of the yellow calcite. "No, I haven't because until now, there was nothing I wanted that I do not have."

"'Until now'?" Eleanor took her hand to examine her ring. "What is it you wish for?"

Fear collided with excitement in her belly. She could wish for a baby on the ring, but it was no more than folklore. And yet she had grown up loving rocks, depending on rocks, and her nerves were telling her this meant something.

She looked at her friends, each one, knowing they supported her.

Eleanor released her hand and gazed at her expectantly.

She held her fingers up and focused on the large yellow stone in her ring. "I love Marianna with all my heart and want her to have a sibling. I wish to have Lord Mabry's child." A shiver raced up her spine after she said the words aloud.

The room was silent as they stared at her in shock, each, except Lissette, knowing her fear of childbirth.

Dory broke the stunned silence and clasped her hands together. "Oh, Elsbeth, you truly must love him."

They all started talking at once about the ring and babies and names, but she kept gazing at the yellow stone, the cloudy, white inside seeming to move like wisps of mist. Blinking, she forced her hand down and lifted her teacup, taking a sip even as her hand shook slightly. The warm liquid calmed her nerves, and she listened to the conversations of her friends.

She only had one more tea with them on the morrow before she and Marianna would leave Town for Teddy's. One more tea with them and her teacher and she didn't want to miss a moment.

ELSBETH SET HER embroidery down on the settee next to her, pleased with the progress she'd made on a dress for Marianna. The time for dinner approached, and she began to worry. Though Teddy often had errands to attend to or friends who wished to hear about his adventures overseas, for the last fortnight, he'd always been home in time for them to share their repast.

That he had Marianna with him told her he must be with one of his relatives, but which one? Joanna and Lady Blackmore lived on the outskirts of London, while Lady Sommerset and Teddy's uncle, Lord Wakefield, lived in Town. His lateness could be caused by them inviting him to stay for dinner.

Disappointed but understanding he hadn't been with his cousins or aunt and uncle for over a year, she accepted that she would be eating her dinner alone. Rising from the settee, she started for the door when the butler stepped in.

"My lady. This came for you." He handed her a letter.

"Thank you." Curious, she waited for the butler to return to his post before flipping it over. It had the Northwick seal. Excited to see what Joanna had written, she returned to the settee. Maybe there was a reading she needed to have completed for tomorrow. Or it could be that the lady wished her to lead a discussion. Joanna often requested one of them to guide the conversation, since Dory tended to bring up other subjects, Eleanor could dominate, and Sophie was just as happy to sit and listen despite her excellent observations when urged to speak. Georgina enjoyed taking the opposing view for fun, but Lissette was the unknown, at least for her. Based on her own tea this afternoon, she'd guess Lissette would ask pointed questions and would not be easily swayed.

Breaking the seal, she unfolded the letter.

My dearest Elsbeth.

I'm sure that you are worried about Teddy, but he and Marianna are safe with us here at Haven House. Unfortunately, he refuses to return home to discuss matters with you. He said he overheard a conversation with your classmates which he interpreted to mean you married him solely to keep a promise to them. Though I find this difficult to accept, my opinion means rather little to him at the moment.

Teddy knew? She crumpled the paper in her hand even as her heart felt as if it had toppled into her belly, which at the moment churned like a mortar and pestle. Frantically, she tried to remember everything that she'd said. Surely, he must have heard that she was in love with him.

What if he hadn't? She'd never told him she loved him. That realization sent a cold chill over her. Why hadn't she? Deep inside, the answer came. She wasn't like Teddy or her mother. She was like her father, who showed his feelings with actions, not words. But Teddy didn't know that.

She needed to tell him she loved him. Immediately.

Rising, the letter dropped to the floor. She bent and picked it up to see if Joanna had had any other insights.

> *Do not come this evening. Teddy needs time to think about what he heard and what he knows. I'm inviting you to call on us earlier than our scheduled Curious Ladies conversation so that you might have time to discuss this with my cousin. I am sincerely hoping that you did not, indeed, simply marry him to save my school. I assure you that I can fight those battles as they arise, if, and only if, I'm told of such threats.*

The testiness of the words were not lost on her. It was clear her teacher was not pleased with her or the girls. As upsetting as that was to her, it paled in comparison to the pain she'd inadvertently caused Teddy. Her chest started to ache at the thought of what he was feeling, what he must think of her. She should leave at once.

Her gaze returned to the letter.

> *Again, I encourage you to wait until the morrow. Teddy is heartbroken and I don't wish to see him put himself in the same position he was the last time he felt so.*

This time, the thrust ran through her at the reminder she'd caused him heartbreak once before, and that he, along with her cousin James, had almost been killed in an alley down by the Thames. Dropping back down on the settee, her eyes filled with tears. Impatiently, she wiped them away with her hand in order to read Joanna's final thoughts.

> *I request that you think carefully about how you feel to-*

ward my cousin and what you will say to him. I will not make him aware that you are coming early. I think it best I don't give him a chance to refuse. Think hard on this, my dearest Elsbeth, and I will hope for a better tomorrow for you and Teddy and Marianna.

Joanna Northwick

Letting the letter fall to the side, she covered her face with her hands and let the tears fall. She thought she'd been helping her friends, but now she could see that her rash promise the night of the ball could very well ruin her happiness forever. How could such good intentions have such dire results?

Finally, she lifted her head and wiped her tears. She was not one to wallow in her misery. She had to figure out what she could say to her husband to make him believe her feelings were true. Chastising herself for not telling him sooner accomplished nothing. But she didn't know how to convince him besides telling the truth, that she'd fallen in love with him aboard ship.

She couldn't turn to Joanna, but she did have one other intelligent woman who was always there for her. Standing, she went to the writing desk and quickly penned a note to her mother. Sealing it with her new seal as Lady Theodore Mabry, she blinked back fresh tears. After penning a note to accept the duchess's invitation to arrive early, along with heartfelt gratitude, she handed both letters to the butler to have delivered immediately.

Needing to keep busy, she sent a maid to let the cook know there would be two of them for dinner. Then she entered the parlor and sat at the writing desk. Glancing at the clock, she estimated it would still be three-quarters of an hour before her mother arrived. Taking out another sheet of paper, she wrote down the words *I love you*. Looking at those three small words, she marveled at how powerful they were, yet how little room they took on the page. It would have been no effort at all to tell Teddy. Even as her heart lurched at the missed opportunity, she swallowed hard. She hadn't and she couldn't fix that. Did he despise her right now?

The answer came swiftly. Yes. Teddy's love was sure and strong. To be betrayed as he thought she'd done would not only hurt him, but turn his regard for her upside down. She shivered and looked to the words on the paper. Her instinct told her they wouldn't be enough. But what else did she have? There had to be something. Even as she sat there, staring at the almost-blank page as ideas bubbled to the surface, only to be discarded as weak or absurd, her failure loomed before her.

How could she have woken so excited with her life this morning, only to destroy it by her own actions and inactions? Near tears once again, she started when the front door opened. Rising, she spun around as her mother swept into the room.

"Elsbeth, what is it? What has happened?"

Suddenly, she was that five-year-old girl again who had lost one of her rocks and she broke into tears.

"Oh, my dear." Her mother strode forward and wrapped her in her arms.

The comfort made her cry that much harder.

Eventually, her mother pulled back and lifted her chin with her hand. "Now, I can't help if I don't know what is amiss. So it's time to stop weeping like High Force Waterfall and tell me what has happened."

She gave a short nod and sniffed before accepting a handkerchief from her mother and blowing her nose.

"Good. Now sit." Her mother led her to the settee then took the chair opposite. "Did you and Lord Mabry have an argument?"

She wiped her nose one more time as she tried to determine where was the best place to start. "Teddy has taken Marianna and gone to Haven House."

"Yes, I know. Joanna told me they would be staying the night. I did find it odd you weren't there."

"Did she tell you why?"

Her mother shook her head. "I assumed it's to visit."

She crumpled the handkerchief in her hand. "No. Teddy went

there because he couldn't bear to be here with me. I hurt him terribly, even though I didn't mean to."

Her mother appeared to relax. "Now, you know Teddy has a flare for the dramatic. I'm sure it is nothing so terrible."

For some reason, her mother's comment angered her. "Mother, remember, he is not the man he was. He is not dramatic. He is practical, kind, and protective."

Her mother raised her brows then seemed to consider. "What you say is true. I forgot for a moment that he has grown into a well-balanced, if determined, man. So it would seem that you are the one being dramatic."

She didn't know if her mother tried to irritate her on purpose or it was just a happy result, but her annoyance helped her reel in her thoughts. "No, I'm not being dramatic. Teddy overheard part of a conversation that was quite damning to my character."

Now she had her mother's attention. "Your character? You have an excellent character."

"Usually." She dropped the handkerchief on the settee and stood, the need to confess while standing too strong to ignore. "Before we traveled to Spain, I promised the Curious Ladies that I would marry before the end of the season."

"What?" Her mother rose as well. "Why would you do such a thing? Is that why you started your list of traits for a husband? You knew I expected you to return to the school for at least a couple more years."

"Two more years? Mother, I would be going into my fourth season by then with barely any hope for marriage."

Her mother wouldn't meet her gaze. "I'm not sure that would be such a terrible fate."

She sucked in her breath. "I thought you *wanted* me to marry. Isn't that what all the training was for, so I would make a good impression on the *ton*?"

Her mother ambled away, finally turning as she reached the writing desk. "It was, but after Joanna opened the school, I saw there were other options for you, if you wished to pursue them."

She stood frozen. She'd had no idea her mother's objectives had changed. She set one hand on her hip. "That would have been helpful to know. Is there some reason you didn't communicate that with me?"

"Yes. You enjoyed your first season so thoroughly, I didn't wish to influence you one way or the other. But then you fairly blossomed at school, making you even more sought after, so I didn't wish to stand in your way."

She threw her hands up. "So all of this could have been avoided if we had simply communicated with each other instead of being afraid?"

Her mother straightened her shoulders and her chin came up a notch. "I was not afraid. I simply wanted you to find your own way. You, unlike many other chits, have intelligence."

She shook her head, still dumbfounded by her mother's revelation. "Not so much intelligence, as it happened. When I made that promise to marry, it was to ensure that Eleanor and Dory and, as I recently learned, most of the others at the school would be able to return this winter. Their mothers had threatened that if one of us didn't marry by the end of the season, they would pull them out."

Her mother's hand flew to her chest. "*No*. Did you tell Joanna?"

She shook her head.

Understanding dawned in her mother's eyes. "You sought to solve the problem by marrying."

"I did. Lord Rushing and Lord Avondale had been showing great interest in me, both of whom were excellent candidates, so I didn't see that it would be a problem. And you've seen how changed all my classmates are for the better since attending."

Her mother sighed and resumed her seat. "You have too kind a heart. I blame myself for that."

She wanted to laugh at the absurdity of the comment, but it was her heart right now that was in jeopardy. "You can imagine how excited they were to hear that I was married and to receive all the details from Dory. Unfortunately, I didn't tell Dory at the wedding that I loved Teddy."

"Oh, good. That's not something you need share with your friends." Her mother's shoulders relaxed.

"No, it's awful. Because I didn't tell her that, all of them thought I had made a great sacrifice. I even think someone stated that it must be terrible."

"And Teddy heard that?"

"I think he did. Of course, I told them how he'd changed and that I loved him. But I fear Teddy didn't stay long enough to hear me."

"But he knows you love him. If he left in a huff, I'm sure he'll come to his senses."

She felt heat rise in her cheeks. "I haven't told him I love him."

Her mother studied her. "Then you need to tell him."

"I know, but I know it won't be enough. He'll think I'm only saying it because he left. That's why I sent for you. Joanna has invited me to Haven House early on the morrow so that I can speak with him. She isn't telling him when I'll be arriving."

"Joanna is very astute." Her mother gave a truncated nod. "And we are quite intelligent. I have no doubt that we can plan how you can mend this misunderstanding in the morning. But first, if I may be so bold, I do believe that you mentioned a repast. If I'm to think, I will need sustenance."

For the first time since reading Joanna's note, she felt a glimmer of hope. "Yes, it will be ready shortly."

"Excellent." Her mother tapped her fingers on the arm of her chair, something she usually did when recalling something.

With her nerves already strained, she couldn't wait. "What is it you think upon?"

"I'm thinking that Teddy's love for you is our best chance for success."

"Not if that love has turned to hate."

"No, I do not think it has. I did not tell you why I gave you permission to marry him, but I think you should know exactly how far the man will go to have you. He practically blackmailed me."

"Teddy?" She couldn't see him doing any such thing. "How could he—oh." All the pieces about her mother's behavior after giving her blessing suddenly fell into place. He'd used her mother's relationship with the captain to force her approval.

On one hand, she was horrified that he would act in such a manner. But on the other hand, she could see where her mother had left him no choice. She also admitted, if only to herself, that his actions to secure her did say much about how deeply he felt. "You refer to your relationship with Captain Gentry?"

Her mother gave a short nod but did not look away. "And don't forget that Teddy insisted on a special license to marry you as quickly as possible. Those two actions alone tell me that we can find a way for him to believe you. But you must be absolutely truthful, no keeping anything to yourself."

"Mother, I will do whatever is necessary. He has my heart."

CHAPTER TWENTY-ONE

TEDDY SENSED MORE than saw Elsbeth as he entered the parlor. Or maybe it was her lily of the valley scent that made him aware of her. He searched the room, almost missing her as she stood next to the maroon curtains of the window, blending in with them in her dress of the same color. He'd never seen her wear that dark a color. It reminded him of mourning and he didn't like it. The dress, to him, symbolized everything he didn't know about her.

Though well aware Joanna wanted him to talk to his *wife*, he was in no mood for games. There was nothing they needed to discuss. Turning around, he reached for the door.

"Teddy, please don't go."

He stilled, fighting the habit of jumping to make her happy. He needed to kill that instinct. "I have more important items to attend to." He had every intention of walking out, but his feet didn't want to move.

"Do you not wish to hear my explanation?" Her voice was soft but clear.

He gripped the door, wishing he could move through it and close it behind him, but there was a very strong piece of him that craved knocking down anything she might say. He had reason to feel as he did, and nothing she could say would dissuade him. Finally, he let the door go, allowing it to almost close. Turning to face her, he folded his arms. "Actually, I do. In fact, I'm quite curious what possible reasons you might give for using me to fulfill the promise you made to your friends and then never tell me about it."

She turned her back on the window, putting her face in shadow. "I know it appears that way, but I assure you, that is not why I married you."

He didn't say anything. Obviously, she was intent on continuing her farce. He had half-expected her to confess and agree to living separately.

"I married you because I love you." She finally looked at him, as if to gauge his reaction.

He couldn't help the sneer that lifted his lips. "That was convenient."

She shook her head. "Actually, it wasn't." She moved to the chair near the fireplace and laid her hands on its back. "I knew you didn't think kindly of me for rejecting your proposal, so as my feelings grew, my promise to my friends became particularly difficult. I had promised to marry, but the man I had come to love didn't love me anymore. That meant having to live in a loveless marriage."

He let out a snort before dropping his arms and moving to the armchair near the door. Sitting, he bent one leg, placing his ankle upon his knee, to preside over her as any good judge. "You'll have to excuse me if I don't quite believe you. If you made such a promise to your friends, you had already decided to live in a loveless marriage for their sakes. I understand helping others, but that is far beyond the pale." A sudden thought occurred and he narrowed his eyes. "Or is it that you *were* in love with someone your family would find unsuitable for a spouse and you planned to simply take your passion elsewhere in our marriage?"

"No! How could you think that?" Her hands clenched into fists and her brows lowered in a scowl which he'd never seen on her.

Despite her obvious anger, he pushed her further. "After hearing what I heard, I can think just about anything about you."

Her eyes glittered with fury. "I am not that kind of woman. I fell in love with you, no one else. Imagine how inconvenient it was for *me*. One moment I'm prepared to make a proper marriage and dutifully fulfill all my obligations when you suddenly appear in my cave."

"*Your* cave?"

She waved her hand to dismiss his comment. "At the time, I thought you were the same as you were when we had last parted, but as we journeyed together, I discovered you were so much more, so much I admired. If you had continued to eavesdrop on my conversation with the Curious Ladies, you would have heard this and more."

His heart took a leap and he ruthlessly squashed it. Flattery was worthless.

"Granted, I didn't realize that was what I was feeling, at least not until the night of the storm."

"The storm?" He frowned. She wasn't making sense now. "I barely saw you that night. If being far removed from me made you love me, I fear our future is going to make you feel far worse."

Her face paled at his words and her shoulders fell. She moved around the armchair to sit.

He should feel triumphant, but he just felt worse.

She clasped her hands together. "No, it wasn't because you were on deck, or rather not at first. When you entrusted me with Marianna and gave me instructions on what to do if you were lost, my heart fairly jumped with fear. After you left, my mother and I made the bed safe for Marianna and waited. But the worse the storm became, the more worried I was for you until I just had to make sure you were alive."

"You left the cabin?" That she had risked her life burned a hole in his gut, and he held his anger back only by clenching his jaw.

"I did. I opened the door to the deck but remained there, searching for you. I saw the wave that sent you across the deck. In that moment, my life seemed to stop because I couldn't envision continuing on without you in it. When the wave passed and I saw the rope about your waist had kept you onboard, I almost fainted with relief—no doubt how Mr. Dodd felt as well. It was then that I knew. I love you. You are my life."

He wanted to believe her. In fact, he *did* believe that she thought herself in love at that moment, but why, then, hadn't she told him? Because the feeling had passed? Was her heart so fickle, then? He tensed, as if he could keep her from hurting him more. "You want me to believe that you fell in love with me but didn't think I was interested in marrying you. Then why did you suggest that we marry?"

Now she looked away and he did smile in triumph, despite the fact that his heart seemed to stop beating, the pain of being so naïve causing the taste of bile to rise in his throat. Obviously, he'd been part of her plan.

"I couldn't stand the thought of you sharing passion with anyone else."

Her words were barely loud enough to hear, but he heard with his heart and it shrunk within his chest. He rose, not wanting to hear any more. "Jealousy is not love, Elsbeth. You mistake fear, loss, and jealousy for love."

He turned toward the door, suddenly aware of voices in the entryway. Damn, he hadn't closed it properly. Best to leave now.

"The dragon teeth."

At her words, he halted but didn't turn. "What about them?"

"The superstition. You agree that it's powerful, this belief that wishing upon a dragon tooth will make the wish come true?"

Unable to help his own curiosity on the relevance of the dragon teeth, he turned back to find her standing. "Yes, for those who believe."

"Well, *I* believe." She held up her hand, the dragon tooth of her wedding band catching the sun. "I believe so strongly that I wished upon the stone in my ring to have your child."

His heart pounded hard, making it difficult to remain still. "Why would you do that? You're afraid to have children. I remember quite clearly our wedding night when I forgot myself that one time. You were none too happy with me."

Her eyes started to glisten with unshed tears. "Because I love you. I want to have your child and give Marianna a sibling to play with."

He might have been able to resist her declaration one more time, but that she thought of his daughter, was willing to face her greatest fear for him, was his undoing. Hope surged within his chest. Still, his mind balked. "How do I know what you say is true?"

The door behind him opened and Lady Dorothea stumbled in. "It's true! She wished in front of all of us."

He looked over his shoulder to see Elsbeth's friends standing in the entryway nodding their heads. Then someone grabbed Lady Dorothea by the hand and pulled her back out, the door firmly closed. He recognized the sound of Joanna's voice as she admonished her.

"Teddy, I would never lie to you. I love you."

At Elsbeth's quiet words, he gazed at her, his heart filling.

He took a step forward then stopped. "And you'll never keep anything else from me?"

Tears started to track down her face as she smiled. "Nothing."

He strode forward and swept her into his arms. As she lifted her face to him, he took her lips with his own and kissed her like a dying man. She may think he was her life, but she was his very breath.

Her arms entwined around his neck and she opened her mouth to his kiss.

Accepting her invitation, he deepened the kiss, his relief, love, and joy filling him. Out of habit, he pulled her closer, molding her body to his.

A knock on the door made him growl.

Elsbeth giggled against his lips before pulling her head back to look at him. "We should probably let them in."

He shook his head and grinned. "Go away!"

This time, she laughed. "They aren't going to go away. Those are Curious Ladies and unless their curiosity is satisfied, they'll continue to harangue us."

"Harangue? I didn't realize how much of a danger they were. I best rescue you, then." Without giving her a hint of his intentions, he scooped her up in his arms.

"Oh!" She tightened her arms around his neck.

He strode toward the door with her. "You may come in!"

As he expected, the door opened immediately and he stepped forward, forcing the crowd of ladies to part.

"Teddy, what are you doing?" Joanna stood with her hands on her hips staring at him.

"What does it appear I'm doing? I'm taking my wife home."

"*Finalmente.*"

At the sound of Consuela's voice, he halted.

The woman elbowed her way between the ladies of the *ton* as if they were no more than palmetto palms. In her arms was Marianna. When she reached them, she grinned. "*Vamanos.*"

He laughed with the happiness filling his heart to have his little family together again. "Yes, we go."

Elsbeth waved and her friends broke out into applause. Even after exiting the house, the sound continued inside. To his surprise, his coach was waiting. He looked to Consuela. "Did you order my coach?"

She shook her head. "Señora Northwick did."

"Your cousin is a very wise woman." Elsbeth kissed his cheek.

He agreed, but he wasn't about to admit it out loud. "She is also a stubborn one."

As he set Elsbeth on her feet, she took his hand. "And I'm so grateful for that."

"I'm grateful for you." Handing her into the coach, he followed then took Marianna from Consuela as the footman helped her alight.

His wife looked out the coach and waved. In the window of the parlor, her smiling friends waved back.

He grinned at her. "Don't worry. You'll have plenty of time to have tea with them this winter."

"I will?" She turned from the window to give him her attention, even as she offered her finger to Marianna, who grasped it and promptly put it in her mouth. Elsbeth laughed.

"Yes, you will. Joanna has agreed to let us live in the dowager house at Silver Meadows so you can continue some of your studies."

Her eyes widened before her whole face softened as she gazed at him with love in her eyes. "Oh, Teddy. You are truly a gem."

"I'd rather be your rock."

Her eyes filled with happy tears once again. "You are. You are my most prized possession."

Marianna let out a loud screech before laughing loudly, batting her free hand at her father's face.

Chuckling, he held his ladies close as his heart filled with joy.

EPILOGUE

Mid-July 1817
London

ELSBETH STROLLED WITH Teddy down Bond Street, watching her mother listen patiently to Dory's animated conversation. Her friend, beautiful in a green day dress, gestured with her hand toward the sky, obviously discussing something far beyond the mortal realm of ribbons and sweets, the impetus for their shopping venture.

She was grateful her mother had been able to wrest Dory away from her own mother for the day and have her meet them for the excursion.

"Have you made a decision yet?" Teddy's deep voice brought her back to her latest dilemma.

She'd been asked to share her findings with Mr. Parkinson, a renowned paleontologist. He was quite interested in the concentration of limestone in the Dragon Caves since fossils were most often found in limestone. On one hand, she felt honored and not a little intimidated by the request. On the other, she was a wife and mother now and did not wish to bring any censure upon Teddy or the Mabry family. "I have not."

"What is it that has you hesitating? You know I'll support you in whatever you decide to do."

She looked up into Teddy's gray eyes, his sincerity easy to read. "I do know that." She squeezed his arm locked with hers. "It's just that Mr. Parkinson, besides being a brilliant scientist, also has rather rebellious leanings in regard to the crown. In addition, my study of geological formations out of interest is completely different from having my results possibly made public. What would your family think?"

His laughter was completely unexpected. "What would they think? I believe they would immediately start making the rounds to be sure everyone knew you had been so honored. Joanna might very well place an ad in the *London Ledger* to be sure no one was ignorant of the fact."

She shook her head, not as sure as he. "It's different for your cousins. They no longer represent the Mabrys. Only you do now, and I don't wish to bring censure down upon you."

Teddy halted, forcing her to stop as well, and faced her. "Ells, I promise you that Mr. Parkinson's acknowledgement of your work will not in any way affect our family."

"Not even Marianna?"

"No, not even her. Your particular area of study is unknown to most, and dare I say it, of little interest to the *ton*. They are far more concerned with the latest debutante's behavior than a married woman's intellectual achievements."

When he explained it in such a way, she realized she'd still been thinking like an unmarried woman. Yet they had been married over a month now and the *ton*'s interest in her and Teddy's love story had come and gone rather quickly. As Dory had stated, in quite a huff, it barely lasted three days before people had moved on to far more interesting subjects. "Then you are saying you think I should agree to share my findings with Mr. Parkinson?"

"What I am saying is that in making your decision, you do not need to concern yourself with my family, which, in case you've forgotten, includes a woman running a feminine Oxford, a famous woman artist, and a lady who trains horses specifically for the fairer sex to ride."

She pretended to ponder his information. "I see. So in other words, I would hardly be noticed if my work was included in a famous paleontologist's book." She bit her lip to keep from laughing.

His brows lowered and he placed his hand upon hers, which to any passerby looked as if he were comforting her, but what she felt was his finger slip beneath her gloved hand and tickle her palm. "You, my lady, are always in my sights."

She finally smiled before turning her hand and capturing his. "Then I believe I will write Mr. Parkinson back and invite him to Silver Meadows after the season ends. I admit to wanting more time with you at the moment and no distractions."

Teddy dropped his hand and started them down the street once again. "My lady, if you look at me in that way, you may find yourself back in the carriage long before you find the ribbon you seek."

She blinked at him as if innocent of his innuendo that they return home posthaste for another passionate interlude. "Truly, Teddy, you forget yourself." She gestured ahead of them to where her mother and Dory had stopped. "We're on an excursion with others. We will just have to wait."

In response, she received nothing more than a low growl, but it was all she needed to know that her husband would prefer they were alone.

"Is that Captain Gentry?"

At Teddy's question, she looked ahead and did indeed see the good captain striding across the busy road, headed for her mother. "I was under the impression he had left England once again, but apparently, I must have misheard."

They did not reach her mother before the captain engaged her in conversation. As they strolled up, Dory looked at her and widened her eyes briefly to alert her that something was amiss.

"That is truly an honor, captain." Her mother's voice sounded much higher than usual.

"What is an honor, Mother?"

The captain turned toward her. "Ah, Lady Elsbeth. I mean, Lady Mabry, Lord Mabry. It is indeed a happy occurrence that I find you here as well."

Teddy gave the man a nod. "It is good to see you, Captain Gentry."

The man smiled warmly at them. "I can see that marriage is quite agreeable to you both."

"It is." She smiled up at Teddy before returning to the conversation she wished to know more about. "And what honor have you done my mother, captain?"

His brown eyes twinkled with undisguised excitement. "I have come to London with the sole purpose of asking your mother if she would be interested in journeying on the *SeaSprite* once again to aid us in mapping an unusual island in the Mediterranean Sea."

She turned toward her mother to find her blushing. *Blushing?*

Teddy spoke before she could. "Lady Astor, that *is* an honor. I didn't realize you had an interest in further voyages."

Her mother swallowed before lifting her chin slightly. "I do. I enjoy traveling and putting to order what I've seen. I've been mapping the Dragon Caves Elsbeth visited. Though I didn't venture in them, her rough drawings and exact measurements have given me plenty on which to base my map."

To be fair to her mother, she did agree. "She's done beautiful work with my scribbles. Mother, is this something you'd be interested in doing?"

"As I told the captain, I need to ruminate on it. There is the school to consider."

Glancing at the sign on the establishment before which they had gathered, she gestured toward the door. "I would very much be interested in hearing more about this adventure my mother could participate in. Captain Gentry, would you like to join us? We were about to enjoy some of Monsieur Armand's delicious confections."

The captain glanced at her mother before replying. "I would be pleased to."

They all turned toward the shop. Once inside, she and Dory sat while the gentlemen conversed and her mother engaged with the proprietor.

Dory immediately leaned closer, keeping her voice low. "I think the captain is quite taken with your mother." Despite Dory's penchant for talking more than she listened, she was rather observant.

"I believe he is also, but I would prefer that we keep that knowledge between us."

Dory's eyes widened, then she nodded sagely. "I understand. I was simply surprised to see your mother blushing so readily. She's so much more circumspect than mine."

She held back a grimace at the mention of Lady Preston, whose roaming eye was not lost on many, but due to her husband's influence in Parliament, she had not been ostracized. Hopefully, Dory would find a match before any outright scandal broke. She laid her hand on her friend's. "I know it's difficult for you sometimes. I understand now more than before, but we needn't worry that my mother will be obvious, whatever decision she makes."

"Do you wish her to go?"

She pondered Dory's question. Did she? She would miss her mother greatly. She also thought her mother's interest in the captain to be below her status, but then again, status could be relative according to her interpretation of Thomas Paine. "I don't know. I believe I will let her decide and support her in her decision." How like Teddy she sounded. Her mother would be much surprised by that.

Her friend sighed. "What a grand adventure that would be. Just imagine traversing the Mediterranean Sea, the place upon which Odysseus sailed and Jason and the Argonauts." Dory paused and shook her head. "Of course, you already have. Was it beautiful, treacherous? I don't imagine there were sirens or moving rocks that could crush ships, but truly, what a place on which to ponder one's existence. Socrates would ask you if you have lived a good life according to his principles. Of course, the question is, do those very principles stand the test of time in our modern, industrial world? I quite imagine that your mother would find much to contemplate on such a voyage."

She was quite sure her mother would be contemplating more concrete objects, such as the captain and his bed. "Do you wish, then, to travel to the Continent?"

Dory pondered the question before finally answering. "I'm not confident in my ability to adapt to life aboard ship. While I would be interested in meeting people from other countries, I think I would prefer they come to England. Though sometimes I wonder if the only place I will find a husband is abroad." She grimaced. "Our countrymen just don't understand how engaging a good conversation can be."

She nodded, though she wasn't sure someone from another country would be able to follow Dory's ideas either. Her mind was quick, and she was very knowledgeable, but her thought process was at times, most times, difficult to follow. She either needed a man who was as quick in intellect or completely baffled by her that he set her above him as something to be treasured. The rest of the Curious Ladies were simply patient with her and responded by choosing one statement or another on which to comment.

Dory leaned away as the rest of their group joined them. Soon, a waiter was taking their orders for hot cocoa. Lady Astor also ordered macaroons, while Dory chose pound cake.

Elsbeth had something far different in mind. "I would like *monsieur*'s caramel ice cream, please." It had been her main purpose for talking the others into shopping. Though she'd enjoyed caramel custard the evening before, it simply wasn't caramel ice cream.

Teddy gave her an odd look but didn't comment, so she turned her attention to the proposal before her mother. Though she would support her parent, she did wish to know the specifics. "Captain Gentry. When do you expect to set sail on this expedition? Is it in combination with a merchant enterprise?"

The captain, who'd rarely smiled on board his ship, seemed much more relaxed now and broke into a grin. "Your understanding of the shipping business is much appreciated. Yes, I will be delivering goods to Malta, but on the return trip, I plan a relatively small detour of a few days to explore Lampion. Like your Dragon Caves, there is much superstition about this island and many sailor stories."

Her mother immediately elaborated. "The captain spoke upon this subject often while we were aboard, and I told him how exciting it would be to map."

"Yes, I believe, Lady Mabry, that even you indicated on board that your mother had done a few maps for you?"

She had glanced over her shoulder, hoping that the ice cream was coming. It was hard to concentrate when it was so near. Turning back, she nodded. "Yes, Captain, she has. At least a dozen so far. She says she's a novice, but I admit that when comparing a map of hers to some I own, hers are quite of equal quality and detail."

The captain practically beamed, his trimmed beard moving with his smile. "Then I fervently hope she will grant my request. I leave in a fortnight and have refused passage to an earl, a viscount, and a lady so that your mother can have a cabin to herself and any other accommodations she needs to make it a pleasant voyage for her." The captain gave her mother a hopeful look.

"Captain, I very much appreciate the invitation, but I must think upon it. My duties at the Belinda School for Curious Ladies are to start in just a couple of months. If I were to travel, I would need to let my nephew and his wife know very soon. I'm not sure they could find someone to replace me."

Now, that was a strange excuse. Joanna could hire someone to take over the literature subject for Sophie and James himself could work with Eleanor on astronomy, her mother's other specialty. Surely, she knew that.

Hearing footfalls, she looked behind her, hoping the server was arriving with her ice cream. But as the waiter approached, she could see he carried only the hot cocoa, which she'd completely forgotten about.

The warm drink was placed before her. She took a sip, but it wasn't what she was waiting for, so she set it down. Surely, the ice cream would arrive next.

Teddy raised his cup to gain everyone's attention. "Lady Astor, Lady Dorothea, and Captain Gentry. I am pleased to announce that my wife has been granted a great honor."

"She has?" Her mother looked at her. "Elsbeth, you must tell us."

She shook her head, not at all convinced anything would come of her correspondence with Mr. Parkinson. "It is not a given as of yet." She paused, listening for footfalls. Hearing none, she continued. "A well-known paleontologist would like to discuss my findings from the Dragon Caves."

Her mother's eyes widened, but the captain appeared perplexed.

As Teddy explained why Mr. Parkinson and his studies of fossils was of import, Dory captured her attention.

"So you have agreed, then?"

She nodded absently, the sound of the waiter returning pulling her attention from the conversation.

"Ells?"

Teddy's question evaporated as the caramel ice cream was set before her. Without another thought, she lifted her spoon, scooped a large amount, and put it in her mouth. She closed her eyes as the cool sweetness cascaded over her tongue.

"Elsbeth." Her mother's tone had her opening her eyes.

"Yes?"

"What flavor ice cream did you choose?"

She took another spoonful of the dessert before answering. It was an odd question, but perhaps her mother had been otherwise engaged in conversation when she'd ordered. Finishing the delectable bite, she responded. "Caramel." She quickly filled her mouth with more, her whole body feeling happy.

Her mother's brows lifted before she broke into a wide smile. "Oh, my. Do you have something else you'd like to tell us?"

Swallowing, she frowned but took another spoonful before looking to Teddy, who shrugged his shoulders. She was about to answer her mother, but she had to take another bite first.

"Elsbeth, what news do you have?" Dory grasped her arm, the one with a spoonful of ice cream, keeping her from taking another bite.

She had the worst urge to jerk her arm away. "I have no other news." As politely as she could, she disengaged her arm and plopped the ice cream into her mouth. Immediately, her mood improved again.

"Lady Astor, perhaps you could enlighten us."

At Teddy's question, she nodded toward her mother. "Yes, please."

"Perhaps I can. Elsbeth, have you been craving caramel ice cream for long?"

Teddy answered for her as she had managed to take another bite of the ice cream. "She's had it at least five instances that I can recall in the last sennight. Why?"

Her mother grinned and her eyes became glassy. "I ask because I craved caramel ice cream when I was with child myself."

She froze, her spoon, which had been scraping the bowl, stilled. "You did?"

"Yes. I couldn't focus on anything until I had my caramel ice cream. I must say your father was quite surprised, considering I rarely enjoyed cold food or sweets."

With child? Could her wish have been granted so soon? She thought back over the last two months. She'd had no courses since they'd married. She looked to Teddy, who stared at her mother with his mouth open, no doubt as equally surprised as she.

Dory squealed. "It worked! The dragon tooth worked!" As her friend hugged her, she grinned at her husband.

Immediately, he rose, pulling her from her chair. "A child. With you."

She nodded, unable to stop smiling.

"Excuse us, Lady Astor, Lady Dorothea, Captain Gentry. Captain, might you be so good as to escort these ladies back after they finish their desserts?"

The captain winked. "It'd be my pleasure."

Teddy clasped her hand and pulled her out of the establishment. Within moments, he was handing her into their coach after yelling to the coachman to bring them home. He sat next to her and took her in his arms, giving her the most loving, sweetest kiss he ever had.

When he set her back, he took both her hands, his gaze searching. "Tell me. How do you feel? Be honest with me. I must know everything."

She squeezed his hands in hers. "I feel like I always feel, except for the need for caramel ice cream."

"I will have Cook keep it on hand. If you wish it for every meal, it's yours."

She chuckled. "I think I might like that too much." She could see herself getting very round with their baby. At that, her old worries returned.

"What is it? You're frowning." Teddy's gaze grew intensely silver.

She shrugged, looking away, her stomach already feeling like the blasted rocks were back. "My happiness is truly sublime, but my earthly worries remain." She locked her gaze with his. "I'm worried about the delivery."

He did not scoff and give her platitudes. "I am too. In fact, I've been thinking about that and had planned to stop in the jewelers today to order a necklace be created with another dragon tooth." He let go of her hand and reached into his waistcoat pocket. He pulled out the small, yellow stone with the white clouds within it. "But now, I think before I do that, I'll make my own wish."

That he had thought to commission another piece of jewelry for her had the rocks in her stomach turning to dust. "What will you wish for?"

He held the stone between them. "I wish that you will have an easy delivery as you bring forth a healthy child."

Once again, as before, she felt an odd sense of calm over the prospect of having her baby. Happy tears itched at the back of her eyes. "I do so love that wish. I feel as if all will go well now."

Teddy's brows furrowed as he stared at the calcite in his hand. "It is odd. I too feel a confidence that all will be well." He raised his gaze to hers. "Do you think…?"

She grinned, her joy at having a baby filling her, squeezing out any more doubt. "I'm not thinking anymore, I'm feeling. I'm feeling happiness, joy, and so much love for you that I cannot contain it!" She laughed, no longer afraid.

Teddy smiled as he closed his hand around the stone and slipped it back into his pocket. "If a wish on a dragon tooth is all it takes, then I suggest we save the rest for our next child and our next and our next."

"Agreed." She leaned forward, and he took her in his arms. Everything felt right as his lips descended once more to hers. She would have never expected that uncovering the lord would prove to be such a worthwhile endeavor that would not only lead her to discovering the strong and confident man Teddy had become but also to finding a love as unchanging as any rock.

The End

About the Author

Lexi Post is a New York Times and USA Today best-selling author of romance inspired by the classics. She spent years in higher education taking and teaching courses about the classical literature she loved. From Edgar Allan Poe's short story "The Masque of the Red Death" to Tolstoy's *War and Peace*, she's read, studied, and taught wonderful classics.

But Lexi's first love is romance novels so she married her two first loves, romance and the classics. Whether it's dashing dukes, hot immortals, sizzling cowboys, or hunks from out of this world, Lexi provides a sensuous experience with a "whole lotta story."

Lexi is living her own happily ever after with her husband and her two cats in Florida. She makes her own ice cream every weekend, loves bright colors, and you'll never see her without a hat.

Website: lexipostbooks.com
Lexi Post Updates: app.mailerlite.com/webforms/landing/c1w1g3
Facebook: facebook.com/lexipostbooks
Twitter: @LexiPost
Instagram: instagram.com/lexipostbooks
Amazon Author Page: http://amzn.to/1IEL2cc
BookBub: bookbub.com/authors/lexi-post
D2D: books2read.com/author/lexi-post/subscribe/1/16171
Goodreads: goodreads.com/goodreadscomLexiPost
Instagram: instagram.com/lexipostbooks
Blog: happilyeverafterthoughts.com
Pinterest: pinterest.com/lexipost77
Email: lexi@lexipostbooks.com

www.ingramcontent.com/pod-product-compliance
Lightning Source LLC
Chambersburg PA
CBHW060440310726
48977CB00001B/266